"You might as well enjoy it," said Vane. "Treat it as the opportunity to try the things you've always wanted."

Enjoy being ruined. "What sorts of things would you suggest?" Eliza asked derisively.

The duke shrugged, and Eliza could *feel* the muscles in his shoulders move under her hand. "You could get rid of the pastels," he suggested.

Eliza trod on his foot. "So sorry about that," she simpered, blinking up at him.

His lightly tanned throat worked as he swallowed a laugh. "Clearly I should dance with wallflowers more often. You're terribly out of practice."

Eliza stepped on his other foot and didn't bother to make it look like an accident.

"Oh, I'm sorry," said Eliza again. "I suppose I am out of practice, but someone did tell me that I should try all the things I've been wanting to do."

"Well met," said Vane. "What else is on the list?"

"To wear something daring," said Eliza after thinking for a moment. "And try brandy. It seems appealingly cathartic."

"Excellent," said Vane, nodding as he spun her down the far length of the ballroom.

Eliza could think of one other addition to her list, but she wasn't going to mention it to Vane, not in this lifetime. *I'd like a kiss*, she thought, curtsying to him as the set ended. If she was going to be ruined and scandalous and doomed to a life alone, she'd quite like to be kissed for the trouble.

Author Note

For all of the changes that the last two centuries have wrought, people themselves really haven't changed. It's the central reason that I return to historical fiction time and time again, both as a reader and writer. Underneath the sense of adventure is a core of timeless shared humanity, and it's those overlaps with our modern experience that keep me at my keyboard when the writing gets tough.

Most of my plot bunnies start with a seemingly innocuous question: How would women in 1815 have dealt with socially accepted sexism? Not only in the small "Well, she could make her voice heard to her husband" sort of ways, but in bigger ways, too. Would she need a coalition of women, like the suffragette movement, or could one woman make an all-out play for respect? Also, as someone who refuses to wear any dress that isn't cut in a classic sheath or A-line myself, what did my fellow anti-empire-waistline gals think when floaty, gauzy empire-column dresses were all the rage?

In Eliza, I rediscovered that, despite changes in technology, fashion and colloquial language, the core needs and drives of the everywoman are virtually the same. We want respect, love, the perfect dress, and a chance to be silly and fun with someone who sees us for who we are.

Thank you so much for reading my debut romance. I hope you had as much fun reading it as I did writing it. Until next time,

Casey

www.CaseyDubose.com

CASEY DUBOSE

———

A Duke for the Wallflower's Revenge

HARLEQUIN
HISTORICAL

ISBN-13: 978-1-335-59581-2

Recycling programs
for this product may
not exist in your area.

A Duke for the Wallflower's Revenge

Copyright © 2023 by Christine Johnson

For questions and comments about the quality of this book, please contact us at CustomerService@Harlequin.com.

Harlequin Enterprises ULC
22 Adelaide St. West, 41st Floor
Toronto, Ontario M5H 4E3, Canada
www.Harlequin.com

Printed in U.S.A.

Casey Dubose writes about kisses, corsets and heroines with an axe to grind. When she isn't writing about historical hotties, she works as a geospatial engineer outside the US capital. Despite her love of historical adventure, Casey is very much the type of heroine who spends her time knitting, arbitrating the demands of her Machiavellian pets and people-watching while gloriously unchaperoned.

Books by Casey Dubose

Harlequin Historical

A Duke for the Wallflower's Revenge
is Casey Dubose's debut for Harlequin Historical.

Look out for more books from Casey Dubose coming soon.

Visit the Author Profile page
at Harlequin.com.

To Violet and Tamara,
my very own real-life internet people.

Chapter One

In some ways, it was as good a day to be ruined as any other.

The summer sky was hazy and blue overhead as Eliza strolled along the footpath, keeping an eye on Aunt Mary and her group of friends as they clustered together off to the side of the Serpentine's footbridge. Mrs Forsyth had just welcomed her first grandchild into the family, and she was regaling the other ladies with tales of the infant's peerless beauty, appetite and ability to sleep.

Eliza marched along, carefully staying to one side of the path before she reached a slight bend. At that point she reversed direction, nodded politely to a pair of promenading young ladies as they passed her, and began walking back the way she had come.

By now, after nearly six full Seasons on the marriage mart, the rules of proper behaviour no longer required her conscious consideration: she was to stay within Aunt Mary's sight at all times. She was not to be too friendly towards any particular gentleman, but neither could she act too frostily. Her bonnet—several years old now—was tied firmly beneath her chin, her crocheted gloves matched the fawn colour of her walking dress, and Eliza knew that she presented a perfectly respectable, perfectly dull façade of spinsterhood to the world.

On the banks of the Serpentine—which was low, for it hadn't rained in more than a month—two young children were playing with a ball and a small brownish dog, all of whom were watched over by a tidy, aproned nursemaid. The little girl, her face creased in an expression of glee, picked up the ball and lobbed it directly towards the water.

The dog sprinted after it into the reeds, barking madly, as the little boy pronounced, 'I could have thrown it further.'

Eliza stopped in the shade of a broad English oak to watch the drama unfold. The nursemaid had hardly begun her prodigious scolding when the dog shot back out of the reeds, covered in water and mud, with the ball firmly clenched in its wickedly grinning jaws.

'Tipton, no!' said the nursemaid, but it was too late.

The terrier dropped the ball at the little girl's feet, grinned in pride, then shook slimy water and riverbank mud all over the three of them.

Eliza grinned, watching as the little girl immediately picked up the filthy ball and hurled it off again, despite the fact that her nursemaid was already towing her and her brother off in the opposite direction. It was a stiflingly hot summer's day—why shouldn't the children be allowed to get a little damp?

Before she could cross the path to re-join Aunt Mary and her cohort, someone grabbed Eliza's arm and yanked her backwards into the shadows of the trees. She stumbled a little over the roots and rocks that pushed the ground up in furrows.

'Let me go—' she began, but she was spun around and pushed back against the tree.

'Hello, sweet,' said the Earl of Abberly, sliding his hand down to grip Eliza's wrist as she tried to tug away.

He was tall and thin, with the kind of pale and mottled complexion that hinted at an over-indulgence in drink and a lack of brisk walks in the afternoon sun. His eyes, a nondescript blue, were quite small and set slightly too far apart, giving observers the uncanny impression of an avaricious frog.

'Unhand me, Lord Abberly,' said Eliza, attempting to shake him off. *Again.*

In the past weeks he seemed to turn up everywhere she went, watching her with calculating eyes and treating her as if her non-compliance was simply a fly to be swatted.

'Come on, Miss Hawkins,' he said, stepping closer and forcing Eliza to lean back against the bark of the tree to avoid his breath. 'You've been on the shelf quite long enough. It's time for you to accept your role— and *me.*'

'I don't know how many times you must hear this,' said Eliza, pitching her voice low to keep from attracting the attention of passers-by. 'But I have no interest in marrying you. Ask someone else.'

Anyone else—it wasn't as though the matchmaking mamas of the ton wouldn't accept a belted earl into the family, even if he was lacking for coin.

If she could just get back on to the path and over to Aunt Mary she could pretend this had never happened, and no one would be any the wiser. If she stayed against this tree with him much longer somebody would be bound to notice. There was no true privacy in Hyde Park, especially during the fashionable hour. Then again—that was quite likely Abberly's plan.

'What's wrong with me?' Abberly asked. 'I'm an earl

and accepted in every drawing room in London. I'm trusted by the Prince Regent. You'd be lucky to have me,' he said, and then leaned in and tried to kiss her.

Eliza didn't think. She didn't try to rationalise her choice, or talk herself into suffering his kiss so she could quietly return to her aunt. Eliza merely reacted. She twisted her face to one side, so that Abberly's lips landed awkwardly along her jaw, and as he leaned back to try to kiss her again she raised her right hand and slapped his face with all the force she could muster.

He released her as his hand flew up to cradle his cheek, clearly shocked by her actions and the force of her blow. But, despite the fact that he'd finally let go of her wrist, Eliza couldn't run back to the safety of the footpath and Aunt Mary's skirts. The sharp crack of Eliza's palm against Lord Abberly's face had drawn the attention of a group of passing noblewomen, and now more and more people were stopping to gawk.

'You'll regret doing that,' Abberly snapped, his beady eyes glittering as he took another step back from Eliza.

He rubbed his cheek once more, and then he smiled—and despite the summer heat, she felt a chill shiver down her spine.

'We would have gone unnoticed if you'd just been quiet. So I suppose this works well for me.'

Eliza couldn't bring herself to have regrets—not just yet. After six Seasons of patience and acceptance and good behaviour, Eliza's patience had finally snapped—although unfortunately she'd caused this scene in the most public venue available. Half of London was out and about, and stopping to act as witnesses to this little scene.

Eliza wiped her gloved hands over her skirts, as

though that simple act could scrub away the last few minutes.

After a long moment of uncomfortable silence, Lady Berkley stepped forward, the feathers on her hat trembling with curiosity. 'Lord Abberly,' she said, pitching her voice like an actor trying to reach the back seats of a theatre, 'are you all right?'

Eliza felt the muscles of her jaw go slack. 'Is *he* all right?' she asked, unable to stop herself. 'He's the one who accosted me.'

He'd planned this. And they were checking on him.

'You struck him,' said Lady Berkley slowly, as though she were explaining something to a very small child.

She *had* struck him—and she would like to do it again. 'He grabbed my arm,' said Eliza, knowing that nothing she said could save the situation. It wouldn't help, but this time, for once in her life, she wouldn't go home and brood over all the things she might have said. 'And he dragged me off the path and into the trees with him.'

Her wrist still bore the red imprint of his fingers, where he'd tightened his grip as she'd tried to tug away. But it was incredibly stupid of her to be saying all this, and she knew it. She was publicly confirming her own ruination: nobody could possibly spin a tale to save her now. But none of this was fair. *She* was the one who had been grabbed. *She* was the one to extract herself from the situation. And they asked if Abberly was all right.

There was a stirring in the crowd, and Eliza's Aunt Mary pushed through to the front of the gathered spectators. 'What's happened?' she asked, looking from Abberly to Eliza to Lady Berkley and back again. Her round face was flushed and she radiated the kind of terrified worry unique to the mothers of adult children whom they could no longer protect.

For a long moment nobody spoke. Aunt Mary was well-liked among her peers, despite her poor fortune and low title. She was a kind and quiet woman who was always willing to lend a sympathetic ear. Society's benevolent toleration had thus far been extended to Eliza, but she suspected that this incident in the trees would bring their tolerance to an end. It would be impolite to condemn Eliza publicly, but nobody was willing to condemn the Earl of Abberly, either.

'Lord Abberly grabbed me, Aunt,' said Eliza, impressed by how steady her voice was. 'These other people watched as I extricated myself.'

Aunt Mary's flushed face went white. Eliza was more than ruined now. She hadn't only been alone with a gentleman, she'd also publicly scorned Polite Society. This was the moment in which she should appeal to the group's charity—there was no real love for Abberly among the ton—but she couldn't bring herself to do it. Not after she'd been ignored and scorned and teased by them for the past six years.

If Eliza had to swallow any more of her pride she'd die choking on it.

'Eliza…' said Aunt Mary, her face ashen.

The crowd seemed to hold its breath, waiting to see if an apology would be forthcoming.

'Come on, Aunt Mary,' said Eliza, walking to her side with a deliberately measured pace. 'I believe I've had my fill of fresh air.'

Eliza looped her arm through her aunt's and steered the other woman towards home.

Low, busy murmurs erupted behind her, and Eliza took one small comfort in her act of defiance: she'd turned her back on the ton before they could turn their backs on her.

As she and Aunt Mary walked along the wide footpath back towards Berkeley Square, she caught sight of a tall gentleman standing beside his horse, just off the path. He seemed to be lazily checking his horse's front hoof for debris, but his attention was firmly on Eliza. As she drew closer she recognised him as the Duke of Vane. He was well built, with dark hair and eyes, though none of his handsome features could reflect the state of his reputation.

The Duke of Vane was living proof that there were no rules for a person's honour. Honour was whatever Society decided to make it, and there were very different standards for men and women, rich and poor, native-born and immigrant. A high-born man could do whatever he wished, and he would still always— *always*—be accepted in the arms of Society.

Eliza had been grabbed in broad daylight, in the middle of Hyde Park, and this was very likely the last time she'd see it for a long while.

As she and Aunt Mary passed by the Duke, he gave her a lazy perusal, his dark eyes moving slowly over her old bonnet to her perfectly practical walking dress and back up again. Eliza knew what he would see: a not so young, unmarried woman with a dearth of suitors and an overabundance of flesh.

When the Duke caught her eye she ripped her gaze from him and stuck her nose in the air, focusing on the gate ahead as if it was the entrance to heaven, guarded by St Peter himself.

Eliza heard someone chuckle behind her—that horrible duke, probably. That was all right—let him laugh. For the first time in her life, Eliza had truly stood up for herself. She wouldn't go home filled with shame and regret and too many finger cakes this afternoon...oh, no. Besides, she'd need to get used to the laughing. She had a feeling she would be hearing a lot of it.

Chapter Two

After a week, Eliza's cheeks hurt from constantly forcing a smile. Aunt Mary had taken them shopping today, to Lady Tottenham's salon, and was generally keeping Eliza frantically busy in an attempt to distract her from the dwindling number of calling cards and invitations on the sideboard in the hall.

And now Eliza and Aunt Mary were attending one of the final events of the social Season—an invitation they'd received well before the incident in the park. These late-Season gatherings usually had an odd air: the debutantes could feel failure nipping at their heels, the bachelors sensed the impending finish line, and the rest of Society seemed almost desperate to enjoy themselves before everyone was scattered across England to various summer house parties and hunting excursions.

In most ways, Lord and Lady Kenworth's ball wasn't particularly different from any other. Aunt Mary was nearby, socialising with the other matrons. Eliza's cousin Helen was dancing with a few of her husband's cronies from Parliament, and Eliza herself was in her assigned spot: on the outskirts of the room, by herself, hiding behind a flower arrangement.

The difference? Not a single person was making eye contact with her, even accidentally. Their eyes flitted past Eliza as if she was wallpaper, telling her with everything but words that she was entirely beneath their notice.

On the other side of the ballroom the Earl of Abberly laughed at something Lady Berkley said, and the sound echoed uncomfortably in Eliza's ears. *His* social standing hadn't changed an inch. Only Eliza's had.

The latest dance drew to a close, and Eliza watched as Helen moved gracefully across the glossy floor. Without seeming to try, Helen was always the most beautiful woman in a room. Her deep red hair was piled high on her head, with a few artful locks trailing over the paleness of her fine skin and highlighting the lithe column of her neck. On another woman the cut of her deep blue dress would have looked severe, but on Helen the silk clung almost lovingly to her curves.

Sometimes it was hard to believe that they shared any blood at all. Helen and Eliza had been born to Aunt Mary's two sisters, and neither of them had had red hair. Eliza had always been conscious of the fact that she looked even worse when standing next to Helen: she was round, where Helen was smooth and angled, her face flushed red, while Helen's complexion remained serene, and her hair— Oh, there was no point in bemoaning her own dishwater hair.

'Hello, dearest,' said Helen, pulling Eliza in for a hug. 'Walk with me, will you? I fear if I'm around for the next dance Lord Stanley will try to claim it.'

Eliza linked arms with Helen, and together they began to stroll around the edges of the dance floor.

'How have you been?' Helen asked, nodding politely to a cluster of Parliamentary wives. 'I would have called, but—'

But her husband rarely let her out of their echoing Mayfair town house unless he was there to watch her.

'Quiet,' said Eliza. 'The worst part has been watching Aunt Mary. It wasn't as though I was popular *before* this happened, but Aunt has all her friends… Maybe she'll let me go to the country alone. Perhaps her invitations will return if she isn't seen publicly supporting me.'

'I could host an event,' said Helen. 'Something small… when the worst characters have decamped for the country. By the time the Little Season begins in the winter, the whole thing will have blown over.'

Eliza thought about it. She should make a few apologies, beg a few favours, and then come back for the Christmas season as if nothing had happened. She should do it if only for Aunt Mary's sake. But… But something *had* happened. It wasn't right that she should have to curry favour from the very people who had turned their backs on her. It made her wonder, in the dark stretches of the night, if there was something she could have done. Some way she could have changed what had happened.

'I can't stop thinking about what I might have done differently,' Eliza said, loudly enough that nearby dancers turned to look at them.

'I could use some air,' said Helen, before steering them both out through the French doors and on to the low balcony beyond. She took a seat on a stone bench and patted the space beside her. 'Now, tell me what nonsense you've dreamed up.'

Eliza sat down, falling automatically into the habit of smoothing her skirts and keeping her back ramrod-straight. Her stays were always cinched tighter for events like this, and she couldn't have hunched her shoulders even if she wanted to.

'I suppose I wonder what would have happened if I'd stayed a little closer to Aunt Mary. Or if I'd yelled more loudly or worn a brighter dress.'

'How would those things have helped?' Helen asked, adjusting her gloves.

'He wouldn't have come as close if I had been near Aunt and her friends. Maybe someone would have stopped him, or they might have seen me more easily… Oh, it sounds so foolish when you make me say it out loud.'

'You aren't foolish,' said Helen, nudging her shoulder against Eliza's. 'This—' she gestured to the glittering ballroom beyond the open balcony doors '—this is foolish.'

'I feel I have let Aunt Mary down,' said Eliza, tracing the embroidered flowers that covered her favourite reticule. 'That's what hurts. When Mother and little Martha died Aunt Mary took me in, and she's been so *good* to me.'

She'd been kind to poor, plump little Eliza even when it had already been clear that she'd never grow into a great beauty. They'd mourned together, and Aunt Mary had always treated Eliza as her own daughter.

'And there's nothing I can do about it,' said Eliza, idly watching the ballroom. 'If I was a man I could meet him for boxing, or fencing, or even start buying up Abberly's markers! But I'm a woman, and the only thing I can do is smile and hope that someone else will stand up for me.'

'But you aren't alone,' said Helen firmly. 'Never forget that.'

Music filtered out into the warm summer night and for a moment Eliza and Helen sat in companionable silence, enjoying this moment of peace away from the scrutiny of Society.

'The next set is forming,' said Helen, rising to her feet and shaking out her skirts. 'Greenville has promised me to Hartley for this dance. But please, darling. Come and see me whenever you need to.'

'I will,' said Eliza, leaning in to press a quick kiss to Helen's smooth cheek. 'I'm so grateful for you.'

'And I for you,' said Helen, blowing Eliza a smiling kiss before disappearing back into the bright ballroom.

Eliza was tempted to linger for a moment longer, but being alone in any capacity could only hurt her reputation more. With her head held high, Eliza stepped back into the ballroom and walked quickly past the refreshments table towards her former spot against the wall. It didn't matter if she was thirsty; lingering near the cakes and punch would only make the other ladies titter at her.

A few minutes after Eliza had resumed her seat behind the lush, fern-heavy flower display, Aunt Mary brought her a cup of lukewarm lemonade. 'Beatrice thinks you've been quite brave,' said Aunt Mary. 'She's glad you're here.'

It would have meant more if Beatrice had bothered to tell me herself.

'I'm glad,' said Eliza, taking a sip of her lemonade. 'Thank her for me.'

Neither Eliza nor Aunt Mary commented on the fact that two of the more status-conscious women in Mary's circle of friends were chatting with other acquaintances on the far side of the ballroom and had made no effort to greet Aunt Mary.

On the other side of the ballroom there was a bit of a stir. A few men had come in late—and not even fashionably late. They were rudely late. Of course one of them was the Duke of Vane. He made a too-deep, nearly mocking bow to their hostess, before clapping one of his fellow bachelors on the back. His dark hair gleamed with russet highlights in the light of the candles, his severe black ensemble was beautifully cut, and all told he looked like the very picture of English bachelorhood: lithe, carefree, and oblivious to life and its consequences.

For a moment, with every particle of her body, Eliza hated him.

Aunt Mary and Eliza watched as Vane worked his way along the edge of the ballroom, smiling and nodding and acting as though he owned the place. Eventually he came upon Lady Knowles, who smiled and turned away from her previous conversational companion as though he'd become invisible.

'People say he's the father of her child,' Eliza whispered, nodding towards Lady Knowles's swelling middle.

Aunt Mary looked affronted. '*I* know that,' she said. 'But *you're* not supposed to know things of that nature.'

Eliza scoffed. 'What? Am I supposed to be deaf as well? I can hear the gossip just as easily as you can, Aunt.'

On the other side of the ballroom, the Duke bent low over Lady Knowles's hand. It was mostly proper, if a bit showy. And then, against all propriety, Vane actually pressed his lips to Lady Knowles's knuckles. That was several inches shy of proper, and Eliza felt a white-hot bolt shoot from the base of her skull right down to her pinched toes.

There was no justice in this world.

She lived in a society where a man could openly, winkingly, flaunt propriety and have his missteps ignored at worst or praised at best. A woman had no give in the tethers that bound her to her honour and her reputation, and if it was taken from her, she had no recourse or option to regain it.

Was this system that valued masculinity above all else the sole fault of the young Duke of Vane?

No.

Had he come to represent all that was unfair and unjust in their society in Eliza's eyes?

Absolutely.

'Eliza,' Aunt Mary whispered, elbowing her sharply. 'Stop wool-gathering. He's coming this way.'

Eliza didn't need to ask who 'he' was. Steadily, with a faint smirk fixed to his handsome face, the Duke of Vane was crossing the ballroom towards Eliza. She took a step to one side, like a hare testing the fox's reflexes, and the Duke's dark eyes followed her, his amused look unwavering.

'What should I do?' Eliza hissed.

But it was too late for Aunt Mary to answer. The Duke was close, and then he bent into a lazy, perfect bow.

'I was wondering if this dance had been spoken for, Miss Hawkins,' he asked, his voice deep and velvety.

They both knew the dance hadn't been claimed. Eliza had stuck her dance card into a potted plant as soon as she'd arrived, and in the potted plant her card remained.

All good sense and convenient excuses fled Eliza— just as they'd done in the park. 'You never dance with wallflowers,' she said, more out of reflex than accusation.

Vane raised an eyebrow. 'Shouldn't we all occasionally try new things?'

Eliza glared at him, and ignored the way Aunt Mary was pointedly flicking her eyes from Eliza to the Duke.

Her message was clear. *Dance with him!* After insulting all the collective witnesses in the park, Eliza couldn't be seen to publicly scorn a duke.

'What do you have to lose?' he asked in a stage whisper, giving voice to the question that had been plaguing Eliza all week.

'Nothing,' she said. 'So I suppose I'd better accept.'

Gingerly she put her gloved fingers in Vane's outstretched palm, unable to shake the sense that she'd just innocently entered into a Faustian bargain—one riddled with fine print.

'Why now?' Eliza asked as they joined the other couples lining up for the set.

What she really wanted to ask was, *Why me?* They'd bumped into one another dozens of times over the years. He was a parliamentary ally of Aunt Mary's husband, Eliza's Uncle Francis, and Society was only so large. Yet over the past six Seasons, he'd never said more than a dozen words to her. Until now.

'You've been staring at me since my arrival,' said the Duke, placing one hand on her back and holding hers with the other.

To Eliza's consternation, she realised she'd agreed to a waltz.

'I wasn't staring,' said Eliza.

'It isn't polite to argue with a lady,' said Vane, as the first strains of music began. 'So I'll agree that you weren't staring. You were glaring—much as you did that day in the park.'

'A gentleman wouldn't bring that up,' said Eliza, even as they began to move together.

He danced beautifully. Of course he did. What Eliza wouldn't give to find one thing this behemoth of a man couldn't do well.

'I have never claimed to be a gentleman.'

'And yet you hold that title nonetheless.'

The Duke smiled at her, and Eliza noticed that a thin white scar trailed down almost perpendicular from his bottom lip…half an inch at most. It was barely noticeable, and only served to draw attention to his full mouth. With that one small imperfection his scar had done what a previous generation's patches and beauty marks had failed to do.

'You were magnificent in the park,' he said, shocking Eliza completely. 'I wanted to tell you that.'

'I gave you the direct cut.'

'And you did it beautifully. You could give lessons to aspiring governesses and companions across the realm.'

'Perfect,' said Eliza as they turned gently to the music. She caught a glimpse of Aunt Mary's worried face over the Duke's shoulder and wished she could reassure her somehow. 'I'll have a budding career to fall back on when this dance with you finishes what Abberly began in the park.'

'You might as well enjoy it,' said Vane. 'Treat it as an opportunity to try the things you've always wanted to.'

Enjoy being ruined?

Perhaps he was mad, as well as scandal incarnate.

'What sort of things would you suggest?' Eliza asked derisively.

The Duke shrugged, and Eliza could feel the muscles in his shoulders move under her hand.

'You could get rid of the pastels,' he suggested.

Eliza trod on his foot. 'Sorry about that,' she simpered, blinking up at him.

His lightly tanned throat worked as he swallowed a laugh. 'Clearly I should dance with wallflowers more often. You're terribly out of practice.'

Eliza stepped on his other foot and didn't even bother to make it look like an accident. She was dancing with a terrible rake who was infamous throughout London for his affairs with bored married women and those unattached among the demi monde. Her shredded reputation was now so much grist discarded beneath the social mill, and she was tired of thinking about it.

'Oh, I'm so sorry,' said Eliza again. 'I suppose I am out of practice… But someone did tell me that I should try all the things I've been wanting to do.'

'Well met,' said Vane. 'What else is on the list?'

'To wear something daring,' said Eliza, after thinking for a moment. 'And try brandy. It seems appealingly cathartic.'

'Excellent,' said Vane, nodding as he spun her down the far length of the ballroom.

The music was drawing to an end, and Eliza almost found herself regretting it.

'To eat cake in public,' she said, jerking her chin higher and daring the Duke to comment.

He did—but not in the manner Eliza had expected.

Instead, he looked truly confused when he asked, 'Why wouldn't you already do that?'

'If you ask me to explain I'll have to do worse than stamp on your foot,' said Eliza. 'And I want—I want to play cards,' she decided, on the spur of the moment. 'Properly. Not just whist at the ladies' table. To see what the fuss is about.'

Her mind was spinning with possibilities—all the things that Society decreed too stimulating or improper for delicate womanhood. In that moment, Eliza wanted to try them *all*.

Vane's eyes twinkled. 'You want to ditch the pastels,

eat cake, gamble and try hard liquor. You're getting into the spirit of the thing,' he said, clearly amused.

Eliza could think of one other addition to her list, but she wasn't going to mention it to Vane—not in this lifetime.

I'd like a kiss, she thought, curtseying to him as the set ended.

Not necessarily from Vane—not from anyone in particular. But if she was going to be ruined and scandalous and doomed to a life alone, she'd quite like to be kissed for her trouble.

Chapter Three

Gabriel Livingston, Sixth Duke of Vane, was not having a good morning.

Firstly, it was the fact that it truly *was* morning. The sunlight was fresh and soft and new—not the bright noon light of Society's 'morning' calls.

And, when Gabriel had slunk into his own home through the back door, he'd found his steward waiting for him in the hall. Dickson had been sipping a mug of tea and serenely reading the newspaper, with his briefcase at his feet and his legs crossed at the knee.

'Good morning, Your Grace,' he'd said, rising to his feet.

Gabriel had sighed and turned into the library. Dickson's presence wasn't unwelcome *generally*…he just didn't want to see him *now*.

That had been the second bad thing.

The third…

'Your mother has exceeded her quarterly allowance,' Dickson informed him, delicately laying a neatly stacked sheaf of papers on the cluttered expanse of Gabriel's desk.

'She always does,' said Gabriel, not bothering to look through the receipts and bills of sale. 'She hosts a house party every year, just as the Season ends. And as we know, she spares no expense.'

'Yes, Your Grace,' said Dickson. 'Usually it is by no more than fifteen percent of her total allowance, but if you'll look—'

'Whatever it is, just pay the bills,' said Gabriel, resisting the urge to rub at his eyes like a tired child. 'Would you be able to manage *your* mother's spending money? To tell an adult woman—the woman who gave birth to you—that you don't approve of her purchases? It's not as if I can't afford it.'

Dickson sniffed. 'I'm sure I couldn't say, Your Grace.'

'Is there anything else?' Gabriel asked, trying not to eye the decanters arranged on the library sideboard.

Dickson passed some more papers across the desk. 'The steward at Sanford Park wants to see you.'

Gabriel scrawled his signature across the invoices and ignored the comment about Sanford. Everyone knew he hadn't been back to his home in years.

'And that's all?' he asked, hope colouring his voice.

'That's all,' said Dickson, managing to hint that there *would* be more, if not for his own not insignificant efforts. 'Good day, Your Grace.'

Dickson showed himself out of the library and Gabriel slouched back against the heavy leather of his chair, gently drumming his fingers against the arm. The library windows were open, and the morning smelled cool and promising…quite unlike the night he'd just experienced.

That brought him to Problem Four.

He'd gone home with Lady Alicia Grice after the Kenworth ball. Alicia had played her usual games, but whereas he'd been charmed and aroused before, last night the entire situation had struck him as cheap. He hadn't wanted to pretend that her husband would catch them at any moment. He hadn't wanted to play at *all*.

He'd helped her to finish as quickly as he could, and all the while tried to forget the feeling of a warm body in his arms and furious golden-brown eyes glaring up at him. It had merely been a dance—*one dance*—and yet he hadn't been able to stop thinking about it.

In truth, he hadn't been able to stop wondering about her since that day in the park…

Gabriel had just decided that maybe he deserved a drink after all when Problem Six—or was it Five? At this point he'd entirely lost count—was escorted into his library by Wilkins.

'Good morning,' said Miss Eliza Hawkins, glancing casually around his library as though she *hadn't* just been shown into a bachelor's residence, alone, at an indecent time of the morning.

Gabriel shot to his feet, and not even he knew if it was out of hard-learned manners or as a protest to her very presence in his home.

Why was she here? He'd encouraged her to pursue the things she'd always wanted, but surely the girl had to be a virgin—and he certainly could *not* be entertaining such thoughts about an innocent, no matter how ruined she was in the eyes of Polite Society.

He had *rules*. No attachments. No responsibilities.

'I'll send a tea tray, Your Grace,' said Wilkins, walking towards the door on silent feet.

'No,' said Gabriel. 'She won't be staying!'

But Wilkins was gone, the door was shut, and it was entirely too late.

Gabriel dropped back into the warm leather of his chair. She was uninvited in his damn house—he saw no reason to stand on ceremony.

'Well, Your Grace,' said Eliza, turning her eyes away from the books and high windows, 'I have a proposition for you.'

'No,' said Gabriel, watching as she sank into one of the chairs on the other side of his desk.

She was wearing a slightly worn day dress and looked all the more comfortable for it. Likely she'd crept out before even the servants would miss her, and had had to lace herself into her clothes.

'Whatever it is that you want, the answer is no. I'll see you out. You cannot be here without an escort—it's beyond ruinous.'

A fact she knew well and had seemingly ignored.

The woman didn't budge.

'I know you're the father of Lady Knowles's bastard.'

Gabriel snorted. 'No, you don't.'

The stubborn chit pressed on. 'And in exchange for keeping this information to myself, you will escort me to Yorkshire.'

'Oh, I will, will I?'

Gabriel crossed the room to the sideboard and poured himself a drink, rudely forgetting to offer one to his un-invited guest. He was experiencing the same odd mix of feelings he'd had last night at the ball, when he'd danced Miss Hawkins across the room and she'd stamped on his feet. She had seemed so…*alive*—a luscious brown-paper-wrapped parcel positively bursting with passion and simply looking for an outlet.

For a moment, as Gabriel retook his seat, he allowed himself to wish that she'd asked something else of him. They were a mere two floors away from his bed, and he knew from experience that he could have a woman out of her stays in less than three minutes, but…

He took a burning gulp of good whisky. But he bedded only married women for a reason.

Eliza Hawkins was watching his stalling tactics with the patience of a born wallflower. Gabriel almost felt guilty: this girl was accustomed to being made to wait.

'Now, then,' she said, with all the starch of a school-marm. 'I'd like to leave as soon as possible, if it's all right with you.'

The sheer nerve of this woman! She could have Parliament on its knees without any real effort at all.

'I'm afraid that doesn't suit me,' said Gabriel. 'As I said—I'm not helping you.'

Miss Hawkins gave him a pitying look, her tawny eyes amused. 'Last year, during the Little Season, you and Lady Knowles disappeared with each other during Lady Constance's musicale. You returned first, and when Lady Knowles came back her hair was in a different arrangement.'

Now that she mentioned it, Gabriel did remember something like that. 'Observant little thing, aren't you?' he murmured.

'You were also seen together at the Christmas ball given at Marbury House. The timing cannot be ignored, Your Grace.'

Gabriel smirked. 'You've been monitoring my whereabouts quite thoroughly, haven't you?'

Eliza snorted. 'What else is one to do at these affairs? I've been banned from bringing my embroidery or reading in the ballroom.'

'So you watch the gentlemen?' Gabriel asked, interested in her despite his better judgement.

'Yes, I watch the gentlemen,' said Miss Hawkins, scorn hanging heavily upon each word that fell from her pink lips. 'Rather as a naturalist watches virulently coloured butterflies.'

Gabriel snapped his fingers and pointed at her in agreement. If he enjoyed her look of frustration…well, that was his business.

'That's it—exactly that. Well done,' he said. 'It's that hungry, hunting look. You've described the expression of every matchmaking mama from here to Scotland.'

'It's not a woman's fault that her entire worth rises or falls on the balance of her marriageability—and no one could know that better than a woman already married with daughters.'

Except a wallflower, thought Gabriel, watching her eyes.

'Regardless,' he said, leaning back in his chair and smiling inside at the way her gaze flicked to the open collar of his shirt. 'I shan't help you with whatever escape it is you have planned.'

'I don't have an escape planned,' she replied. 'Abberly will be in Yorkshire, hosting an elaborate summer house party. I plan to travel there and challenge him to a duel. You will assist me, and in exchange Aunt Mary and I will keep your…secret.'

Gabriel set down his heavy crystal glass with a thump. 'A duel? You're mad.'

She had to be. If she was bold enough to shoot at a peer of the realm, they might hang her for it.

'No,' said Miss Hawkins, holding eye contact with him. 'I'm not.'

'Women don't duel.'

'There are lots of things that women aren't *supposed* to do,' she replied.

The only sign of nerves he could see was the way she traced her index finger over the floral embroidery on her reticule, over and over in a self-soothing little pattern.

'But just because we aren't *supposed* to do something doesn't mean we *can't* do it.'

'Well, you can't do this,' said Gabriel. 'Because I won't be helping you. Do you have any idea what your request—' *your blackmail scheme*, he added to himself '—will entail? Paying for transportation, food, board, supplies... Not to mention the time and scandal involved.'

'Money won't be an issue,' said Miss Hawkins, a little more forcefully than necessary.

She opened her reticule, extracted a bulging coin purse, and tossed it onto the desk in front of him. The purse landed with a solid-sounding *thump*.

'If you took this from your family—'

'I sold my trousseau.'

Gabriel stared at the woman in front of him while the force of her words dissipated into the room like so much smoke. She'd sold her trousseau. She'd sold her trousseau to pay for a trip north so that she could challenge Abberly—duel him for her own honour.

It was simultaneously one of the maddest, bravest and saddest things he'd ever heard. That trousseau would have held everything that Miss Hawkins had intended to take to her future husband's home. How many hours had she spent embroidering sheets, crocheting lace, admiring any small pieces of jewellery she might have been given?

That trousseau would have been its own little Pandora's box, unique to the girl who possessed it. Even girls without dowries—girls like Miss Hawkins—clung to their trousseaux. One thing held trousseau chests in common: hope. And apparently Miss Hawkins had sold hers.

'I got a good price for it,' said Miss Hawkins, her voice level and her eyes dry. 'I know the worth of fabric, and a discreet down the street from our milliner who is willing to accept a piece here and there. There's more than enough money to get us to Yorkshire and back.'

Gabriel was finally starting to understand that Eliza wasn't acting impulsively. She'd clearly lain awake at night contemplating her future and what would happen to her when the Season ended. She'd looked at her options and had chosen this: a man she only knew casually, a pouch of coins and a dream of revenge.

'You're serious about this? About the duel?'

'Quite serious, Your Grace. And I *will* tell people about you.'

Gabriel drummed his fingers along the arm of his chair. He knew he wasn't the father of Lady Knowles's child: he'd never properly bedded the woman. Even if he was, Lady Knowles was a married woman—any child of hers would legally be the offspring of her husband. Eliza was bluffing, with no cards in her hand, and *that*—that was the act that betrayed her fear and desperation.

It was also a manoeuvre worthy of Wellington at his finest, and Gabriel couldn't help but admire it.

'I won't help you,' said Gabriel, with no small amount of regret. 'I apologise if what I said during our dance made you feel as though I was making light of your situation. But I cannot, and will not, let you do this to yourself and your family.'

Eliza narrowed her eyes and he could sense her marshalling her arguments.

'You have two young cousins,' said Gabriel, not

leaving a space for Eliza's protests. 'And while they are male, they will still require connections when they come of age. Your aunt has her group of friends, yes, but they will not be able to stand by her when Society discovers your trip to Yorkshire, let alone your intention to duel with an earl. You could hang, Miss Hawkins, if you killed a peer of the realm.'

'We'd delope!' she protested. 'Nearly everyone does. I wouldn't actually shoot him.'

Gabriel pressed on. 'Your uncle holds a barony, and as such would be able to continue voting in the House of Lords, but what would his peers think if he were unable to control a spinster in his care? How would it affect his reputation, Miss Hawkins? And, for all that you seem to believe the worst has already befallen you, what would the execution of this plan do to your own?'

She'd be worse than ruined. Even if she found a home in a tiny village in the northernmost reaches of Scotland, nobody would speak with her in the churchyard. No letters would find their way to her door. Laughter would be a thing of the past, along with companionship and human warmth.

It would be a grey, short, bleak life, and Gabriel didn't want that for anyone.

Especially not for her—not this woman who seemed to vibrate with purpose and wit and vivacity.

Just minutes ago Gabriel had been contemplating the emptiness of his life: to vote, to dance and to indulge. Here was his antithesis: a woman with nothing but a purpose and the willpower to see her plan through.

'I'm sorry,' he told her, and watched the last of her desperate hope fade from her eyes. 'I truly am. But I won't help you with this.'

Eliza stood from her chair, her movements abrupt

and jerky. 'Thank you for your time, Your Grace,' she said, her eyes focused on something in the middle distance, beyond Gabriel's left shoulder. 'I'll see myself out.'

Gabriel practically leapt out of his chair. 'Absolutely not! Good grief, Miss Hawkins, you could be seen. Or robbed. Or seized. Or…' He trailed off, thankful all over again that he'd decided not to take on the responsibility for one of these creatures. The world was full of terrible things waiting to befall them. 'I'll call for the carriage and a maid and I will escort you home.'

Eliza sighed, but followed him out of the library and through the house towards the mews, where he called for his enclosed carriage.

'It seems reasonable on paper,' she said, as the horses were backed into their spots in the traces. 'I don't have a male family member who would defend my honour, so I should at least have the option of defending my own. Some of us women have ended up saddled with junior cousins and older uncles who can't be prised out of their studies even with a big stick. What are we supposed to do?'

When she said it like that, it did make a certain amount of sense, he supposed.

'You aren't going to try to rope some other man into this scheme, are you?' Gabriel asked, horrified by the thought.

Maybe he should tell her uncle. Maybe she needed a tonic from a surgeon, or—or something.

Eliza sent him an expression so scornful it could be used to strip wallpaper. 'Of course I'm not going to ask someone else,' she said. 'You're the only one the idea would have worked with. Uncle Francis likes you, and you've visited the house often enough in your political scheming that I know your reputation is mostly exaggerated. But, since you *do* have a terrible reputation, it would have worked in your favour when you refused to marry me afterwards.'

Gabriel sent her an admiring glance. 'Where were you when we were fighting Napoleon? You'd have sent the Corsican home long before old Wellington ever did.'

She really might have. Despite the utter recklessness of her plan, the breadth of her daring was admirable— as was the calculating fashion with which she'd triangulated him as her ideal accomplice. For a moment, as the carriage was wheeled in front of them, Gabriel knew a moment of regret for what might have been.

Yes, he thought, looking at Eliza's determined face as she stepped into the carriage. *It would have been a glorious duel.*

Chapter Four

The carriage ride home was quiet. It was still fairly early, and it didn't take long to drive from His Grace's fashionable St James's home to the more commercial neighbourhood where Uncle Francis lived during the Season.

Eliza risked a glance at Vane, who was looking out of the small window with an expression of bored indifference. The upstairs maid, temporarily borrowed from her duties in his townhouse, sat rigidly next to Eliza, caught in a social situation she'd probably never anticipated.

Eliza could sympathise. The silence inside the carriage was like they were in a funeral procession. It felt sombre, containing a collection of people never usually found together and inspiring thoughts of mortality.

At least Vane hadn't laughed at her. She wouldn't have been able to stand that—not after he'd so effectively stamped out Eliza's hopes and dreams. And he wasn't wrong—barrelling up north to challenge Abberly to a duel *would* absolutely end Eliza's life in English society.

'You're being awfully quiet,' said Vane as the carriage came to a gentle stop. 'It has me rather worried. What are you thinking about?'

Failure.

'Consequences,' said Eliza.

She couldn't shake the tightness that was gathering in her chest: this was the end. She was staring down the barrel of a gun—though not in a duel. She had to accept what had happened. Her reputation was besmirched, she'd insulted Polite Society, and there was nothing she could do about it. She was well and truly powerless.

Vane shook his head in amusement and swung down out of the carriage before offering assistance to Eliza and the maid. The pavements were deserted, and the narrow street free of other carriages, but nobody knew which neighbour might be peeking through their curtains. At least this carriage wasn't an entirely unusual sight: Uncle Francis and His Grace were both Whigs, so Vane had a history of dropping by to iron out various political plans.

'You're coming in?' Eliza asked as he pushed open the front door.

She foolishly hoped he wouldn't. Aunt Mary might not even be out of bed yet, and—

And there she was, in the front parlour, dressed in her favourite morning gown, though her hair was still in a loose, slightly messy chignon.

'Your Grace!' she said, setting her teacup down with a click. 'We weren't expecting— Eliza, where have you—?'

Well. That was that, then.

'I had business to discuss with Francis, and thought I'd escort Miss Hawkins inside. Lovely morning, isn't it?' Vane commented politely.

Eliza stared at him. He was so charming, and so effortlessly charismatic, even *she* nearly believed him. The effect was, unfortunately, rather undermined by

His Grace's attire: last night's formal evening wear, slightly rumpled and entirely unbuttoned at the throat. She'd just marched into the man's library, attempted blackmail, and imposed upon him for a ride home in his carriage. She'd done all that, and now he'd escorted her inside for the purpose of covering for her.

'He's lying, Aunt Mary,' said Eliza, not wanting the Duke to get any more mired down in the disaster that was becoming her life. 'I slipped out to ask His Grace if he would escort me to Yorkshire. I wanted to duel Abberly. I still do.'

Maybe now her aunt would take Eliza's feelings seriously. Maybe now she'd stop advising Eliza to be patient and hopeful.

Aunt Mary blinked, for once without a quip or an encouraging word.

Eliza charged on. 'His Grace has talked me out of it. I can't do that to you, or your boys, or to Uncle Francis. I know that life isn't fair, and that justice isn't real…but it isn't *right*, Aunt Mary. Men can do whatever they want, hurt anyone around them, and everything is forgivable simply because they're men! I wanted to confront Abberly in a way that would make him listen, and there isn't much that is louder than a gun.'

Eliza took a shaky breath: if she said one more word, it would turn into a sob.

'Oh, Eliza…' said Aunt Mary.

Next to Eliza, Vane shifted uncomfortably.

'Abberly has even invited us to his stupid house party,' said Eliza, snatching a piece of heavy card from the mantel. 'He's still invited us to his house party— as though he hasn't just humiliated me in front of half of Polite Society. It's as if he's rubbing it in my face.'

'The Prince Regent will be at that party,' said Vane.

'If you'd taken up arms against a peer there, it might very well have led to an accusation of treason. Who would say you weren't hoping to hit the Prince?'

Eliza heard her own mouth saying, 'That's ridiculous…' even as her thoughts whirled like tossed dice.

The Prince Regent was attending Abberly's house party.

Abberly was a notorious social climber—one of the reasons it was so inexplicable that he'd set his sights on Eliza. The Earl, despite his lack of ready funds, would leverage every last bit of credit on impressing the notoriously spendthrift Prince. This party would make or break Abberly's social reputation—and now Eliza knew exactly which way she wanted things to go.

'I think we should attend his party,' said Eliza slowly. 'And I think we should ruin it.'

'Dearest,' said Aunt Mary. 'You loathe the man. Attending his house party would serve no purpose. Besides, you know your Uncle Francis won't travel. He's busy with the boys while their tutor is on holiday. Eleven and nine are such boisterous ages…'

'Travel where?' asked Uncle Francis, walking out of the dining room with his pipe in one hand and a cup of coffee in the other. 'Vane, good to see you. What brings you here?'

The Duke sent Eliza a helpless look.

'I was just thinking that His Grace could escort Aunt Mary and myself to a house party,' said Eliza, feeling a twinge of guilt for misleading her affable, bookish uncle. She tried to remind herself that what she'd said was technically the truth.

'A house party? You should, Mary. You know I always feel bad for keeping you in Town after all your friends have left for the country.'

'But…'

Vane raised an eyebrow at Eliza, and she could *feel* the repudiation.

She sighed. 'Uncle Francis, I'm afraid it's not just a house party. It's got rather complicated with Abberly and—'

Uncle Francis cut her off and sent her an affable smile. 'Your Grace, you know where to find me when you finish planning with the ladies,' he said, walking into his library and closing the door behind him.

Aunt Mary looked at the library door, then at the visibly uncomfortable Duke standing in her hall, and finally at Eliza, her freshly minted family scandal.

She sighed, and gestured towards the sunny front parlour. 'I suppose we should have a chat, shouldn't we?'

Eliza felt a surge of affection for Aunt Mary. She was the kindest, steadiest, most optimistic woman Eliza knew, and it killed her that she'd inadvertently harmed Mary's standing with her friends.

Eliza sat next to Mary on the low sofa and watched as Gabriel awkwardly perched on the arm of one of the cosy wingbacks near the fire.

'Tell me,' said Mary, and Eliza marshalled her thoughts, trying to decide where to begin.

'Abberly shouldn't be able to get away with this,' she said. 'And with the Prince planning to attend Abberly's house party, it's my one chance to harm his social reputation the way he has ruined mine.'

'All of the risks will still exist,' said Vane. 'Your family's reputation would still be in jeopardy.'

'It wouldn't need to be public,' said Eliza, desperate to make them see that this was her best option—the only alternative to doing absolutely nothing and accepting her fate just as she'd already passively accepted so much before. 'All I'd need to do is prevent the Prince from being impressed with Abberly's efforts.'

'Nobody should get hurt,' Aunt Mary warned, in a tone that she usually reserved for scolding her rowdy young sons. 'And you'd need to be incredibly discreet.'

'Of course,' said Eliza, feeling hope leaping behind her breastbone.

'I admit I wouldn't mind seeing Abberly taken down a peg or two,' said her aunt, idly drumming her fingers on the arm of the sofa. 'He strung Margaret's daughter along for two seasons before deciding to ignore her completely. She managed to marry a viscount's youngest son, but she was heartbroken to have lost her chance to be a countess.'

'He's a pest,' Eliza agreed with vehemence.

Embarrassing him wouldn't be enough—nothing would—but it would be so much better than doing nothing.

'Pranks were rather common when your mother and I were girls,' said Mary, nodding at the downstairs maid as she carried in a heavy tea tray.

She poured a cup for His Grace before balancing a slice of morning cake on the edge of the saucer and passing it over to him.

'We'd put pebbles in each other's walking boots, or switch the sugar for the salt. The ladies' punch bowl would be spiked...we'd add saucy prompts for charades... Things were more relaxed in those days. Though I don't at all miss powdering my hair.'

Vane and Eliza shared a look, and for the first time in her life Eliza knew *exactly* what a man was thinking. Mary's assumption of innocent plans was sweet, but entirely out of character for Eliza. Vane was looking at Eliza the way a spectator might look at a flaming firework fuse—with the knowledge that either the firework would go off or someone would get burned.

'Is that the sort of thing you had in mind?' Vane asked. 'Putting frogs in the bathwater or hiding the billiard cues?'

Eliza didn't have any firm plans in mind. 'Pranks, by definition, need to be executed as opportunities arise,' she said. 'I can only tell you that I want to call Abberly's ability to host into question. I'll make sure not to be caught.'

'It doesn't sound particularly harmful to me,' said Aunt Mary. 'And with the Prince Regent there…it could be an excellent opportunity.'

Nobody needed to say that merely being seen in his presence would lend Eliza's reputation some much-needed repair.

'If we do this, everything will go back to normal as soon as we return home,' said Aunt Mary in her sternest mama voice. 'You'll make peace with what has happened and you will behave yourself at all future public events.'

Hope bloomed anew. 'Yes, of course,' said Eliza.

'Well, you've convinced me,' said Mary. 'Your Grace?'

He sent them the kind of look that usually graced the face of a cornered rabbit. 'I'm not sure this is a good idea…' he said, shifting his weight on the comfortably worn cushion. 'It could be quite dangerous. I'm not the sort of escort you need.'

Eliza eyed him. Anything less than utter confidence was out of character for the Duke. Did he not think he was proper enough? Or capable of playing nice?

'Oh, we're very low maintenance—don't you worry,' said Aunt Mary. 'We won't be forcing you to take us shopping or to provide entertainment. Just a carriage and an open mind about Eliza's motivations. You won't have to put up with us for long.'

'I wouldn't think of it as *putting up* with you,' said Vane, briefly locking eyes with Eliza before glancing away again.

She felt a jolt of something shoot through her, and hoped that she'd managed not to blush.

'Who could resist such a call to action?' he asked, looking at Eliza once more.

And then, the cheeky blighter, he *winked*.

Eliza almost—but not quite—regretted dragging him into her schemes.

After an adulthood spent watching the behaviour of Polite Society, she felt she had most of the men neatly sorted into a few simple categories. There were dignified older gentlemen, and aged lechers who never outgrew the randy schoolboy phase. There were devoted family men in competent and incompetent varieties, as well as inveterate bachelors at all levels of domestication.

Eliza had long had Vane neatly labelled: *bachelor for ever, well socialised, barely house trained.* This thoughtful and very nearly responsible side of him was one she'd never seen, and once more she had the sensation of standing on the edge of a steep drop she hadn't seen coming.

'Well, then, that's settled!' said Mary, clapping her hands together and startling Eliza out of her reverie. 'Your Grace, I'll send a messenger over this afternoon with suggestions for our travel plans. Thank you so much for agreeing to be our escort—Francis does speak so highly of you. A house party,' she said on a little sigh, relaxing back into the cushions. 'You know, I can't remember the last time we had a proper holiday. This might be rather fun.'

Fun was not the word that Eliza would use to describe their upcoming trip. But, as Vane rose to his feet and made proper farewells, Eliza couldn't help the little bubbles of excitement that were fizzing in her stomach.

This was it. Her chance for revenge. A shot at deciding her own fate. And maybe—just maybe—she'd get to explore those butterfly feelings she got when arguing with the Duke of Vane, too.

Chapter Five

Much like the Duke himself, Vane's larger carriage was dark, oversized, and surprisingly uncomfortable.

Though it was well past noon, and London had fallen behind them in a cloud of smoke and heat, Eliza still couldn't quite believe that this was happening. She was sitting next to her Aunt Mary as they travelled north to Abberly's house party, where Eliza would have her chance to mar his social reputation just as he'd besmirched hers.

She'd been half afraid that Vane would come to his senses, realise what an imposition it was, and fail to follow through with the plan. But he'd come, silent and brooding, and they'd rattled away the morning.

It hadn't rained in weeks, it seemed, and the dusty heat of the road made even talking seem an onerous task. Eliza had embroidered until even that had given her a headache, Aunt Mary had read and dozed, and ever since they'd stopped to switch horses at noon they'd all been content to jounce around in silence.

Next to Eliza, Aunt Mary gave a little snore and slumped more heavily against the far window. Now she couldn't even ask if her aunt would like to play cards.

Well, as she and the Duke had been given this little moment of privacy…

'Why married ladies?' Eliza asked, her voice breaking the quiet between them like shattering glass.

Vane slowly pulled his gaze from the window to Eliza's face. 'What kind of a question is that?'

'One of the more interesting ones, I expect. Unless you'd prefer me to talk about the weather?'

Vane glared at her, and Eliza spared a moment to wonder why she so enjoyed frustrating this big, powerful stranger. It went against all common sense—he held all the social and physical power in this situation—but she did enjoy shocking him.

'I don't have the faintest idea how you have passed yourself off as a wallflower for…how many Seasons, is it?'

'Six and a half,' said Eliza promptly.

'Shocking…'

He still seemed rather annoyed to be escorting her on this trip—but, then again, he'd been badgered into it. Some annoyance was to be expected.

'I'm held up as an example of proper behaviour,' said Eliza. 'Or at least, I was.'

'And you enjoyed that?' he asked.

No. Of course she hadn't. It had hurt to be held up as the ideal for dealing with disappointment and shattered domestic aspirations. Why was it that women were expected to deal with their disappointments graciously, while men could start whole wars over them?

In the distance, thunder rumbled, low and ominous.

'Of course I didn't,' said Eliza. 'Season after Season I watched other women get married and start families, and I was expected to smile and be gracious and hope that some man would settle for me. It's not that I didn't want to make friends, or to have some measure of success. I just wasn't...' She swallowed thickly. 'I suppose I wasn't pretty, or thin, or rich enough to fall in with my peers. And when they all started having children, the younger ladies treated me as though spinsterhood might be catching.'

'If you wanted a family, you should have thought of that before coming on this trip,' said Vane, his eyes oddly sad. 'Some rich man from trade would have been happy to take you. It would have meant marrying down, and perhaps another scandal, but you could have had children.'

Could have had children.

Past tense—as though her womb were as dead as her prospects.

'If I'm going to marry down, I might as well do it after embarrassing Abberly,' said Eliza. 'I'm not going to get caught.'

'Have you thought about what might happen afterwards?' Vane asked as the carriage rocked and the thunder rolled.

'My dowry is a piece of land somewhere in Brighton. I could go there and be comfortable enough. Maybe I could invite other scandalous women and we could all live together? Swilling tea and brushing cat hair off the furniture.'

She said it only half in jest. Truly, having a houseful of women who had also been cast off from Society sounded like a refuge. Eliza would no longer be on the outside of the group; she would have friends and confidantes.

'I suppose we should be glad we live in England now,' said Vane dryly. 'In the Middle Ages you would have been burned alongside the rest of this coven you're proposing.'

A burst of wind rocked the carriage, as though in agreement with the Duke.

Eliza felt herself grin. 'If you're trying to offend me, it isn't working.'

'Minx,' said Vane, smiling for the first time since they'd left London.

The first few raindrops plunked down on the roof of the carriage and Eliza smiled in relief. 'Maybe the storm will cool things off,' she said, peering out of the window.

'Is this what you want to talk about now?' Vane teased. 'The weather?'

'I am British,' said Eliza. 'We solve everything with a hot cup of tea and we spend our lives discussing the weather.'

'And that's what you plan to do?' Vane asked, his dark eyes impenetrable. 'Live in the country with a flock of fallen women, discussing the weather and drinking tea?'

'Or brandy,' said Eliza. 'I haven't decided.'

'Very well,' said Vane, pitching his voice so she could hear him over the pounding of the rain. 'And cake too, wasn't it?'

A familiar tension coursed through Eliza—a sudden physical awareness of her softness and how much space she inhabited. But it didn't seem necessary. Vane wasn't scoffing at her, or scolding her for enjoying sweet things. In fact, he sounded almost encouraging.

'Yes,' she said, tilting her nose into the air. 'Yes, it was. What about you?' she asked, emboldened by Vane's questions. 'Why haven't you begun work on your succession?'

Vane made a face. 'I have brothers, so there's not so much pressure—' he began.

Without warning, the carriage lurched to a grinding halt. Vane, riding in the backwards-facing seat, was pitched forward into Eliza. She had only the briefest impression of the weight of his body and the warm, soapy smell of his skin before he righted himself.

Eliza smoothed a hand over her collarbone. If she allowed herself to think about it, she could still feel the warmth of his hand as he'd caught himself against her.

'What in the world…?' Aunt Mary asked, righting herself and clinging to the leather strap with the other hand. 'Did we hit something?'

'Are you hurt?' Vane asked, now perched on the edge of the seat opposite Eliza. 'Did I—?'

'I'm perfectly fine,' said Eliza, though she was touched by his concern.

'I'll go and see what's happened,' said Vane, swinging out of the carriage, leaving Eliza and Aunt Mary in the gloom of the coach.

'I was having the most lovely nap,' said Aunt Mary, absently fixing a few hairpins. 'I have always loved the sound of the rain.'

Eliza nodded, wondering what was happening beyond the carriage walls. It wasn't bright enough to pull out her embroidery, and she didn't have a tinder box to use on the unlit lanterns hooked to the wall.

When she heard their trunks being handed down, Eliza gave up on waiting. She swung the door open and squinted into the driving rain.

'Rutted down in the mud, miss,' said the coachman, passing their trunks to the tiger, who stashed them on the grassy verge at the edge of the road.

'Yes,' said Eliza, looking down at the muddy morass that had once been a road, 'I can see that.'

Behind her, Aunt Mary muttered, 'Oh, dear…'

Vane appeared out of the rain. He'd lost his hat somewhere along the way, and his hair was slicked back sharply from his face. It only drew attention to the high planes of his cheekbones and the sharp angle of his jaw.

Not that Eliza was noticing.

'Get back inside the carriage,' he said, his eyes fierce.

'I'm already wet,' Eliza pointed out. 'And you need the carriage to lose as much weight as possible so the horses can pull us free.'

Vane stopped a few feet from Eliza. He was in mud nearly up to his knees, his shirt had gone translucent with rain, and his eyes were cold and angry.

Certainly Eliza's pulse was thundering with nerves, nothing more.

'Lower the step and I'll hop down,' said Eliza, trying to keep her voice cheery.

It wasn't *her* fault they were caught in the biggest storm of the summer… Except she *had* been the one to blackmail him into leaving London, today of all days.

'If you catch lung fever,' he said, taking her weight and swinging her out of the carriage and onto the verge, 'I'm taking us back to London and damn your revenge.'

For a moment it was all Eliza could do to blink up at him. He'd picked her up and spun her over the mud as he might a child, and had done it without even changing the pattern of his breathing. It was clear to anyone who saw him that he was tall and wonderfully built, but—

'Are you all right?' Vane asked, peering down at her.

Eliza's mouth went dry as he roughly pushed a sodden lock of hair back from his forehead. 'Fine,' she said, her voice embarrassingly squeaky. 'Just fine.'

Vane poked his head into the carriage to explain what was happening to Aunt Mary, before closing the carriage door and rounding the vehicle, going to the back, where he joined the coachman and the tiger.

A few moments later Eliza was surprised that her

now soaking dress wasn't steaming like a warm horse on a frosty morning. He'd put his shoulder to the carriage with the other two men, straining against the load while the horses stamped and pulled.

Eliza didn't know where to look first—except that wasn't quite true. She *should* look away, like a good spinster maiden. But, Lord help her, she didn't think she'd be able to avert her gaze for anything less than a rain of snakes.

Vane's breeches were plastered to thighs well-toned by riding and exercise. The muscles of his shoulders and arms bunched as he shoved at the carriage. His behind was no longer obscured by his coat, and his handsome, sharp jaw was set in furious determination.

Eliza held her breath, her heart pounding along with the drumming of the rain, as the carriage lurched. Of all the plays and dramatics she'd witnessed in her twenty-five years, Eliza had never been as captivated as she was by the performance in front of her now. The three men shoved, and one of the big bays nearly went to its knees, knocking the tiger off-balance as well.

Vane grunted and bared his teeth, and Eliza groped behind her for the top rail of the fence. Vane's preternatural attractiveness was a force to be reckoned with... Looking at him right, wet and labouring, was like trying to walk into a gale-force wind.

This was no gentle fancy...no internal registering of someone's fashion or pleasing face.

This was attraction, primal and urgent, and it couldn't have come at a less helpful time.

The carriage lurched again. The horses scrambled, the men strained, the wheels shifted—and something snapped.

Vane staggered back from the coach, turned his

flushed face up to the thundering sky, and proceeded to swear, softly and emphatically, mostly under his breath, before ending with, 'Of all the bloody, benighted, damned things to happen!'

Eliza must have made some kind of noise, because as the Duke's eyes snapped open he started walking— no, *stalking*—straight towards her. She hardly had time to make note of the curses.

'Get in the carriage,' he said through clenched teeth.

'Why?' asked Eliza, taking a step back from the man's pure, menacing fury.

She didn't think he would hurt her, but... Well, what did she really know about him? He certainly looked capable of violence.

He also looked *delicious*. Eliza wanted to lick the damp notch between his shadowy collarbones. And what a time for her to lose her mind—just before she could finally realise her revenge.

'Because the tiger and I are going to walk to the nearest village. I will find a conveyance there, rent it, and come back here. And then,' he said, stepping so close that she could smell the warmth of his skin, 'I will put you and your aunt in it, drive back to London, and try to forget that you ever wandered into my life.'

'Your Grace,' said Eliza, trying to maintain what little dignity she had left, 'you'll think much more clearly once you're dry and warm. Why don't we both walk to the next village, secure rooms, and discuss this reasonably?'

'Don't you "Your Grace" me,' said Vane, looming. His voice was pitched low, and all the more alluring for it. 'Don't think to trick me with the pretty manners you use on the rest of the world. You're a harridan in deep disguise. A skirted harpy. A silk-wrapped albatross.'

'That's still better than being a wallflower, *Your Grace*.' Eliza's usually bottomless patience was running quite short in the presence of this arrogant man. 'None of those creatures you name are boring. None of them will be told what to do.'

He growled. The man actually growled. And at his sides, his big hands clenched. 'Get. In. The carriage,' he said, his dark eyes snapping.

Eliza could feel a flush from her forehead to the centre of her decolletage. 'No.'

Without a word, Vane turned and started walking up the road. 'If you want to stand out in the rain until you die of lung fever, I won't stop you. Your aunt is the one responsible for your behaviour, not me.'

Eliza dashed to the door of the carriage. 'We're walking to the village,' she panted, dragging her valise off the seat and into her arms. 'The coachman will stay with the vehicle. Come on!' she urged, towing Aunt Mary out of the coach and onto the verge.

'Eliza!' Mary called, but it was too late.

This trip was Eliza's great rebellion, and she scurried after Vane's tall form. She had to convince him not to turn back for London now—especially since she knew he'd been reluctant to escort them in the first place.

They walked along in the pouring rain until the carriage was out of sight, with Aunt Mary and the tiger trailing along behind them. If not for the chafing of her soaked half-boots, Eliza wouldn't have thought it terribly unpleasant.

Better than sitting at home with no callers or invitations, thought Eliza, hiking up her valise a little higher. Better than wondering when her life would actually start.

'Why are you following me?' Vane had turned to watch her, with his hands on his narrow hips.

'I'm not following you, Your Grace,' said Eliza, marching right past him. 'I'm merely heading in the same direction.'

Maybe she shouldn't be antagonising him, but it seemed as though part of him enjoyed being challenged.

'And? You think to convince me to continue on this foolhardy journey?'

Absolutely.

That was why she'd dragged her beloved aunt out of the dry carriage and into the rain. She needed to convince the Duke before he worked himself up into such a state that he actually *did* send them home.

'I don't need to convince you,' lied Eliza. 'You can either continue to assist me or you can go back to London and face whatever scandal I can cause for you. But I *will* be going on, Your Grace. I am perfectly capable of hiring a carriage for Aunt Mary and myself. And, failing that, the postal coaches will come through eventually.'

Vane fell into step beside her, matching his longer strides to Eliza's, hampered as she was by her height and heavy, sodden skirts.

'You're serious about all this, aren't you?'

Eliza sent him a look that might have curdled milk. 'No, Your Grace, this has all been a grand lark. I'm quite content with my tiny life and ruined prospects. I am in positive delights about remaining a burden and a blot on my family name for time immemorial.'

Vane was quiet for a while as they walked along. Then, 'Why is this so important?' he asked. 'If you're caught, it will only make the scandal worse. Embarrassing Abberly will not save your family or your prospects. What's done is done.'

Eliza swiped a sodden, loose strand of hair away from her face. 'It's…'

How did she put it into words? How did she explain what utter powerlessness felt like to this man who was the embodiment of power in England?

'It's not about me—at least, not entirely. It's so much bigger. Abberly and men like him can go around ruining women and squandering fortunes and beating their horses and nobody blinks. Nobody *cares*. Do you know how that feels? To have about the same level of rights as a horse?'

'No,' said Vane. 'But men—gentlemen—should never treat their women like horseflesh. There are *rules*.'

'There are,' Eliza replied. 'There are rules for women. There are…' she searched for the right word '…guidelines, for men. Suggestions. And if they don't follow those guidelines, nothing will happen to them. Their stupid, venal, greedy lives go on.'

'So you're to make an example of Abberly?' said Vane, as though he were turning her plan this way and that. 'To show him that sometimes there will be consequences?'

'Yes,' said Eliza, angrily pushing her hair out of her face again.

She felt ugly like this—wet and angry and unkempt. She felt ugly in comparison to the Duke, who looked like an oil painting of a modern Poseidon, lord of the sea and everything he touched. And worse than feeling ugly—which had essentially become Eliza's routine state of being—she felt *silly*.

'You have cousins, don't you? Your uncle's heir and spare?'

'I have three cousins,' said Eliza. 'Helen, who is also

burdened with mere womanhood. And my aunt and uncle's two young sons, yes. They're aged nine and eleven.'

'Couldn't your family have…done something?'

'Done what?' asked Eliza. 'Don't you think I have considered all my options?'

'They could have done more than this!' said Vane, his face going red. 'Leaving you with me! Your uncle didn't even offer to bring you north!'

'Don't talk about my family like that,' said Eliza, rounding on him. 'They have loved me when I felt nobody else would!' She couldn't ask any more of them. 'I've already explained to you why you were—*are*—my best option.'

'That is quite possibly the saddest thing I've ever heard,' said Vane. 'I am the worst possible last resort.'

Eliza didn't care. She could make out smoke from a house now, and knew they couldn't be far from somewhere comfortable and dry.

'Look,' she said, gesturing ahead. 'We're almost there. Don't you want to dry off and find something hot to eat?'

Vane glowered at her before begrudgingly admitting, 'Yes.'

'As do I,' said Eliza. 'So let's find an inn, and have some tea, and discuss this like adults.'

'Fine,' said Vane, striding on ahead of her. 'But your stalling tactics won't work. I still intend to find a carriage and leave for London tonight.'

Chapter Six

She had no idea how much danger they'd been in.

That was all Gabriel could think as he roughly tow-elled himself dry in the small room of the coaching inn. Eliza had come leaping out of the carriage and into the rain with absolutely no thought of what might have gone wrong. She hadn't listened to a word he'd said, and it had never crossed her mind that in other circumstances the breakdown of their carriage might have been a trap.

It was the oldest trick in the highwayman's book: drop a tree across the road, or otherwise ensure that the carriage came to a stop. Once the vehicle was at a stand-still the highwayman—with or without his henchmen—would take charge of the horses, divest the passengers of their money and valuables, and *usually* let the vic-tims leave—without their dignity, but with their lives.

Best-case scenario.

Gabriel's family was unfortunately acquainted with precisely the very worst-case scenario for highway rob-bery gone wrong, and being trapped in a carriage fea-tured heavily in Gabriel's nightmares.

He couldn't believe he'd ever agreed to this plan. He must have lost his reason back in Lady Stanley's parlour: it was the only explanation for how he'd ended up not only responsible for two proper Society ladies, but escorting them in his carriage as well.

Now dry, back in his trousers and wrapped in a borrowed dressing gown, Gabriel couldn't help but think about the women—or, more specifically, the one wallflower in particular—in the room next door.

Gabriel stared at the innocent wooden door with dread and fascination. The innkeeper had given them adjoining rooms...

Eliza had marched up to the man, plunked down the requisite coin, and demanded two rooms, a bath and a meal. She'd been calm and self-assured, as though she travelled every day, and Gabriel's interest in her had only grown—much to his own frustration.

Now, if he held his breath and listened intently, he could just make out gentle, watery, bathing sounds from the room beyond. He would probably hear those gentle splashes in his dreams... No, in his nightmares. Frustrated, flesh-hued nightmares.

This trip had been one of his most foolish ideas. Not even a full day from London and Eliza had already been drenched by the rain and marched along miles of road. For all he knew she was next door contracting a terrible cold after the day's misadventure, and there was nothing he could do to stop it.

God only knew what trials awaited them if they kept on with this folly—and yet the thought of turning back to London filled him with dread, too.

'I am the worst possible last resort.'

His own words echoed back to him as he roughly dried his hair with the small, slightly frayed towel. He should be no one's last hope. He'd always been useless at dealing with a person's less tangible, more emotional needs. He'd proved that time and again. He should re-fuse to be a party to anything like that. It was the only responsible thing to do.

He *should* refuse…but he didn't want to. So here he was, having made himself responsible for the care of a loose cannon of a spinster and her middle-aged aunt, no matter the brevity of the commitment.

He was terrified something was going to go wrong, yes, but part of him was also enjoying it. It was the thrill of the unknown, and also the unlikely experience of someone seemingly having complete faith in him. She trusted him to get them to Yorkshire safely and with a minimum of fuss.

Theoretically, he could do just that.

A few moments later there were loud footsteps in the room next door—the maid removing the tub, most likely—followed by a steady thump on his door.

'Are you decent?'

Not one bit.

'Yes,' Gabriel called.

He immediately regretted it.

Eliza pushed open the door. She was back-lit by the fire in her chamber, and the doorway framed her like a painting—a naughty, erotic painting that Gabriel wouldn't mind hanging over his bed.

Her hair was down…long and dark and curling around her shoulders. Her face was flushed from the warmth of her bath. But neither of those things were particularly out of place. Oh, no. But the blasted woman was wearing nothing but too-tight trousers, a loose white shirt, and a fringed shawl that had to belong to her aunt.

'Where—?' he croaked. After swallowing hard, Gabriel tried again. 'Where did you get those?'

'The clothes in my valise were soaked,' said Eliza

airily, assessing Gabriel's room. 'So the innkeeper has loaned me these.'

'But the maid...?'

'Certainly her clothes wouldn't fit me,' said Eliza. 'The trousers are a bit odd, but the whole ensemble is rather comfortable. Far superior to a lady's stays.'

She looked like the better sort of Baroque painting. All glowing skin, voluptuous thighs and beautifully curved hips. She might not have been built for the slender, gauzy styles of today's fashions, but she had certainly been built for *him*. At least in Gabriel's opinion.

Finally those honey-gold eyes landed back on him. At the sight of *his* borrowed clothes, she added, 'I rather think I got the better end of the deal.'

Gabriel leaned back on the bed, letting the slightly worn blue dressing gown gape open over his chest. If she wanted to look at him, he'd be happy to allow it. After all, turnabout was fair play.

It was clearer than ever why Society would never allow women to stroll about in trousers: the city would grind to a halt within minutes. Every drover and hackney driver would run their wagons and carriages into buildings and one another out of sheer distraction. Her arse was so shapely...and the slightly translucent material of the shirt highlighted the gentle, unassisted curve of her waist.

Gabriel watched as Eliza's eyes slowly trailed over his form, and so focused was her attention that he could practically feel it like a caress. Her cheeks pinkened, her lips parted... And Gabriel had to think very hard about the smell of London in the summer. A cock-stand could only ruin the moment.

She just looked so damned intrigued...curious and luscious and ripe for the plucking.

But not by him, Gabriel reminded himself. Never by him. He didn't dally with innocents, he didn't spend time with his dependents, and he took every pain to ensure that he didn't acquire any more. Even agreeing to accompany Eliza this far was putting that final dictate in danger.

'Enjoying what you see?' Gabriel asked.

He had to clear his throat to get the words out. He'd been with so many women, in so many varied ways, and yet this rank novice, with soft curves and sharp eyes, had him fighting down an unwelcome erection.

Eliza gave him a hot look and a coy little shrug. 'Perhaps.'

'Did you have a reason for knocking?' he asked, unable to ignore the way candlelight pulled out the deep bronze tones of her hair.

'Supper has been brought up,' she said, sauntering back through the door to her room. 'I thought you'd be hungry.'

He was—although watching her arse in those trousers was inspiring a different kind of hunger entirely…

He got up and followed her, and when Eliza sat herself down without waiting for Gabriel's assistance he was both thankful and annoyed. Helping her to her seat would have given him an excellent chance to look down the gaping collar of her shirt.

'Good evening, Lady Stanley,' he said, nodding at Aunt Mary, who was already seated at the small round table.

'Good evening,' she said, pouring wine into his glass. 'I'm so sorry about your coach. Do you think it will take long to repair?'

'I have asked one of the men in the stables to ride down the road and help John Coachman,' said Gabriel, setting a slice of roast beef onto Eliza's plate before serving himself. 'We'll know in the morning if the wheel is serviceable.'

'And if it is repaired will you try to drag us back to London?' Eliza asked, spooning boiled carrots onto her plate.

That was the question Gabriel was asking himself. The venture had sounded entertaining and simple enough when he'd been perched in Lady Stanley's parlour: he was to escort a polite Society matron and her belligerently independent ward to a house party. It was a task that could be accomplished by nearly any wet-behind-the-ears young fop, and yet here he was, dubious as to his own abilities.

Eliza might go rogue and wander off into all sorts of unknown danger. Lady Stanley might take poorly. Their feelings might be hurt—that would be worse than all the other risks combined.

Hell. Gabriel hadn't been trained for this. He did rather like the idea of scooping Eliza up and dragging her off—but his attraction to her was another risk he hadn't foreseen. He'd previously found her appealing... pretty, in a cuddly sort of way, and admirable for the chin-up attitude with which she'd faced Society. But then he'd discovered her clever mouth and her round behind, and everything had changed.

'I haven't decided,' he told the women now, pouring water into Lady Stanley's glass, then Eliza's, and finally his own. 'It may not be advisable.'

'Do you have any particular concerns, Your Grace?' asked Eliza, cutting her meat into small, polite bites.

Gabriel pointed his fork at her in accusation. 'You're doing it again—but you can't fool me.'

'Doing what?'

'Wearing your wallflower disguise.'

Lady Stanley snorted, and then covered that faux pas with a sip of her wine.

Eliza huffed and looked up at him with exasperation. 'I *am* a wallflower. I am quiet and boring and everything Society wants me to be. You're the only one who doesn't believe it, Your Grace.'

Lady Stanley coughed.

'Other than my family,' Eliza amended.

'Gabriel,' he said, leaning back in his chair. 'My name is Gabriel. I'm inviting both of you to use it.'

He could practically see her thoughts playing out across her face: she wanted to argue with him, though she was tempted to invite him to use *her* name, but most of all she wanted to convince him to continue on their journey north.

'Eliza,' she said.

'And I'm Mary, just as I've told you before,' her aunt said, spooning more potatoes onto his plate.

'The trip will be long and uncomfortable,' Gabriel warned.

'Like every ball I've ever attended,' said Eliza cheerfully, taking a bite of carrot.

'If we run into more trouble—highwaymen or wild animals—you need to do as I say.' He was fencing with spectres, and they all knew it. The decision was as good as made...

He only hoped it wouldn't come back to haunt him.

Lady Stanley gave him a sharp look. He wondered how much she knew...how much of his tragedy had become common knowledge.

'I'll agree to that—but only because I think the likelihood of meeting wild animals on the Great North Road is deeply unlikely,' said Eliza, soldiering on.

She was laughing at him, the little harridan. Her eyes were twinkling, and her lips were quirked, and Gabriel caught himself wanting to kiss the expression right off her silly, smug face.

'I simply want you to know what you're getting yourselves into,' he said. 'I won't be held responsible if you're savaged by badgers.'

Or worse.

There, on her own head be it.

Mary leaned back in her chair, watching the conversation with apparent relish. 'Badgers are nocturnal, dear. You should be more concerned about snakes. Or maybe rams. They butt quite aggressively.'

'I don't see why you're making such a fuss about this trip,' said Eliza, taking a sip of her wine. 'I need you for your knowledge of the roads, your carriage, and your ability to keep a secret. The trip should cost you nothing but time.'

Why *he* was making such a fuss?

'You make me sound like an elderly aunt who deplores travel but refuses to be left at home.'

'Well…' said Eliza, smiling down at her plate. 'You said it, not I.'

At this point Mary was openly grinning. He'd walked into that one. He liked her clever mouth and secret smirks: he liked *her*. And she was telling the truth, wasn't she? She truly didn't need him to care for her, or to reassure her, or to smooth her way. She didn't want him around for his prestige or his title or his dukedom. She wanted— Well, *him*. A man who could be trusted with a secret and wouldn't try to force her to marry him at the end of this adventure.

He could enjoy this. He *would* enjoy this.

Had he ever spent time with a woman purely for the

pleasure of her company? It didn't seem likely. What a novel trip this could turn out to be.

'It would be a shame to miss out on seeing Abberly brought down a peg or three,' said Gabriel, rocking his chair back onto two legs.

'So you'll do it?' Eliza asked.

She was talking over Mary, who commented, 'I quite agree, Your Grace.'

'We'll press on,' said Gabriel, loving the way his words made Eliza's face light up.

He knew a moment of terror—so many things could go wrong!—but ignored it. He couldn't let old fears dictate this aspect of his life any more. Eventually he'd have to travel with his mother and sister, or with his future wife. This would be good practice for that.

'Thank you,' said Eliza, practically bouncing in her seat. 'You won't regret it.'

'But Abberly will,' said Gabriel, raising his glass in a toast. 'To justice.'

'To vengeance,' said Eliza, lifting her own glass.

'To holidays!' said Mary, her eyes twinkling.

They all finished their last mouthfuls of the wine that had been served with their dinner. 'Well,' said Gabriel, rising to his feet, 'if we're to do a proper job of this, it's time for your first lesson.'

'Lesson in what?' Eliza asked, pulling the shawl more tightly around her shoulders.

'Freedom! Living life to its fullest! Just as we discussed during our dance.'

'Eliza, you didn't tell me any of this,' said Aunt Mary.

Eliza blushed. 'It was just a conversation,' she muttered.

'You had a list, I believe?' said Gabriel, knowing full well that they both remembered her heated little speech.

'Eating cake in public, drinking brandy, and trying your hand at a proper game of cards—was that it?'

'You know it was,' said Eliza, glancing at Mary.

'Then tonight's lesson in rakish about-towning will cover one of my favourites: brandy.'

'That would be just the thing after a wet day,' said Mary, covering the dinner dishes and setting their plates aside.

This close to London, many of the taverns kept a few prized bottles of brandy stashed away, in case the gentry came calling. It wasn't as fine as what he kept at home, but it would do, and it had warmed him up nicely while Eliza had her bath.

He fetched the bottle and returned to the women.

'Brandy is rarely consumed at the dinner table,' he said, dragging his chair over to the fireplace, where two rather worn armchairs awaited him. 'We must away to the fire.'

'Of course,' said Mary, giving him a teasing curtsey as he guided her to her seat.

'I can see this is going to be a serious business,' said Eliza, splaying her hands on her thighs. 'Yet you gentlemen always make drunkenness look so simple.'

'A gentleman is never drunk!' said Gabriel theatrically, rinsing out their wine glasses and pouring a measure of brandy into each. 'He has merely over-imbibed. Gentlemen can be tipsy, sloshed, wrecked, three sheets to the wind, pissed, plastered, and entirely off their heads, but they are never drunk.'

'Hear, hear!' said Mary, graciously accepting her glass from Gabriel.

Eliza smiled serenely up at him as she took her own. 'Then what were you two years ago, at Lady Hampton's masquerade ball, when you ripped away Lord Warren's headpiece to prove he wasn't actually a minotaur?'

Gabriel winced. 'All of the aforesaid. But once again I have to observe that you've been keeping awfully close track of me. Maybe when we return to London I can hire you to maintain my social calendar. You'd likely know it better than I do.'

Eliza waved her hand airily, as though his concerns could be brushed away like dust motes. 'I might need a position…but certainly not as a procurer for the ladies of the *ton*.'

A spluttering noise came from Aunt Mary, who dabbed at her watering eyes with the corner of a handkerchief. 'Eliza!' she said. 'You really shouldn't say such things. At least not when I have a mouth full of brandy,' she added after a pause.

Gabriel wanted to applaud. No governess could have so ruthlessly set him in his place. Eliza in full steam was magnificent. Her plain gowns and proper demeanour hid a mind that could fire back rebuttals more efficiently than most members of Parliament.

'Point gloriously made,' he said. 'But you've distracted me from our purpose here this evening. Lesson one: never gulp your brandy. These aren't quite the right glasses, but you should cup the bowl like this, and gently swirl the brandy, letting it warm to the temperature of your skin.'

Eliza watched him carefully and mimicked his motions. On Gabriel's other side Lady Mary sipped her brandy like a stately old man who'd long held the custom.

'Is this where we talk about the weather and complain about our spouses?' Eliza asked, her voice accompanied by the gentle crackle of the fire. 'I assume that's what the gentlemen do while they drink their brandy after the ladies have removed to the drawing room.'

'Quite likely,' said Vane. 'Or they discuss the latest horse race, or any interesting bets placed on the book at White's. What do you ladies talk about after you withdraw?'

'It depends on the kind of lady you are,' said Eliza, and Mary made a noise of agreement. 'Sometimes it's innocent enough. Dresses and dances, and how everyone's relatives are getting on. Sometimes we drop hints to each other about you lot. Lord So-and-So is particularly lecherous tonight. Mr Someone is smarting from a failed courtship and took it out on the lady next to him at dinner. And sometimes we discuss books and plays and the weather—just like you.'

Gabriel couldn't stop himself. 'Have you ever discussed me?'

Eliza blushed, which fascinated Gabriel no end. How far did her blush go? Did it match the colour of her nipples, or was the flush of warmth over her skin of a rosier hue?

Mary made a noise that, had it come from anyone else, Gabriel would have called a snigger. 'Why don't you withdraw with us next time and find out?' she asked.

'I believe I can live with my curiosity,' Gabriel replied. 'I hadn't realised you ladies have a…a spy ring of information.'

No wonder Eliza remembered so much about his various activities. He hoped his past bed mates had kept at least a few of the details to themselves: it was disquieting to imagine one's amatory efforts being casually discussed over tea and biscuits.

A look passed between Mary and Eliza, and Gabriel

could feel that the tone in the room had shifted, but he wasn't sure where he'd gone wrong. Blast it—this was why he didn't socialise with women. He always said the wrong thing, hurt their feelings, and could do nothing but make it worse if he attempted to make amends.

'What did I say?' Gabriel asked.

'What would you have us do?' Eliza asked, looking into her brandy. 'Let each other get pinched and teased and set down by you "gentlemen" with no warning?'

'No,' said Gabriel, taking an unthinking swallow of his own drink. 'Maybe you should start a circular. Call it *Fashion Plates Monthly* and rest assured that none of us would ever open it.'

'I didn't take you for a revolutionary, Your Grace,' said Mary, leaning back in her seat.

'I quite like your imagination,' said Eliza.

Oh, if only she knew.

'Secret lady printers…skulking through the dark. But in the meantime—am I meant to be holding this brandy, Gabriel, or drinking it?'

The sound of her saying his name passed through him like a blessing…like a curse. When was the last time he'd heard his given name from an attractive woman's lips? Perhaps when he'd seen Lady Gorsing for the Christmas holiday…

The brandy. That was how all this had started in the first place.

'Once you've warmed it through, take a small sip. Don't gulp it, but don't hold it on your tongue either. Most good brandy will have a sharp, smoky taste, but the finish is a little like wine.'

Eliza swallowed and made a face. 'It's hard to imagine that anyone would enjoy drinking enough of this to become plastered, sloshed or pissed.'

Gabriel settled into his seat and stretched his legs out towards the fire. 'Give it a moment.'

The silence that encompassed them was warm and companionable. Gabriel found himself relaxing into the heat of the fire and the quiet of the women's presence. Eliza was witty and clever, and more than a little alluring, but Gabriel didn't feel the need to fill this silence between them to prevent the moment from turning awkward or ripe with tension. It simply felt right.

'It does get better as you go,' said Eliza, her voice low and smooth. 'It's not particularly tasty, but one does get a lovely warm tingle.'

Gabriel topped up his own glass, poured a refill for Mary's, and added a drop to Eliza's as well.

'Just the thing for a body caught in the rain,' said Mary, still idly watching the flicker of the fire.

Not that Eliza looked as though she'd been caught in a storm just hours previously, he thought. Her skin was pink from the liquor and the warmth of the fire. Her hair shone like polished oak, and where the ends had dried it was beginning to curl. Her posture was relaxed without her stays, and she looked...*well*. Very well indeed.

Eliza swirled her drink contemplatively. 'Who taught you to drink brandy?' she asked.

'My father taught me to drink it,' said Gabriel. 'My schoolfriends taught me to hold it.'

Eliza murmured a soft acknowledgement.

'My father—I still think of him as the Duke, most days—took my older brother Matthew and I aside one evening after dinner. He'd noticed the decanter was suspiciously empty, and he told us that if we were going to be drinking anyway, we might as well learn to do it properly. And then he sat us down in the library and poured us our first paternally approved brandy.'

'He sounds like a patient man,' said Eliza, taking another slow sip.

'He was,' said Gabriel, staring into the fire. 'Patient and fair. You'd have liked him.'

And every day I feel a little more as if I'm letting him down.

Eliza rocked her glass back and forth, occasionally sneaking glances at him from the corner of her eye. Mary peacefully took sips of her own glass and seemed content to watch the fire, letting the conversation move at its own pace.

'You said your brother Matthew was older...'

It was phrased like a statement, but Gabriel understood it for the question it was.

'Yes,' said Gabriel shortly. 'I was fifteen. There was an accident.'

As much as opportunistic murder could be considered an accident.

But he wouldn't think of it now—not when brooding might make him lose his nerve all over again.

'It was tragic,' said Mary quietly. 'Your poor mother...'

Eliza nudged him, her soft fingers briefly resting over Gabriel's sleeve. 'I'm so sorry. I think your father would be proud of you now. Just look at you...passing his lessons on to strange women.'

It was just the right thing to say—sincere and light-hearted at the same time. But Gabriel found it too much...too dissonant with the inside of his own head.

He knocked back the rest of his brandy—breaking his own 'no gulping' rule—and rose to his feet, suddenly itching to be away from Eliza's presence.

Who was she to say that his father would be proud of him? She hadn't met him. Or perhaps she was too restful. He was finding himself thinking of things he hadn't pondered in years, and then blaming her for it.

'I've taken up too much of your evening. My thanks for your company. Enjoy the rest of your drink with my blessing.'

'Goodnight,' said Mary, giving Gabriel a look that once more reminded him why he didn't socialise with nice women. They were *observant*.

'Thank you for the lesson,' said Eliza, looking up at him with a little furrow between her brows.

'Goodnight,' said Gabriel, stepping back into his own room and closing the adjoining door with a solid click.

As he unknotted his cravat and peeled off his coat he couldn't help but reflect on where he was once more: staring at a door, all the while contemplating what lay beyond it. He was tempted to push a chair under the doorknob, but that wouldn't help. It wasn't as though a barricade could keep out his thoughts of her.

And thoughts of Eliza—and of the past—were the danger that Gabriel had never seen coming.

Chapter Seven

At least, Eliza thought, Gabriel had the decency to look guilty.

'Ah…' he said, modulating his voice and making it a little lower. 'Should have warned you about this.'

'Never again…' said Eliza, closing her eyes.

Breakfast had taken care of most of the vague nausea she'd woken with, but thus far her headache had only grown.

'I will never let you serve me another drink. How do you make it go away?'

'Food, tea, or more of what ails you,' said Aunt Mary, patting Eliza's knee.

Vane tipped his flask towards her helpfully.

Eliza shuddered and pushed it away. 'No, thank you.'

Vane frowned at her, a little divot forming between his eyebrows. 'I truly didn't think that two glasses of brandy would do this.'

Eliza closed her eyes and tipped her head back to rest against the curved wall of the jolting carriage. That position only made her head pound more insistently, so she forced her neck up.

'I had another after you left—it was early, and there wasn't anything else to do.'

'Ah… The third glass. The first is a little tingly, so you have another. The second makes everything feel distant and warm. And the third…'

'The third is toxic,' said Eliza, pinching the bridge of her nose tightly.

'You poor thing,' said Gabriel, sounding disgustingly cheerful. 'You never forget your first.'

'First drink?'

'First hangover. Matthew and I were spectacularly sick behind the stables our first time. We'd found the stable master's gin bottle, and to this day I can't stomach the smell of gin without gagging.'

'Please…' said Eliza, as close to begging as she'd come in her adult life. 'Please, no more talk of gagging.'

'My apologies,' said Vane, and then, blessedly, was quiet.

They jounced down the road, and Eliza swore never to touch the demon drink again. It was hard to believe that men went out and imbibed the stuff on purpose.

At noon they stopped to change horses, and Vane jumped out to stretch his legs. The bright sunshine only threatened Eliza's head still further, so she curled up as best she could on the narrow bench seat, thankful that for the moment the conveyance was still.

'All right,' said Vane when he returned. 'Up you get.'

'What?' Eliza asked, slitting one eye open.

Vane waited at the carriage door while she dragged herself upright, and then presumed to take the forward-facing seat next to her.

And when Aunt Mary arrived with cheese sandwiches, did she voice a complaint about this newest of Vane's ventures into impropriety? No. She merely tucked a sandwich into Eliza's lap and took the rear-facing seat with a cheerful expression.

'Here,' said Vane, propping her up and passing her a small corked jug.

'I can't,' said Eliza, trying to press it back to him.

Vane sighed, reached around Eliza, and flicked open the earthenware bottle.

A gentle, welcome smell trailed up to Eliza's nose.

'Peppermint tea?' she asked, taking a tentative sip.

It was cold and fresh, and suddenly it was all Eliza could do not to guzzle the whole thing down in one go.

'Oh, thank you. Thank you so much.'

Vane looked almost *pained* at her thanks. 'I felt slightly responsible for your predicament,' he said.

With a lurch, the carriage rolled into motion.

'It was my own fault,' said Eliza, daring to look at Aunt Mary's cheese sandwich. The crust was firm and the centre of the bread looked soft. It didn't immediately turn Eliza's stomach, which she took as a good sign. 'I was adventurous. Like Icarus, I flew too close to the sun.'

Gabriel looked amused. 'That was where you were adventurous? Not turning your back on Society or wearing trousers to the dinner table?'

'No, those things I don't regret. It was the hubris of drinking without counting that was my downfall.'

Although in truth, she hadn't thought those decisions through either. All of them had seemed like a good idea at the time.

'She gets quite tragic when she's ill,' said Aunt Mary, pulling out a book and turning to the ribboned page. 'I think she read too many Greek myths as a child.'

It took everything in Eliza to keep from sticking her tongue out at her aunt.

Beside her, Vane nodded gravely. 'I quite understand. My younger sister went through a Shakespearian stage, and to this day she starts speaking in couplets when she's well and truly furious.'

'It could be iambic pentameter,' said Mary, settling more firmly into her seat. 'That's much worse.'

'What about you?' Eliza asked, not willing to be the sole target of this gentle teasing. 'How did you entertain yourself on rainy days when you were a boy?'

The Duke eyed her before shaking his head and capitulating. 'Beowulf,' he said, his voice filled with resignation. 'Matthew and I would fight over who would be Beowulf and who would be the dragon.'

'Eliza broke the spine of *The Odyssey* exactly where Odysseus is reunited with Penelope,' said Aunt Mary, continuing to pretend to read her book.

Eliza gasped. How could her aunt do this to her? 'You're the one who dog-eared *Memoirs of Emma Courtney*!'

Vane shook with silent laughter next to her. 'Dare I ask about the works of our lovely Miss Austen?'

'You dare *not*,' said Eliza, thankful that she had left her treasured copy of *Sense and Sensibility* at home. If he found her dog-eared copy, she would simply have to change her name and move out of the country.

Vane held up his hands in mock surrender. 'I'll leave Mr Darcy in your capable hands,' he said with a wink.

Eliza huffed, faux annoyed, and relaxed into the rocking of the carriage. The storm had chased away the worst of the summer heat, so the day was pleasantly warm, and the last of her headache had faded away.

They fell into a comfortable silence, listening to the rhythmic rattle of the carriage and the occasional snort from the horses. Green hills and stone fences were rolling past the windows, and she thought it was the sort of late summer day that children dreamed of: warm and overflowing with possibilities.

It was only when Eliza's chin hit her chest that she realised she was nodding off. Mary appeared to be doing the same on the seat opposite, though she'd wedged herself into the corner and had one leg stretched out the length of the seat.

Suddenly, with Mary asleep, Vane's presence seemed to fill the carriage. It was easy to forget that he was such a tall man—the vehicle had been built for him, with the man's dimensions taken into account. But now, despite the plushness of the seats and the added height of the enclosed space, it suddenly seemed cramped.

Eliza was mentally alone with him, seated so close that she could very nearly feel the heat of his body.

No, she wasn't just close…she was touching him, half slumped against him as she dozed again, lured in by his stability and his heat. When she managed to wake herself up she would be mortally embarrassed, she was sure of it. What an imposition she was, flopping onto him like an overly familiar hound…

'Sorry,' she mumbled.

'Come on,' said Vane.

And then his big hand was tilting her shoulder towards his own…and her cheek fitted so nicely against the extra-fine wool of his coat. This was the most time she'd ever spent in close proximity to a man, and she thought perhaps they were good for something other than escorting one about the ballroom. He smelled lovely—like bergamot and orange soap—and resting against him like this was just the thing to cut down on the jolting of the carriage.

As Eliza's eyes fell closed once more she finally put words to this sensation: she felt comfortable and safe.

And, considering how she'd ended up in this situation, that was a very novel sensation indeed.

Gabriel had had every intention of staying as far away from Eliza as possible for the remainder of the evening. He'd grown too comfortable with her curvy little body resting against him so trustingly. The scent of her hair had been an incessant torture in the still air of the coach. With his luck he'd associate the smell of lilac soap with Eliza for the rest of his natural life.

In all his thirty-one years, Gabriel had never spent this much time with a woman who wasn't a close blood relative. He hadn't wanted to. He chose to spend his time with lonely wives and merry widows—the kind of women who knew how to conduct a proper affair. They played their games, and had their fun, and could expect a kiss on the cheek and a pinch on the behind as he donned his hat and headed for the door.

As he rolled through the Midlands with Eliza's head on his shoulder, the transactional nature of those other encounters began to make Gabriel uncomfortable. He hadn't wanted to spend any time with those women with their clothes on, nor to hold a conversation with them as equals. Oh, he'd talked to them—he wasn't a heartless cad—but he'd been careful to keep their talk to the opera, or recent public debates, or innocent stories of families and children and light-hearted blunders. Any discussion of one's deepest hopes and dreams would have been out of the question.

Here, with Eliza, he was enjoying the presence of her company even while she slept. That knowledge was cloying—like a cravat that had been knotted too tightly. He'd get out of the damn coach, escort her to her room at the next inn, and then… He didn't know what he'd do. He only knew it wouldn't involve Eliza.

The Crofton Fair put a stop to any plans.

Small booths and canvas canopies spilled out of the village in all directions. The air smelled of food, the streets hummed with laughter and haggling and humanity, and there was absolutely no way the carriage could make it through the press of people gathered in the road.

'Are we there?' Eliza asked, suddenly jerking awake beside him.

A few little wisps of hair were sticking out from her head, and Gabriel was reminded of a startled barn kitten who hadn't set its fur to rights.

'In Yorkshire?' he asked, amused. 'Not likely. Some village is holding a fair, and I don't think there's any getting around it. Not until early tomorrow, quite probably.'

Eliza had her nose very nearly pressed to the glass of the window. 'Can we attend? Do you think there's room at the inn?'

Gabriel laughed, and gently nudged Mary awake. 'Where there's money to be made, innkeepers tend to find a way.'

Eliza beamed at him, and Gabriel tried and failed to ignore the pleasure he took from her joy. She was simply so easy to please, that was all. Surely that was it. A kind word here, a human gesture there, and she beamed at him as though presented with jewels. It made him want to see what she'd do with other gifts. How would she look if he brought her flowers? Or ribbons? Or leaned in to give her a kiss?

But those were thoughts for another time. His first order of business was to secure them a room. Second? To see what kind of mischief Eliza could get up to at the fair.

Chapter Eight

Eliza stood outside the inn, absorbing the giddy air of frivolity and joy that surrounded her. The breeze carried the smell of savouries and sugar, the twilight hummed with conversation and laughter, and around her dust motes spun in the golden light of evening as lanterns were lit and everything looked gilded with honey and bronze.

There was simply only one problem: no matter how long they stayed, Eliza would never be able to experience it all.

'Now,' said Gabriel, swinging his arms at Aunt Mary and Eliza with a roguish grin. 'I have two lovely ladies accompanying me and the night is young. What shall we do first?'

'I want to do everything,' said Eliza, watching as a sideshow performer contorted himself though smaller and smaller hoops. 'I couldn't possibly choose.'

'The maid at the inn said this fair started as an annual cheese festival,' said Mary. 'If I'd known about that, I'd have dragged Lord Stanley out of London a bit more forcefully.'

'The cheesemongers it is,' said Vane cheerfully, and set off through the crowds.

Eliza allowed herself a moment to enjoy her place on Vane's arm. Just this one moment—and then she'd remember that this was at best temporary, and at worst something she'd never be able to acknowledge again after the house party was over and everyone had returned to London. But for now she would enjoy the ease of Gabriel's company, and the way he stood a head taller than most of the crowd; easily navigating them through the throngs of people shopping and haggling and chatting together.

There was a silversmith with a portable forge, and a weaver selling wicker baskets. One man was roasting early hazelnuts, and a woman had fine soaps for sale. And spread throughout were stalls selling every shape and colour of cheese.

'This is the one,' said Aunt Mary, breaking off a morsel to give to Eliza.

Eliza made a face. 'You know I don't like blue cheeses, Aunt. They smell so awful.'

'But they taste wonderful.'

Vane, for his part, had politely sampled one or two of the cheeses before declaring himself hungry for *real* food and buying a meat pasty from one of the many tables they'd passed on their wandering.

Mary had acquired a flagon of small cider, which she and Eliza shared between them, and Vane seemed oddly content with his pint of summer ale. He'd lingered over the leatherworker's table, and Aunt Mary had been quite taken with the display from the Staffordshire Potteries. Eliza, though, had been able to resist those goods with nary a temptation.

It was the currant buns that got her. She smelled them before she saw them—all cinnamon and butter and sugar, floating in the air like fairy magic, guaranteed to lead her astray. The three of them had made it into the heart of the pretty stone village now, where bunting criss-crossed the alleys and was draped over doorways and windows. More lanterns had been lit, and somewhere ahead some musicians were tuning up. Mary was haggling over embroidery thread nearby, and Eliza couldn't help but drift over to the bakery table, where round baskets displayed pies and pastries.

'One bun for a penny, miss,' said the woman working at the table, deftly wrapping two meat pies for her current customer.

Eliza debated, pretending to look at the sugar biscuits. A penny was a terrible price for one bun, but all the prices seemed to be inflated for the fair. Plus it *was* bigger than her palm, and the currants looked sticky and delicious.

'All right,' she said, passing over the coin and tucking her gloves into her pockets. 'One of the buns.'

She was practically tingling with excitement as the bun was placed on a square of paper and passed across the table to her. It was still warm on the bottom, and the sugar glaze had run down into the cinnamon-filled spiral of dough.

'You're looking at that bun as if you've never seen one before,' said Vane, appearing out of the crowd.

Eliza held her treat more closely to her body, out of sheer instinct. 'Never one this big,' she admitted. It could be used as a tea saucer.

'Worthy of the fair indeed,' said Vane, taking his place by her side as they wandered down the street.

Aunt Mary had moved on to yet another cheese vendor, where she appeared to be conversing quite passionately about goats. The vendor had brought one of her goats along, and every so often she had to nudge its head away from the table, her coin purse, and the rope with which it was tethered.

Vane and Eliza found an empty spot on the opposite side of the road and waited for Aunt Mary to finish.

'What's next?' she asked, taking a reasonable and ladylike bite of her confection. It tasted of butter and spices and practically melted on her tongue. It was all she could do not to moan.

Vane clicked open his pocket watch and then shrugged. 'We discover what is at the opposite end of the street or we head back to the inn. Someone mentioned there was a man with a ferret. I'm not sure if that was supposed to be a warning or an invitation.'

'It depends on the man. And the ferret,' said Eliza around another mouthful of sticky-sweet bun and currants.

Vane tipped his pint glass towards her. 'Are you sure you don't want a taste?'

Eliza wrinkled her nose. 'No. I am just starting to feel human again.' The sticky bun was helping that along nicely.

Vane grinned down at her. 'You won't be able to resist for long. No young buck—or young lady, in this case—can resist curiosity for long once they've tasted freedom.'

'It wasn't freedom I tasted,' said Eliza. 'It was perfidy.'

He laughed, and Eliza felt warmth welling in her chest. Why couldn't the other men of the ton be like this? Vane was so easy-going and unpretentious. It didn't matter that she was...well, *her*. He seemed to like her well enough anyway.

Someone rounded the corner while talking over his

shoulder and nearly crashed into Eliza, tripping over Vane's shoes as he went.

'Sorry, there,' said the stranger, righting his pint of ale before straightening up and looking at the Duke. 'Vane? Is that you?'

'Hello, Robertson,' said Vane, brushing spilled ale from his trouser leg. 'I didn't expect to see you here.'

'I was travelling north and caught wind of this lovely little affair. Joffrey is around here somewhere… We decided we'd stop and see what fun there was to be had.'

This Robertson fellow looked vaguely familiar to Eliza. He had to be in Society one way or another, so she'd likely have met him. Lord Robertson, heir to the Earl of Something-or-Other.

He looked over at her, slowly perusing her straw bonnet, rumpled travelling dress and plain face. Eliza wanted to kick him in the shin.

'Not your usual type,' said Robertson, dismissing Eliza and turning back to Vane. 'But I see you've found your own sort of fun—though she isn't worth leaving London for.'

She was standing next to him! Did he think women were deaf?

No, of course he didn't. He thought that women were powerless to do anything about his boorish behaviour, and he was right.

Eliza took an aggressive bite of her bun, silently daring the man to turn his head and make eye contact with her.

'Wait a moment,' he said, whipping around to look at Eliza again. 'You're the Mad Maid! Half of London is wondering where you have gone.'

'The *Mad Maid*?' repeated Eliza, offended and worried as to the origin of that nickname.

Robertson waved a hand dismissively. 'You were all the talk at the clubs…only nobody could remember your name. The Mad Maid seemed to fit.' He turned back to Vane. 'I see the appeal now. The mad ones are always the best in bed.'

Eliza spluttered, but no words came out. How dared he assume she was caught up in some affair with—with Vane? Not that Vane wasn't handsome—he was—but… She was getting off topic. How dared he imply she was mad?

Vane looked surprised by his friend's drunken forwardness, flicking his gaze from Eliza to Robertson and back again. Eliza looked away, studying the pattern of the brickwork on the building next door. This was where Vane would laugh awkwardly, agree with his friend, and try to pretend the whole incident had never happened.

She was still holding half her bun, though she'd lost interest in it now. How pathetic would that be? Standing in the corner, quietly eating her pastry, while two Society bachelors stood by and talked about her supposed madness.

She'd never live it down.

'It isn't like that,' said Vane, and Eliza's attention snapped to his face. 'Eliza and her aunt required an escort, and I needed a break from London's smoke.'

When he reached for her, hooking her arm through his own, Eliza was so shocked she stood by and watched as though it was happening to an entirely different woman.

'We're friends, Robertson. Spending time with a woman is a novel distraction. You should try it.'

And then, while Eliza was still agog over his casual declaration of friendship, he steered her out into the street and steered them over to Aunt Mary, who had finally completed whatever transaction and/or bonding ritual she'd been conducting with the goatherd.

'Ready to press on?' she asked, unaware of the tension that had followed Vane and Eliza across the street. 'I heard there's dancing up ahead.'

'Of course,' said Vane, offering Aunt Mary his other arm. 'Onwards.'

As Vane led them towards the sound of fiddle music, Eliza felt as if she might float away without Vane's heavy arm to anchor her. When had anyone defended her like that? And so simply! He'd declared them friends, cut off the odious man, and walked away.

'Are you all right?' he asked quietly as they skirted a group of women buying cut flowers.

'Yes,' she said, smiling up at him. Probably he hadn't expected Eliza to be grinning like a fool, but she simply couldn't help it.

One of those bold, nearly black eyebrows rose. 'Why are you smiling at me like that?'

'Smiling about what?' Aunt Mary asked as they walked into the village square. 'Oh, how lovely. Eliza, you simply must dance.'

'I will if you dance too, Aunt,' she replied, thankful for the change in conversation. It wouldn't do to dwell on the way Gabriel made her feel.

The square was bedecked with bunting and flags, and lanterns hung overhead and in every doorway. Tapers sat in glass jars all around the central flower planter at the heart of the square, and on the far side an overturned wagon had been turned into an impromptu stage for a fiddler and a hand-drummer. An upright pianoforte had been carried outside, and together they were cheerfully playing fast-paced country dances.

In Eliza's eyes it was better than any ball she'd ever attended. Couples of every age and class were dancing together, dressed in everything from mended canvas work clothes to their Sunday best. Two laughing women were dancing together near the centre of the square, and a handful of school-aged children had formed a chain and were whirling around on the outskirts of the dancers.

It wasn't about status, or being seen, or presenting only one's best features. It was joyous, and shared, and *fun*.

A short man in a vicar's collar, with laughter lines around his eyes, walked up to Aunt Mary, gave her a flourishing bow, and asked her to dance. She laughed and accepted, and suddenly it felt as though Eliza was very much alone with the tall man at her side.

'Do you dance?' Eliza asked, taking one of his big hands in hers.

She wasn't wearing her gloves and neither was he. They'd munched on the food for sale as they'd wandered through the stalls and booths, and neither had bothered to don them again. She'd never done this before—touched a man bare-handed. It suddenly seemed more intimate than any conversation or dance could possibly be.

His hand was warm, and slightly rougher than her own. His knuckles were heavier than hers, and Eliza spared a thought to wonder how they'd feel interlocked with her own fingers. For now she would enjoy the sensation of pressing palm to palm, lifeline to lifeline.

'You know I dance,' said Vane, looking down at her severely.

No matter. His brooding mood wouldn't bring her down—not this night. Maybe he was put out that his friend had seen them together…or maybe he was regretting coming on this trip with her entirely.

But now, in this one warm, sugared moment, it didn't matter. Someone had defended her unequivocally—even if he did regret it. No polite avoidance, no uncomfortable laughter, no abrupt change of topic. No. He saw her. For that one moment at least, Vane had seen her as a person—one worthy of respect.

'I didn't know if dukes learned country dances,' said Eliza, taking another bold step closer to him.

She could smell the warmth of his body now. That bergamot and soap smell she'd come to associate with him. They were standing too close for propriety—but then, they'd left that behind when Eliza had shoved her way, unchaperoned, into his library.

Around them couples were starting to dance, leaving Eliza and Vane as a still, quiet island in a sea of revelry. Vane held Eliza's eyes for a moment too long. Maybe…

But she wouldn't torment herself with maybes. She was Eliza, a ruined wallflower, and he was a duke. Those things were immutable.

Chapter Nine

Eliza and Vane stood on the edge of the village square as music silvered the air and couples whirled. 'Do dukes learn country dances?' Vane scoffed, before stepping confidently into the dance, guiding Eliza along with him. He didn't miss a beat, quickly and easily moving them through the throng of dancing bodies. 'Of course I have learned country dances,' he said, his tone almost scolding. 'Every boy who finds himself infatuated with a barmaid learns them—though I also remember rather long hours spent with a dancing master and my mother.'

'An infatuation?' Eliza teased, only breaking eye contact with him for a giddy spin with the neighbouring couple.

She felt almost drunk on the sound of the fiddle. She would have sworn that her joy was unspooling in the air behind her like so much ribbon.

'The Duke of Vane with a crush on a barmaid?'

'What did you expect?' Vane asked, his fingers momentarily tightening on hers. 'That I sprang from the womb a full-grown man?'

'The Athena of our times? It doesn't seem likely,' Eliza teased back. 'The goddess of wisdom you are not.'

Vane pulled her closer still. If Eliza took a deep

breath her chest would brush against his, and for a moment she wanted to look around to see if anyone was watching them. This could never have happened in London, and yet…and yet she felt safe in this crowd. Nobody would know by looking at them that he was a duke and she was a fallen wallflower.

Vane bent over her, his lips by her ear and his breath warm on her skin. 'So…by your logic I'm a god?'

Eliza couldn't help the shiver that ran through her, and she stumbled a little as Vane led her into another tight turn. He steadied her—goodness, those hands— and Eliza decided to toy with him right back.

She pursed her lips in mock-thought, humming a little. 'Hmm… I wouldn't say that. What's the phrase? If at first you don't succeed…?'

Vane's cheeks flushed and his expression turned incredulous. 'You think—? Oh, sweetheart. Practice, as they say, makes perfect. There's a reason I'm not turned away from any bed in London.'

Eliza jerked her attention away from his lips. 'Novelty is a powerful lure,' she said, her voice breathless. She blamed it on the reel, which had just drawn to a close. Vane had danced them to the edge of the square, and the shadows made Eliza feel bold.

'I assure you…novelty is only one of my appealing qualities,' he said.

Vane hadn't stepped away from her. They were still posed for dancing, pressing hand to hand, but then Vane moved. Instead of ornamentally pressing his palm to hers, he slid his hand down to wrap those big fingers around her wrist. Eliza flushed, aware of how quickly her heart was beating.

'I think we can safely rule out humility as one of your virtues,' she said, her voice high.

Slowly, deliberately, Vane ran his thumb over the soft skin of Eliza's wrist. When had that innocuous bit of skin become so sensitive?

'I never claimed it was,' he said, his voice low and tempting. 'Neither is restraint, minx. So don't tease.'

'What happened to enjoying a woman for her companionship?' Eliza asked, trying not to watch the way his lips moved when he talked.

'I can enjoy more than one thing simultaneously,' said Vane, dragging his thumb over her wrist once more. 'One of my many skills.'

'I've heard rumours,' said Eliza, not willing to be the one to back down. Not now...not with him.

'Rumours never live up to reality, sweet. I hope you know that.'

'Hmm... In my experience, reality rarely lives up to the imagination.'

'So you have imagined me?' he purred.

He had her there.

'You?' she said, as dismissively as possible. 'I don't think so.'

His eyes flared hot, whether in arousal or jealousy she didn't know. She'd be sure to revel in that later. The idea that she could make any man feel attracted or jealous was novel and delicious.

'So you do have fantasies? Virginal and white, I assume. You'll have to tell me about them.'

Eliza experienced a shiver of nerves at having stepped into a game she didn't know how to play, with stakes she wasn't sure she could meet. Still, the only way out was through...

'There are too many people about for any of that.'

And somewhere in the crowd was Aunt Mary. Eliza didn't know if she was hoping her aunt would come to save her or give her just a little more time to flirt with danger.

'As if that would stop me,' said Gabriel, stepping even closer.

Eliza had to tilt her head back to maintain eye contact with him, as tall as he was.

'Your education on illicit affairs is lacking,' he told her.

She shouldn't be surprised that Gabriel had seduced women in public places. Having experienced the full force of his attention for herself, she couldn't blame those other ladies one whit. He really was a most excellent rake. She should know better than to reply.

'Are you offering to teach me?'

Gabriel froze like a fox that had realised it was well and truly cornered: predator turned prey. His fingers tightened incrementally on Eliza's wrist, and then he released her completely.

'Are you adding that to your list of lessons?' he asked, his voice low and raspy. 'To drink, to gamble, to play bed games with me?'

'What if I am?' Eliza asked, thankful that she sounded more confident than she felt.

Tonight, when Vane had dismissed Robertson while maintaining Eliza's dignity, she'd finally realised not only how many things she'd missed out on, but also how many of those deprivations were still to come. She'd never been to a village fair like this, and once she returned from the house party she likely never would again. A wallflower could only turn down an earl so many times, and she'd already turned her back on Society once. With women, Society was notoriously unforgiving.

Until Eliza had gone out into the world she hadn't

realised how much of it she was intending to give up. That knowledge alone had made her brave. But Vane? He teased her and laughed with her and he saw her— really saw her—so *of course* she wanted him. Him and his stupid expressive eyebrows and that tiny scar on his lip…

'If you're asking me to add ravishment to your curriculum, I'm going to need an assessment of your current skills,' he said.

Cupio, cupis, cupit—*I want, you want, she wants.*

Of course Eliza wanted him to do that—but she hardly had time to wonder what he meant by 'an assessment' before he'd tugged her around the corner of the building and into the shadowed alley alongside the square.

'Your Grace!' Eliza squeaked, peeking over Vane's shoulder to see if anyone was watching.

It was one thing to flirt with him and daydream about more…it was another thing entirely for him to whisk her off into a dark alley with the intention of…of…

Vane's big shoulders shook as he laughed. 'Oh, your face, minx! I just wanted to kiss you, but we can go and find your aunt if you'd like.'

She pinched him in retaliation for scaring her, and then couldn't help but allow her attention to drift to his lips. One kiss wouldn't hurt, would it? She might not ever get another chance.

'Yes,' she said, tightening her fingers in the material of Vane's waistcoat. 'I think I'd like that.'

'I should make you ask nicely,' he said, so close that his breath feathered over Eliza's cheeks. 'But I can't wait.'

It was not how she'd imagined her first kiss. It wasn't in a pretty garden somewhere, with a gentle fair-haired man who would press his mouth to hers and then promise to make her happy for ever after.

No, it wasn't the way she'd imagined her first kiss.

Because never in her wildest dreams could Eliza have imagined something like this.

Gabriel kissed her as if he wanted to devour her, cupping her cheek to hold her still, tracing her lips with his tongue and teeth, and always pressing for more. When Eliza tried to move with him, to learn the steps to this ancient dance, the kiss only deepened. He swept his tongue over hers, all warmth and confidence and man, and Eliza dug her fingers into his shoulders, bracing herself as if she was caught in a storm.

And she was.

Gabriel was acting as if he would be content to kiss her here, in the shadows near so much gaiety, until they were found or they expired from lack of air. Her head spun, and for a few glorious seconds Eliza forgot that he was a duke and she was herself and this was but a brief stop on a road that could only end in frustration or tears.

She'd wanted a kiss. She'd found so much more.

'Come on,' he said, and Eliza realised she was leaning into him, still chasing his mouth with hers. 'It's time to find your aunt.'

'Yes,' said Eliza dazedly, following Gabriel back into the square. 'Of course.'

'Here you are,' said a red-cheeked Aunt Mary, appearing out of the crowd and waving happily at the retreating vicar. 'Just where I left you. Wasn't that a lovely dance?'

'Oh, yes,' said Eliza, knowing she'd have agreed even if Aunt Mary had asked if the sky was green. 'But I'm afraid I'm a bit fatigued.'

Mary huffed out a breath. 'Thank goodness. I didn't

want to be the old lady ruining the young people's fun, but I'm quite ready to be off my feet.'

'Of course,' said Gabriel, swinging his arm at Mary. 'My apologies for not thinking of that sooner.'

'You're not the least bit old,' said Eliza, walking on Mary's other side.

It was definitely for the best that Mary had come on this trip, Eliza decided. She needed a buffer between herself and Gabriel—otherwise how would she ever sort these feelings out? Attraction felt an awful lot like affection...which didn't make any sense whatsoever.

'All right, perhaps I'm not *old*,' said Mary, oblivious to Eliza's internal debate. 'What about stately? Or mature?'

They debated Mary's youth and lack thereof all the way back to the inn, where Gabriel bade them goodnight and entered the room beside their own.

Mary and Eliza unhooked each other's dresses, just as they always did, and after brushing their teeth and saying their prayers Mary crawled into the narrow bed and flopped back onto the pillow.

'I'd forgotten how tiring a holiday can be,' she said. 'Though I'm having so much fun.'

'Good,' said Eliza. 'You certainly deserve it.'

Eliza sat up for a few moments longer, slowly brushing out her hair and contemplating why both she and Mary felt better away from London. It wasn't as though attending musicales and balls and afternoon teas was a taxing activity—they were lavishly catered, filled with friends and acquaintances, and didn't require much more than polite behaviour and some light socialising.

Maybe it was simply the novelty of being away and out of their normal routine. She felt as though she had permission to try new and different things.

Like kissing one's escort…an attractive and affectionate duke.

What had she been thinking? And *why* was she dying to do it again?

From the bed, Mary gave a light snore, and Eliza slumped back into the room's one hard, wooden chair. She wanted to kiss Gabriel again now, and she wanted it so badly that her lips were tingling. She hadn't had a chance to properly enjoy it back in the alley…she'd been worried that they would be caught, or Mary would come looking for them, or…

She didn't know. She was making excuses. And Gabriel was just next door!

Eliza set the hairbrush down with a thump. Mary didn't twitch. As Eliza braided her hair and wrapped herself in her shawl, the pattern of light snoring didn't change one whit.

She took her candle and, at the threshold, looked back one last time…and then she crossed the hall to knock on Gabriel's door.

'Yes—? Eliza!' he said, backing out of the way as Eliza quickly shoved her way into his room.

She might be willing to walk into a man's bedroom while wearing only her shawl and her shift, but she didn't want to be seen doing it.

Gabriel turned, then seemed to realise what Eliza was wearing, and she was able to watch as his eyes dilated and his jaw muscles jumped. That did all sorts of warm things to her insides.

'Were you serious earlier?' she asked, pulling the shawl more tightly around her shoulders. 'When you asked if I wanted to add bed games to our curriculum?'

There was something predatory about Gabriel's languid movements as he crossed to room to sit on the low settee shoved against the far wall. 'Oh, I was quite serious, minx. But that doesn't mean it's a good idea.'

'Why not?' Eliza asked, twisting the edge of the shawl in her fingers.

'Because you don't know what you're getting into,' said Gabriel, his eyes glinting in the light of her candle.

Eliza poked her nose into the air, crossed the room, and stood toe to toe with this vexing, beautiful, kissable man.

'And that's exactly why you should show me.'

Chapter Ten

Eliza's presence filled the inn's little bedchamber the way Cicero's teacup held a tempest. She was flushed, her lips looked as if she'd been gnawing on them—and Gabriel was nearly paralysed with wanting her.

He was sitting on the thread-worn settee in the inn's little chamber, and Eliza was standing between his legs, looking uncharacteristically nervous.

'Light the candles, minx,' he said, running the pad of his thumb over her bottom lip, trying—and failing—not to imagine those lips touching him in all sorts of places. How much had she overheard from her side-lined position in Society? How many glib conversations had she pieced together?

Eliza was looking down at him with dark, pleasure-bright eyes, and the pad of his thumb was still pressed against her slightly parted lips.

'The candles,' he reminded her, removing his finger. 'I want to see you.'

She blinked. 'Is that…optional?'

If only she knew how badly he wanted to see her.

'How about this?' he said, running his knuckles over her jaw. 'If I undress you, and then you want to blow out the candles, we can. But give me that much.'

Eliza worried at her bottom lip with straight white teeth, and Gabriel couldn't help but kiss her. She kissed him back with a kind of stunned incredulity that Gabriel found intoxicating. He wished he could pull her into himself and tend her like an acolyte to a flame.

A better man would have kissed her gently, sent her back to her own room, and poured cold water over his head. Gabriel, quite thankfully, did not consider himself a better man.

As Eliza padded around the room, lighting the candles from her own, Gabriel was quick to yank off his coat and waistcoat and cravat, which he'd loosened when he'd got back to his room. His trousers remained firmly in place. Despite her bold mouth and needy kisses she was new to this game, and he'd need help to keep his patience. After all, he had no intentions of taking this *too* far—all she needed was a taste.

When the room glowed, and reddish candlelight caught in Eliza's kiss-mussed hair, she glanced shyly over at him.

'Come here,' he said, tapping the rug before him with the toe of one boot.

Eliza narrowed her eyes at his order but complied. Oh, the power of curiosity… This must be how unsuspecting travellers felt when they were lured off the straight and narrow by fairy folk.

'Now,' said Gabriel, leaning towards her. 'I would very much like to know how much of this business you understand.'

Eliza blushed furiously, and suddenly Gabriel hated her practical shawl—hated that it kept him from tracking the progress of her blush as it crept from her cheeks to her throat to her chest. Were her nipples the same soft pink? Or tawny, like her eyebrows? It wouldn't matter to him either way—he simply wanted to know.

'Aunt Mary explained things to me a long time ago, Your Grace,' she said, rebuking him with his title.

Gabriel couldn't allow that—no, he couldn't.

'Oh?' he said, running his hand up her arm and pausing at her throat, doodling little nothings with his fingers over the place where her pulse fluttered. 'So she explained *soixante-neuf*, did she? Or how a man can take a woman from behind? Or how she might ride him like a jockey in the Derby?'

God help him, he wanted to introduce her to all of it. He wanted to claim all her firsts for himself, selfish bastard that he was. He wanted to give her all the fond memories she would need to see her through the rest of what was likely to be her solitary life.

Eliza's eyes had gone round and her hands were clenching the material of her shift. 'No,' she said, her voice high. 'Just that…his part…it goes in the woman's—'

'Pussy?' Gabriel asked, using one hand to draw Eliza closer and letting the other slide down over her breast, the curve of her belly, to the body part in question. He cupped her there, and maybe it was only his imagination, but he thought he could already feel her heat.

Eliza squirmed. 'Yes.'

'A rakess would say the word,' said Gabriel, leaning forward to press a quick kiss to her linen-covered stomach. 'Or I could supply other options if you prefer?'

Her soft hand smacked over his mouth, though her eyes had gone warm and dark.

Gabriel pressed a kiss to her palm before guiding her hand away. 'All right, minx. We can save that for lesson two. Do you know of anything other than the mechanics?'

While she thought about her answer, Gabriel reached up and began unbuttoning her night shift, parting the fabric with a growing urgency to see her clad in nothing at all.

'The maids complain about men grabbing their—' She gestured to her breasts, where Gabriel now had her dress gaping open.

'Breasts?' he supplied. 'Really, pet, that one isn't even naughty. The word certainly appears in the Bible.'

'Not like that!' said Eliza, scandalised.

Gabriel ignored her, and started peeling her shawl away from her body. Task accomplished, he pulled her closer, stroking her hip through the thin muslin of her shift. 'What else?'

Eliza picked at one of her cuticles and stared down at the floor by his boots. 'Well… One of the maids said the junior footman knew what he was doing.'

'With…?'

'Breasts,' said Eliza, flicking her gaze up to catch his own. 'And kisses,' she added.

There she was. The girl who would apparently allow no one and nothing to go unchallenged. He wondered if she'd goad him on like that in bed…if she would drive her heels into his back and urge him on.

'Well,' said Gabriel, and his voice had gone dark and low, 'we'll have to find out what you think.'

Before she could protest, he scooped her up and tugged her into his lap, more than pleased to have the soft, warm weight of a woman against him again.

She braced herself against his chest and gave him her best, most poisonous, governess-in-training look. It didn't work on him—not any more. He knew that underneath that prodigious glare was a woman who wanted to experience everything the world had to offer...including him.

'Much better,' he announced, holding her by the waist. 'Now, on with our lesson. You mentioned kissing?'

Eliza nodded and leaned forward, and Gabriel met her halfway. With every little shift of her weight her thigh rubbed against his raging hard cock, and it was taking all of Gabriel's meagre patience not to rock himself up into her soft body, desperate for release.

When he lifted her breast free from her shift and ran his thumb over her nipple she groaned and broke the kiss, arching a little more firmly into his palm.

'That's nice,' she told him, breathless.

Gabriel lifted her other full—magnificent—breast from her clothing and toyed deliberately with her nipple while he rucked up the material of her shift.

'Here,' she said, sliding onto the floor.

She took a deep breath, yanked her chemise over her head, and then scrambled back into his lap—an armful of soft, curious, pink woman.

God help him, she was beautiful. The cream of her skin, the pink of her nipples, the mix of defiance and nerves in the set of her chin and the furrow of her brows...

'You're stunning,' he told her, cupping her arse and urging her closer to him. 'Magnificent.'

Eliza shifted uneasily before muttering, 'Thank you.'

He grinned, and pressed that smile to her mouth, nibbling his way along her lip before she opened to him properly.

'So polite,' he mumbled, not bothering to lift his mouth from hers. 'All right,' he said eventually, leaning back and cupping the weight of her breasts in his palms. 'What other naughty things have you overheard? What do you like?'

Eliza paused in her slow stroking of his chest. 'Why do you think I know what I like?'

Ah… Not an outright denial. 'You're a clever woman,' said Gabriel, pinching a little bit harder at her nipple. 'There can't be much for women to get up to on winter evenings. All those warm baths…'

Eliza somehow went even redder, and Gabriel realised he'd inadvertently struck the truth—or at least a piece of it.

'Oh…' he said, drawling out the syllable long and low. 'You *have* played in the bath, haven't you?'

Don't picture it, you randy goat. Don't picture her relaxed in the bath, with one leg swung over the side so that only soap bubbles obscure the heaven between her legs.

Eliza jutted that stubborn chin into the air. 'I was curious…and it felt good.'

'What did?' Gabriel asked, kneading gently at one of her breasts.

Her nipples had gone hard and tight, and he desperately wanted to suck them into his mouth, to feel her begin to rock in time with his tongue, but that wasn't the game.

Patience.

'I touched myself,' she said. 'With my fingers.'

'Here?' he asked, rewarding her boldness.

When he cupped her mons she was hot and damp, and only started a little.

'Yes,' she said. 'Which is how I know that it can feel nice. It doesn't have to hurt, the way some people say it will.'

'You,' said Gabriel, kissing the tip of her nose, 'are absolutely right.'

Carefully, slowly, he slid the tips of his fingers through her curls to part her hot flesh for his exploration. She was soft there…women were so magically soft…and Gabriel knew he would happily spend the rest of his life trying to accurately describe the joy of attending to a slick, silky pussy.

Eliza jolted a little when his fingers found her nub and began circling, but he kissed her self-consciousness away, enjoying the way she always—every time—chased his mouth when he broke the kiss. Soon she was rocking into his hands, subtle little grindings of her hips, and she was starting to go wet under his fingers.

'What else?' said Gabriel, looking up at her.

He could feel his heartbeat in his cock now—he didn't think he'd ever been so hard in his life—but every time he reached the end of his tether he found just a little bit more patience waiting there for him.

'I once saw Lord Harlow with a woman bent over the table in Lady Alicia's library, but…'

Gabriel groaned, imagining the way he would cover Eliza in that position…just rucking up her skirts and sliding into her molten heat.

'But I don't want you to be…inside me like that. I can't have a baby.'

Her cheeks were pink, the odd lock of long hair beginning to curl around her face, and yet she looked so seriously down at him.

'You won't,' he said, his heart softening at the amount of trust she was placing in him. 'I won't be inside you. I haven't been inside a woman for years. But there are plenty of other things we can do,' he said, and he slid a finger inside her.

She immediately moaned, low and throaty, and Gabriel was quick to add a second finger. He could come like this. With her grinding in his lap and him imagining that his cock was in the place of his fingers… He could come in his trousers like a boy—which would be incredibly embarrassing.

Better to think of something else.

'What about here?' Gabriel asked, pinching a nipple harder than before. 'Has anyone said anything about kissing you here?'

'No,' said Eliza. 'But I'd like it if you did.'

She hadn't finished the final syllable when Gabriel took a hard nipple into his mouth and flicked it with his tongue. Eliza gasped, and one of her hands slid up the back of his neck to clench in his hair. He'd always loved a woman who took her pleasure seriously, and with Eliza he couldn't think of anything else.

He pulled away, but before toying with her opposite nipple he asked, 'Did anyone ever say anything about a man making his lover come?'

Her hand tightened in his hair, almost to the point of pain, and Gabriel loved it. She would be the type of lady to mark his back, to demand her pleasure of him, and he couldn't wait. He'd keep her in bed for a week… he'd feed her from his own hand—as many pastries as she wanted—give her brandy and wine, and clothing would be banned after sunset.

Well, he would do that if she was his. But she wasn't, and he needed to remember that.

'Yes, Gabriel, please,' she said, her back bowing, and Gabriel's world narrowed to her breast under his mouth and her slickness around his fingers.

His own arousal was a bit like the ocean: immense, distant, and with no relevance to the current situation.

Eliza's thighs were trembling, and her rhythm was jerky now, as if she was not sure what her ultimate destination was, but was heading there anyway. Gabriel splayed his free hand over her back and leaned away from her, tipping his face up so he could see hers.

Her eyes were only half open, just like her lips. Her cheeks were pink, and sweat was making her hair curl around her face. She was perfect. He could live a thousand lives and not forget this night.

Finally, with a keening sound, Eliza came. He could feel her channel seize his fingers, and she slumped forward onto his chest as she shivered with aftershocks.

For a moment, neither of them spoke. Gabriel gently extracted his fingers from inside her, which made her twitch, and then they were both content to catch their breath for a handful of heartbeats.

'Nothing I had heard,' said Eliza eventually, pushing herself up from his chest, 'would have prepared me for that.'

Gabriel smiled up at her—the grin of a predator with a willing victim. 'Happy to oblige.'

As Eliza looked thoughtfully down at him, all Gabriel's long-suppressed arousal came roaring back—with interest. His trousers felt as though they might do him permanent damage.

He was only distantly aware that he might be absolutely scandalising her as he nudged her backwards and tore open his trousers. His cock sprang free, angry and hard, and when he grasped it, it was nearly as painful as ignoring it had been.

'Can I...? What do I do?' Eliza asked, looking down at his cock with wide eyes.

It was flattering that she was looking at him like that, but Gabriel had no time for flattery.

'Would you like to help me?' he asked, feeling his pulse in his groin. 'I'll just need your hand, minx.'

'Oh, yes,' she said, nodding quickly, still staring at his arousal.

'Here,' he said, grabbing her wrist. He guided her hand between them, down to her core, wetting her fingers with her own slickness, and then wrapped his fingers over hers around his cock. 'Just like that,' he mumbled as she started to stroke.

'That looks painful,' said Eliza, watching as the head of his cock disappeared and reappeared from her fist.

'I just want you so damn much,' said Gabriel, rolling his head back to rest it against the settee.

'Oh…' said Eliza, drawing out the word into a sort of thoughtful hum.

'Those soft tits and your pretty eyes…the little noises you made for me. Hell,' he said, thrusting up into her hand.

It seemed like only seconds more and he was coming, hot seed spilling over their hands and onto his belly. The orgasm was so strong as to almost hurt, and he swore his balls ached afterwards. But it was worth it… so worth it… Because Eliza was looking at him with a flush on her cheeks and wonder in her eyes.

'That was my best lesson yet,' she said, scooting off his lap and flopping onto the settee next to him.

'You say that as if you're surprised,' said Gabriel, taking in a few deep breaths before forcing himself to stand and wander over to the pitcher and basin. He cleaned himself up with a few economical strokes, then rinsed the cloth and carried it back to Eliza.

She blushed furiously, but tidied herself up and made use of the screen while Gabriel turned down the coverlet.

Panic and renewed lust mingled in his gut. He couldn't wait to teach her everything, to surprise her over and over again—and that was the problem. He didn't have women over and over again. His affairs were always brief, both parties understood the arrangement, and they parted ways sooner rather than later as amicable friends.

He'd have to do the same with Eliza. He'd have to. He was already breaking too many of his own rules as it was. No promises, no unmarried women, no strings. It was for her own good. He could give her a romp, could give her kisses and pleasure, but there it had to end.

'Goodnight,' she said with a blush.

To Gabriel's surprise she went up onto her toes to kiss his cheek, before quickly slipping out through the door and back into the bed where she actually belonged.

As he lay down on the cold sheets it took all Gabriel's willpower to remind himself that the bed where Eliza belonged most definitely wasn't *his*.

Chapter Eleven

They were well over halfway through the journey, and being in the carriage was starting to pall for all parties. Vane's jaw was tightly set and he kept shifting his weight, as though his back ached. Aunt Mary had a damp cloth pressed to her brow, and if anyone had bothered to ask Eliza she'd have said that might never be able to stand straight again.

'This carriage is too big,' she said. 'I can't even brace my feet against the floor to keep myself in place.'

To demonstrate, she kicked out her legs, letting her heels swing against the box of the bench seat. *Thump-thump.* The carriage had been built to Vane's proportions, which meant there was room to sit without being crushed together. But it also meant that Eliza and Mary couldn't put their feet on the floor.

'Well, let's see *your* carriage, then,' said Vane, opening one eye to squint angrily at Eliza. 'Since you seem to have so many opinions on mine.'

'I don't have one,' said Eliza. 'I'm just saying that for those of us who aren't built like Richard the Lionheart, maybe you could have put in some straps or something.'

'*"Straps or something",*' Gabriel mimicked. 'I'll send a note along to the designer, shall I?'

'Children!' said Aunt Mary sharply, glaring at them from beneath her damp handkerchief. 'Stop it, both of you.'

An expression of vague shame filtered over Gabriel's face. 'I apologise, Lady Stanley. None of us is at our best today, I'm afraid.'

'I'm sorry, Aunt,' said Eliza, turning to look at Mary, who was sitting beside her.

Underneath the linen handkerchief and the shade of her bonnet, Aunt Mary was looking quite pale.

'Are you all right?' Eliza asked, patting around the seat, looking for the flask of water. 'You don't look well.'

'I think I could do with a short stop,' said Aunt Mary, closing her eyes. 'Just for a few minutes...to let myself settle.'

'We should be at the next village in a few hours,' said Gabriel, pitching his voice low. 'We'll be sure to give you as much of a rest there as you need.'

'I'd much prefer a break now,' said Mary.

'We shouldn't—'

'We really should,' said Eliza, thumping on the roof of the carriage to signal the driver.

Aunt Mary did not look well.

Gabriel tensed, but nodded curtly. 'A short break, then.'

There was a heavy jolt as the carriage was driven onto the verge, and then they came to a stop. Before Gabriel could reach for the door it swung open and the young tiger's face poked inside. He was of an indeterminate age, thought Eliza—perhaps twelve, and had spent too much time in the sun, or fifteen, and in need of feeding up.

'Everything all right, Yer Grace?' he asked, squinting as his eyes adjusted to the shade inside the carriage.

'Fine,' said Gabriel. 'The ladies are in need of a break.'

The tiger nodded and swung down the steps. Gabriel hopped out of the carriage, then assisted Aunt Mary and Eliza with their descent.

'Lovely,' said Aunt Mary, keeping hold of Gabriel's arm. 'A nice place to rest.'

'Lad, fetch one of the blankets from the coach,' said Gabriel, patting Mary's hand.

The tiger hopped into the carriage, and Eliza looked around at their resting place. Rolling hills stretched out beyond a stone fence, and here and there small stands of trees broke up the fields and the horizon. A little stream fed into a dark, reedy pond, and above it all floated fat clouds.

All in all, it was the picture of an ideal summer's day.

'Where are we?' Eliza asked as the tiger spread out one of the heavy wool blankets. Fields and streams were lovely, but they weren't exactly a defining geographical landmark.

'Somewhere in Yorkshire,' said Gabriel, settling Aunt Mary in the shade of a stone wall before ducking back into the carriage.

Eliza wondered at his curt behaviour—she didn't think he'd said more than the bare minimum since Aunt Mary had asked to stop. Was he really so concerned about their timetable?

When Gabriel stepped back out of the carriage, he had an elegant duelling pistol in each hand.

Eliza felt her eyebrows crawl up her forehead. 'What in the world are you doing with those?' she asked. She thought to tease him, and ask if he'd reconsidered her request to duel with Abberly, but he didn't seem to be in a teasing mood.

'Standing lookout,' said Gabriel.

He passed one of the guns up to the coachman, and tucked the other he into the waistband of his trousers.

Eliza took another look around at their surroundings. Just fields, stones and tall grasses as far as the eye could see. There weren't even any trees close enough to present the threat of hidden danger.

'Er…lookout for what? I was joking when I teased you about wild animals.'

'One never knows what might happen on the road, far from help,' said Gabriel. 'I won't risk it.'

'Leave him be,' said Mary. Her colour was slowly returning to something close to normal, though she was still holding her now very wrinkled but mostly dry handkerchief to her forehead.

'Let me freshen that for you,' said Eliza, gently taking the neatly embroidered cotton. 'There's a stream just over the fence.'

'Oh, that would be lovely,' said Mary. 'I'm afraid the heat and the ruts in the road are getting to me.'

'It happens to the best of us,' said Gabriel. 'Eliza, allow me to escort you.'

'It's just over there,' said Eliza, pointing. 'If you'll give me a boost—'

Gabriel put his hands on the curve of her waist and boosted her rear up onto the flat top of the drystone wall. Eliza blinked at him; she hadn't been expecting that.

'Gosh. Thank you,' she said. Then she swung her legs up, and over, and slid down into the field beyond. There was another thump, and to nobody's surprise Gabriel was standing beside her.

'I'm coming with you,' he said. 'Since I doubt you'll stay here if I tell you to.'

'Quite right,' said Eliza, setting off. 'It feels good to do a bit of walking after being trapped in your carriage.'

'Understandable.'

'The stream is only fifty yards from here, and there's nothing impeding your view,' said Eliza. 'You really didn't need to come with me.'

She was babbling. His odd silence and obvious tension were worrying her.

'Is this because of…you know…?' she said. She wasn't quite brave enough to directly reference what they'd done in Gabriel's bedroom after the fair. 'I don't have any designs upon your person. I know it was just fun.'

It had been fun. But it wouldn't have been worth it if Gabriel was unhappy with her now. His easy company and casual flirting were part of what she so enjoyed about spending time with him. Thus far he'd treated her like just another person, with thoughts and ideas of her own, and she'd treasured the experience.

Gabriel's face scrunched into a comedically confused expression. 'What…? Oh. No, of course it's not that,' he said. 'How can you even think about that at a time like this?'

Eliza stretched out her hand so that the tips of the dry grasses could brush against her palm as they walked along. 'I wasn't. It was just a guess as to what might be bothering you.'

'Why do you think something is bothering me?'

Eliza gestured pointedly to the polished butt of the gun that poked out of his waistband.

'Ahh…' he sighed. 'Yes.'

They paused at the edge of the little stream, and Eliza crouched down to immerse the handkerchief in the cool, clear running water. It was tempting to take off her shoes and splash her feet, but that wouldn't be fair to poor Aunt Mary.

'So?' she said, standing up and cupping the sodden piece of fabric in the palm of her hand.

'My father and brother were killed by highwaymen in a robbery,' said Gabriel, scuffing the tip of his boot against the bank of the stream.

'That's terrible,' said Eliza almost without thinking. 'I'm so sorry.'

She had several follow-up questions, but now really wasn't the time. She could see that.

'It was awful. And I know that something like that isn't likely to happen twice, but...' He shrugged helplessly. 'It's worrying.'

'I understand,' said Eliza, reaching out to briefly squeeze Gabriel's hand. 'You've been very patient with us, and we'll be at Abberly's before you know it. Nothing is going to happen to us.'

'I know you mean well, but that doesn't really help,' said Gabriel as they began to walk back. 'Nobody ever thinks something bad is going to happen to them.'

'Because that's no way to live your life,' said Eliza. 'You do your best to be prepared, and then you deal with the situation in front of you.'

Gabriel looked broodingly at his feet.

Eliza bumped him with her shoulder and asked, 'So, what made you decide to face your fears with a Society matron and a wallflower who had been pushed to the edge? Did you want to get the most difficult scenario over with right out of the gate? A bit of a sink-or-swim situation?'

Gabriel managed to crack a smile. 'The entertainment factor did seem likely to outweigh the downside. And it's been quite good value for money thus far.'

'Why, thank you,' said Eliza, giving him a mock curtsey. 'I aim to please.'

'No, you don't,' said Gabriel.

Did he sound almost...fond? she thought.

'You aim to do exactly what *you* please,' he said, 'while convincing everyone around you that it was their idea in the first place.'

Eliza made a face. 'I don't do that...much. It sounds terrible when you put it that way!'

Gabriel laughed for the first time since they'd set out from the last inn. 'It's a skill, minx. Use it judiciously.'

'Maybe it's like rabbits having sharp teeth, and horses kicking a man through a wall,' said Eliza. 'Everyone needs *something* which others should fear.'

'Nature seems to find a way,' said Gabriel. 'In your case, you're one of those lovely little unassuming flowers that turns out to be covered in thorns as soon as someone grips it.'

'I like that,' said Eliza.

Gabriel was the opposite, she thought. He appeared to be nothing but privileged fluff, but upon closer investigation he had previously unsuspected depths.

'I'd be a thorny violet quite happily.'

'Of course you would,' said Gabriel, smiling over at her. 'I've got your number now.'

Eliza was pleased that she'd been able to lighten Gabriel's mood—even a little. She'd assumed that his anxiety came from the time it was taking to escort them to the house party, or even from the liberties the two of them had taken after the Crofton Fair. Instead she'd discovered that he was facing an existential fear—for what seemed like very little reward.

Gabriel boosted Eliza back over the fence, and Eliza folded the sodden handkerchief and gave it to Mary, who'd completely removed her bonnet. Mary's pallor was better, and she was twirling a clover flower between her fingers.

'Oh, thank you, dearest,' she said, pressing the linen to the side of her throat. 'I'll be right as rain in a bit.'

'Don't rush,' said Gabriel, fetching a jug of cool tea from the carriage. 'I'll check with the coachman…perhaps we can water the horses.'

Aunt Mary sighed as Gabriel walked off. 'He's so considerate. He'll make some young lady very happy one day.'

Eliza wouldn't think about that. She wanted Gabriel to be happy, for certain, but the idea of smiling at some as yet faceless woman and addressing her as the Duchess of Vane was vaguely upsetting. Gabriel was *her* friend.

'How much of his family history do you know?' Eliza asked, pitching her voice low.

'Only the gossip and what appeared in the papers. He's very brave, isn't he?'

'Both the former duke and the heir killed,' said Eliza. 'How awful.'

'Quite,' said Mary, tilting her head back and closing her eyes.

Eliza spent the next quarter-hour lost in thought. It has been hard enough when her own parents had died. She'd been devastated, and her lovely world had been turned upside down. But she hadn't suddenly become the head of her family. She hadn't inherited a title and all the responsibilities that came with it.

She'd been a grieving daughter—Gabriel had been a grieving brother and son, but also a young duke.

Maybe his habit of eschewing responsibility came from having it thrust upon him at too young an age.

Or maybe Eliza was reading too much into the entire situation.

Still, she thought as she helped Mary to her feet and folded the blanket. *Perhaps I am not the only one on this journey with a score to settle.*

Chapter Twelve

Two nights later their little travelling party arrived in York, a mere morning's drive away from Abberly's estate. They were very nearly at their destination, and Gabriel could not wait to spend his days outside the hot, bouncing carriage. Not that his current accommodations were anything to sneeze at...

After four nights in cramped inns, their travelling party had stopped at Burton's Hotel in York. Dinner had been braised trout with fresh greens and boiled potatoes, raspberry tarts had been served as dessert, and now a group of guests were mingling comfortably in one of the upstairs parlours.

Gabriel swirled his brandy and pretended to listen to the talk of cigars and shipping being conducted by two of the men nearby. Mary was seated among a cluster of women near the fireplace, enthusiastically talking with a wealthy Frenchwoman who had been eager to return to England after the wars.

And Eliza...

She was inexplicably sitting alone at a small table near the darkened window, playing a desultory game of Patience. As Gabriel watched she flipped over a card and glared down at the knave of hearts. The card stared unseeingly back.

For a moment Gabriel debated what he should do. It was clear that Eliza was in some sort of distress, and a good man would go over to see if he could offer some sort of assistance. But as much as Gabriel wanted to be a good man, he wasn't sure if was capable of actually cheering her up.

That kind of delicate emotional work was precisely the sort of thing he worked very hard to avoid.

She flipped over another card and merely looked at it—clearly not what she needed to complete her run.

With his decision made, Gabriel topped up his brandy, poured her a glass of sherry, and crossed the room.

'Goodness, Eliza. What can that card have possibly done to you?' Gabriel asked, taking the seat across from Eliza at the small round table by the window.

Below them the gardens of the hotel rolled away. The candles and the firelight were reflected in the window glass, and he had to admit that the hotel was a pleasant change from the coaching inns at which they'd stopped along the road. It was lushly appointed, with pleasant bedchambers, two dining rooms, and several parlours where guests could socialise and help themselves to the decanters.

Gabriel passed her the small glass of sherry, from which she absently took a sip.

'I can't complete this hand,' she said, looking down at her arrangement of cards.

'Then why bother?' Gabriel asked, scooping up the expensive cardstock and shuffling. 'I have never seen the point of playing Patience.'

'Of course you haven't,' said Eliza, taking the cards back and stubbornly turning out a new game. 'You had siblings and private tutors and an estate at your disposal.'

'True,' said Gabriel, taking the three of spades from her fingers and laying it down on the two. 'But I don't think you're all in a snit because our childhoods differed—are you?'

'I'm not in a snit,' said Eliza with a little sniff.

Gabriel gave her a pointed look.

'Well, if I am, I have reason.'

'I know better than to argue with a lady on such a topic,' said Gabriel, shaking his head at the impossibility of Eliza finishing this hand of Patience either, 'but I'm here if you'd like to talk about it.'

He sipped his brandy, and Eliza sipped her sherry, and they both flipped over the playing cards as he gave her a chance to marshal her thoughts.

'What's really bothering you?' Gabriel asked.

Eliza sighed. 'You'll think it's silly.'

'Only one way to find out.'

He knew he wouldn't find it silly. Because nothing about Eliza was silly. Stubborn, reckless, funny, wry and impulsive, perhaps, but not silly.

'I'm afraid that this will backfire—that by agreeing to go to his stupid party I'm playing right into Abberly's hands. It will look desperate…as if I've chased the man who ruined me all the way to Yorkshire.'

He'd never seen her looking so glum.

'Nobody could consider you desperate,' said Gabriel, giving up on the game and stacking the cards into a complete deck once more. 'From another angle, it will look as if you're taunting Abberly with what he can't have.'

That was how Gabriel would interpret it. That was a little how Gabriel felt just now.

That idea seemed to cheer Eliza. She perked up and said, 'That could be true…'

'But…?' Gabriel prompted.

Eliza heaved out a sigh, and he watched her look sightlessly through the black glass of the window to the night beyond, where only her reflection stared back at her.

'But even if I do manage to besmirch his reputation, none of it will matter. Even if he isn't bosom friends with Prinny by the end of the party, he'll still be an earl. He'll still be *important*.'

She looked away from her reflection, turning to Gabriel instead.

'Why *did* you agree to take us on this trip?'

He should have expected that. Eliza instinctively understood that the best defensive tactic was to immediately take up the offensive.

Gabriel swirled his brandy while he thought of an appropriate answer. 'I liked the idea of being included on your quest for revenge. And I was right, too—it has been the perfect distraction after the hubbub of the Season.'

His answer obviously hadn't been what she wanted to hear. Her expression never flickered, but something in her eyes went flat.

'I'm glad you've enjoyed the trip so far, then,' she said.

If Gabriel hadn't known her better, he'd have assumed her comment was sincere.

'I'd hate for you to have come this far and regret it.'

Gabriel pinned Eliza with a look modelled after his own mother. With weight behind his words, he said, 'I'd hate for you to feel that way, too.'

Eliza looked away.

Gabriel fought for something to say—something sincere that would actually make her feel better. He hated seeing her so drained of confidence. This wasn't who she was. Eliza was sure of herself, and full of conviction for her cause. This unsure woman made his heart ache.

And then, suddenly, he knew.

'This is just stage fright,' said Gabriel, setting down his glass and picking up the deck of cards. 'Tomorrow you begin your role of a lifetime. Even a professional actress would be nervous.'

He had her attention now.

'Well…it will take quite an effort to disguise my utter loathing for the man.'

'That's the spirit,' said Gabriel, fiddling with the cards. 'We both know you're an excellent actress. You had the entire ton convinced you were nothing more than a wall-flower.'

Now they were back on familiar territory.

'I *am* a wallflower. Wallflowers exist on the edge of ballrooms and social gatherings—which, as we know, is my natural habitat. They aren't sought-after guests. They're agreeable, they avoid drawing attention to themselves, and they feel comfortable with their own small group. Which part of that doesn't sound like me?'

Clearly Eliza had a skewed vision of herself. She did spend most of her time on the edges of a room—but that was only because she was pretending to be a co-operative, meek young woman.

He knew exactly which part of her little diatribe didn't sound like her actual personality.

'Most of it, now that I'm getting to know you,' he said, setting the deck in the centre of the table. 'Agree-able, you most certainly are not.'

Though *he* found her much more than simply agree-able.

And suddenly he knew *exactly* how he would dis-tract Eliza from her doubts.

He shuffled the cards once more, before dealing them two each.

'Perhaps your presence brings out the worst in me,' said Eliza sweetly.

Gabriel grinned, relieved that she was back to boldly insulting him. 'I know. I rather enjoy it.'

'What have you dealt us?' she asked, picking up the two cards that had been placed before her.

She held the cards neatly, sitting in her chair with good posture and a ladylike demeanour, but she wasn't fooling him. Oh, no, Gabriel had got to know the real Eliza Hawkins, and he knew she was going to enjoy this.

'Vingt-et-Un,' said Gabriel, picking up his own cards. 'The object of the game is to build a hand that is valued as close to the number twenty-one as possible without going over.'

'You remembered?' said Eliza, looking down at her hand, which came to a measly thirteen.

'Yes,' said Gabriel, drier than cheap gin. 'I have managed to remember an impassioned list that contained only three items: cakes, liquor and gambling. An impressive feat, to be certain.'

'Well, you are gaining in age,' said Eliza primly. 'I'm sure I saw at least three grey hairs when we stopped to change horses at lunch. They do shine so.'

God, he loved—*liked*—her clever mouth.

If she hadn't blushed while laying down that little insult he might have been a touch worried. As it was, he had no doubt as to how attractive she found him.

'I'll get you back for that comment. Now, pay attention.'

He explained the betting mechanisms, and about asking for additional cards, and then told her that in this game everyone's hand was visible.

'There are only a few cards in play, which means you can mostly calculate which cards are still in the deck. Roughly half the deck would get you close to twenty-one, and the other half would put you over. It's your call, minx.'

'Another card,' declared Eliza.

She was dealt a queen and went over twenty-one. Gabriel's total came to sixteen, and he won the hand.

'I think I've got it,' said Eliza. 'This time don't help me.'

She lost the next two hands, and then finally earned herself a win.

'This is admittedly better when there are more players,' said Gabriel. 'You can see which cards are on the table and have a better chance of calculating your odds.'

'It's better than whist!' said Eliza, tapping the table for another card and then groaning when she went over the limit. 'At least I'm not disappointing my partner.'

If someone were to show Gabriel a man who would be disappointed by having Eliza for a partner, Gabriel would show you a fool.

'Whist has its place, and room for strategy,' he said. 'This is different, and in a way simpler.'

'There's an element of speed,' said Eliza, 'And keeping track of which cards are already in play. I'll have to teach some of the other ladies, so we can have a group to play with.'

Eliza wasn't a fox let loose in the henhouse—she was a hawk cleverly disguised as a chicken.

'Don't win all their pin money,' said Gabriel. 'A gentleman—or in this case a budding rakess—is always sporting.'

'We don't bet anything, if you haven't noticed,' said Eliza. 'Most of Aunt Mary's acquaintances don't have pin money, anyway. We have to wager something else.'

'Like what?' Gabriel asked, grunting a little when his cards added up to twenty-three. 'Earbobs? Decorative cushions?'

Eliza gave him another of her deeply scornful looks, and Gabriel couldn't help but smile. He'd started to wonder what he could do to make her look like that while sitting astride him in bed...but those were thoughts best avoided.

'No,' she said. 'Secrets is a common thing. Treasured recipes or favourite shawls. Small things husbands won't notice. Sometimes we might wager a favour, but those are rarely called in.'

'Or not that you know of,' Gabriel said, dealing another abysmal hand. They really did need more players if Eliza was going to get any better at this. 'Most people don't announce it when they need to call in a debt.'

'True,' said Eliza, looking sceptically at her cards before deciding to hold. At seventeen, she'd made a very good choice and won the hand. 'But word always gets around.'

'If word always gets around, why are you willing to risk everything here—and in front of the Prince Regent, no less?'

Eliza huffed out a breath and gave him a tight-lipped expression. 'Because it will be worth it. Because if I have to lose nearly everything, Abberly should lose *something.*'

Gabriel sensed that he'd pushed her hard enough, so he played another two hands before he asked, 'What would you wager, if you were to play this with your gambling ladies?'

'There's not much I have that they'd want. Embroidery, perhaps.'

How incredibly boring.

'And if *we* were to wager something?'

Heat flared in Gabriel's belly as Eliza's focus drifted down to his mouth. Her little pink tongue darted out to lick her bottom lip, and Gabriel shifted uncomfortably in his seat. It had been years since something so innocent had affected him like this, and he'd reached the conclusion that it was simply Eliza who did it. Her mixture of boldness, innocence and curiosity was too powerful to resist.

Eliza swallowed. 'I imagine I have even less that would be of interest to you,' she said, her voice throaty.

'You know better than that, minx.'

Eliza meticulously straightened her cards before glazing up at Gabriel through her lashes. 'A dance?'

'I do enjoy dancing with you…' he agreed neutrally.

'A kiss?'

Oh, she sounded so hopeful.

'I get kisses free,' he said, with a wink.

Eliza narrowed her eyes at him. 'I'm not doing *that*.'

Gabriel had to cover a laugh with a cough. 'No, sweet, of course you're not. And I wouldn't enjoy being with you under those circumstances.'

Eliza looked at her cards, looked at Gabriel's cards, and then sighed. 'You want a favour from me, don't you?'

'Of course I do,' Gabriel purred, imagining the sort of thing he'd use such a favour on. He'd love to get his mouth on her…or ask about her deepest, darkest fantasies…

'On this hand?' Eliza asked.

'On this hand,' he said.

Eliza nodded, doing her best not to smile. God, she was cute. Anything daring immediately caught her fancy.

'I'll hit,' she said.

He dealt her a card, but neither of them flipped it.

Gabriel surveyed his cards. 'I'll hit.'

He pulled a card from the deck and turned over a three.

'Seventeen,' he said.

Eliza turned over her own cards. 'Eighteen, Your Grace.'

'I owe you a favour,' said Gabriel. He hoped she'd call in something interesting.

'Hmm...' said Eliza, theatrically drumming her fingers. 'I think I'd like some information.'

'Oh...?'

This couldn't be good, he thought.

'When you were sitting across the room, staring at me over your glass of brandy, what were you thinking?'

'I wasn't staring,' Gabriel spluttered.

Eliza gave him a dismissive expression.

'I could tell you were upset,' he said reluctantly. 'I was trying to determine if there was anything I could do to help.'

Perceptive little thing, wasn't she?

'Really?' she asked, looking genuinely surprised. 'But you always know what to say.'

'No, I don't,' said Gabriel.

'Yes, you really do,' said Eliza. 'You don't think it's just your title that has women hanging on your every word, do you? Not to mention all your gentlemen compatriots. You're clever, Gabriel. And you're good with people.'

He snorted. 'I must respectfully disagree with you.'

Eliza crossed her arms, and Gabriel stole only the briefest of glances at her bosom.

'Tell me *one time* when you well and truly mucked it up,' she said.

Maybe it was the brandy. Maybe it was the knowledge that when this trip was over he'd never have to converse with her again. Or maybe it was simply Eliza, her clear thinking and honest interest, that made him confess one of his most shameful memories.

'When I inherited the title I was a few months shy of my sixteenth birthday. When the day came, the family was still in full mourning, and the funeral was only a few weeks past. A winter storm blew through the county, and a tree fell on one of the tenant cottages.'

Gabriel watched as Eliza swallowed, worrying where this was going.

'The tree went through the roof, which was due to be replaced in the spring. It killed a woman and her infant child, leaving a widower with no home and five children to tend. He came up to the Hall, hat in hand, to ask what I would be doing about it.'

'I'm so sorry,' said Eliza.

They were meaningless words, made smooth like river stones through sheer time and repetition. But it was clear that she meant them, and Gabriel appreciated the empathy she was showing towards his much younger self.

'I didn't know anything. I still felt like a child, flapping around in his father's borrowed boots. And suddenly people were looking to me for answers. I hadn't been able to help my mother plan the funeral, I had no idea how to properly instruct the estate managers on their work… And now a tenant farmer, who depended on me as his landlord, was standing in the library of my childhood home, calling me "Your Grace".'

It was a scene that seemed perfectly preserved in the

annals of his memory. The room had smelled like dust, woodsmoke and over-stewed tea. The tenant's hands had been chapped red from work and the cold, and his boots had looked like great edifices of sartorial grandeur: hobnailed, wide enough to fit thick wool socks, and oiled to a shiny, waterproof patina.

Here in the present, Gabriel swallowed down the hot shame that still crept over him. 'I told him that I didn't know what to do. That he'd be better off talking to the steward or someone at the church.'

'You couldn't have known,' said Eliza, quick to defend him.

Gabriel wanted to get the conversation over with. He regretted bringing it up, and he wished to move on as quickly as possible. He shuffled the cards again—anything to keep from looking at Eliza's pretty, sympathetic face.

'My mother heard it all from where she'd been keeping an ear out, by the door. She came rushing in with her black crepe dress flapping. She apologised for me and said that I didn't have the sense I'd been born with. She told him she would take care of everything. Then she sent him home with a basket of blankets and biscuits.'

She'd taken over nearly all of the ducal responsibilities. Gabriel had quickly claimed the accounting and logistical tasks, but he had left his mother with the diplomatic role for far too long.

'I know that in your head you believe that one critical error as a child set the tone for all future interactions,' said Eliza. 'I still go a little mad each time one of the family gets a cold, thinking that I'm going to be left alone again. But you must see that you've long outgrown it.'

To Gabriel's mind, this conversation had long overstayed its welcome.

'It's in the past,' he said, with a cheer he did not feel. 'Fancy another game?'

Eliza gave him a long look, and Gabriel experienced the sensation of being studied like a captured butterfly.

'Rest assured that you have cheered me up perfectly well,' she said. 'And, while I appreciate the lesson, I really should retire.' She glanced over at Aunt Mary, and then back at him with what looked like regret. 'Thank you for a lovely evening, Gabriel.'

He stood when she did, and took her hand in his. He could feel the warmth of her skin even through their gloves as he kissed the air above her knuckles. If only they weren't surrounded by people... After three nights in small, cramped inns, this return to Polite Society was a jolt.

'Pleasant dreams, Eliza,' he said, low enough not to be heard.

She left the room with a swish of skirts, and he managed to look away before she closed the parlour door behind her.

With a sigh, he poured himself a second brandy. It was the first night in three that Eliza hadn't given him a goodnight kiss, and he refused to acknowledge that it felt like loss.

Chapter Thirteen

As the coach rolled down the beautifully gravelled drive of Abberly's Yorkshire estate, Eliza couldn't help but think that some people had all the luck. The drive was lined with old elm trees, beautiful green hills rolled across the landscape, and at the centre of it all stood Gordyn Manor, a redbrick Elizabethan house boasting an army of chimneys, what looked like a rooftop walkway along the parapets, two sprawling wings, and massive symmetrical bay windows that stretched from the first floor to the third.

'Look at that house,' she said as the carriage crested a gentle hill. 'I can tell just by looking that it has a gallery and a library. And probably a music room, too.'

'Ooh, and an orangery...' Aunt Mary sighed.

'The village didn't appear to be doing very well,' said Gabriel. 'There were several empty cottages.'

'And the Home Wood has been recently timbered,' said Aunt Mary with a knowing expression. 'He must be quite desperate for coin.'

Eliza scowled. 'All that while he gets to live in this—this *castle*!'

'Don't set the place ablaze until the end of the party,'

said Gabriel, stretching out his legs. 'I'd quite like a chance to enjoy the house before we have to get back in this blasted…er…benighted carriage,' he said, with a guilty look at Aunt Mary.

'I'm not going to burn the house down,' said Eliza.

'Of course you aren't,' said Aunt Mary, replacing a few stray hairpins as the carriage rounded the front of the house.

Only because brick won't burn, Eliza added in the privacy of her thoughts. *And there will be too many innocent people at risk.*

A mixture of excitement and dread churned in her stomach. This was it. This was her chance to reclaim just a little of her independence and dignity, even if only in her own mind.

The carriage came to a stop and Gabriel hopped out of the vehicle even before the tiger had lowered the step. He helped Mary and Eliza down, and for a moment the three of them enjoyed a moment of contemplative silence as they looked up at the manor's façade.

'Good luck,' said Gabriel as the doors opened and Abberly's butler and housekeeper descended to greet their guests. 'It's the role of a lifetime.'

Eliza glanced up at him as the nerves in her belly melted away into something sticky and warm. He seemed to know her so well, and yet only a week ago he'd been nothing but a distant acquaintance. She wanted to thank him. Or ask what happened next. Or hustle him back into the carriage so she could stay in that liminal world where he was all hers.

'Most of Lord Abberly's guests are in the drawing room, having tea,' said the housekeeper as a footman whisked away their bonnets. 'Some of the gentlemen are out for a shoot, and I'd be happy to have one of the grooms escort you to their location, Your Grace,' she added to Gabriel.

He waved away the offer. 'A spot of tea sounds lovely.'

Their little group was shown into a large, formally appointed drawing room. The walls were cream, and although the dark maroon draperies and heavy furniture were currently out of vogue, they fitted in with the deep-set fireplace and the air of history radiating from the old building. People were gathered here and there throughout the spacious room. A cluster of ladies sat around the tea table, and others were gathered at a card table near the corner windows. The Marquess of Merlon was asleep in a chair near the fire, and Lady Beatrice was crocheting near the piano while Lady Cecelia practised.

Eliza paused behind Aunt Mary, automatically seeking out a seat in the corner, where she'd be able to go unnoticed. As she looked around the room again, she thought it quite likely that she was the only guest without at least a courtesy title to her name. All the pillars of Society were represented.

She'd been right. This was Abberly's great social gamble...and she'd be there to ensure that it did not pay off.

'Gabriel?' one of the unfamiliar women said, interrupting the butler's announcement of his presence.

Eliza felt Gabriel tense beside her. 'Mother,' he said. 'What a lovely surprise.'

The Dowager Duchess of Vane stood up from the couch, looking gracefully and effortlessly elegant in a green-and-cream-striped muslin day dress.

'Who have you brought with you? Make the introductions, dearest.'

Without any external sign of discomfort, Gabriel

turned and said, 'Mother, this is Lady Stanley and her niece, Miss Hawkins. Lady Stanley, Miss Hawkins… the Dowager Duchess of Vane.'

Eliza and Aunt Mary curtsied, and then Her Grace looped her arm through Aunt Mary's and guided her over to the sofa. 'I'm sure you must be ready for a cup of tea after all that travel. Summer is simply the worst time to be enclosed in a carriage.'

'So true,' said Aunt Mary, watching wide-eyed as the Dowager Duchess handed her a cup of tea.

They chatted about the weather, and the superiority of the country over the city, and joined in with a few of the other ladies discussing shared friends.

'Now, Gabriel,' said Her Grace, with the presence of a woman who has never tolerated being ignored, 'do tell me how these lovely ladies convinced you to come north and socialise.'

Gabriel had been sitting oddly still on a too-small, tufted Queen Anne chair. He reminded Eliza of the way a rabbit froze in the early-morning woods, pretending that if it didn't move, the hounds wouldn't discover it was there.

When his mother addressed him, Gabriel set down his teacup with a clink and rested his hands on the arms of the chair. 'Eliza and Lady Stanley received an invitation from Lord Abberly, and Lord Stanley thought I could serve as escort. He and Lady Stanley often host me for dinner between Parliamentary meetings.'

The Dowager Duchess paused a second too long before responding brightly, 'Well, they're absolutely lovely. I'm so glad you brought them.'

Eliza nudged Aunt Mary's ankle with the toe of her slipper. Whatever was going on, it was between the Duke and his mother. No grown man over the age of

thirty wanted to hear a Society matron compliment-
ing his mother on how well she'd brought him up, and
Eliza could see those comments forming in Aunt Mary's
mind already.

Of course Eliza was dying of curiosity. Gabriel clearly
hadn't seen his mother for some length of time. Never-
theless, the Dowager seemed perfectly aware of the fact
that Gabriel didn't frequently keep the company of rep-
utable ladies—not that Eliza counted as one any more.

The house party was growing more interesting by the
minute.

As the Dowager commented that Aunt Mary and
Eliza seemed 'absolutely lovely', Lady Partridge sniffed.
'I'm surprised you came,' she said, faux brightly. 'One
hardly expects to see you at these more refined events.'

'We received an invitation from Lord Abberly, just
as you did,' said Aunt Mary.

Someone else muttered, 'I suppose there's no accounting for taste.'

Eliza suspected it was Lady Berkley—the woman
who'd come to Abberly's defence in Hyde Park. She was
among the group playing cards. Perhaps Eliza *did* want
to discover just how well brick might burn.

Before the room could become openly hostile, a footman opened the door and stepped inside. 'Lord Abberly
has asked me to inform you that the shooting party has
returned, and His Highness's carriage has been spotted
turning into the property.'

Someone gasped. 'But he's a day early!'

'We haven't dressed for his arrival!' said another.

Eliza looked down at her rumpled travelling ensemble with dismay. She hadn't even had a chance to comb
out her hair.

'Out we go,' said the Dowager Duchess.

Gabriel offered his mother his arm, and Eliza wondered where the cheerful, winking, good-natured rake had gone. This quiet and proper duke seemed to be someone else entirely.

The guests spilled out into the sunshine of the late afternoon, mingling with the men dressed in their riding breeches and Hessian boots. Eliza and Aunt Mary ended up mostly hidden, near a plant pot the size of a wine barrel, for which Eliza was grateful. She saw Abberly snap something at a footman, who scurried inside just as the royal carriage rounded the house.

In the bright light it seemed to be nearly all gilt, from the golden spokes of its wheels to the filigreed trim and the large royal seal on the door. Here and there it was possible to make out a spot of red paint, but the overall effect was that of a fabled lost city of gold.

The four-horse team of matched greys pranced to a stop, and one of Abberly's footmen scrambled across the gravel to flip down the carriage's step and pull open the door.

It was the first time Eliza had been so close to the Prince, and it was something of a disappointment. He was a large, overdressed man, with flushed cheeks and thinning hair. He was extravagantly dressed in tight buckskin breeches, Hessian boots, and a collar so high it nearly covered his ears. His cravat was a complex knot, tucked into a scarlet waistcoat, over which rested His Highness's navy jacket.

He looked like any other man.

Eliza had known this about the peerage for most of her life: that they looked and acted just like any other people alive. Yet she'd still expected a bit more royal gilding. Here was a bloodline that had ruled for centuries. That had to count for something, didn't it?

Instead he looked…well, middle-aged, overdressed and under-slept.

As Abberly stepped forward to greet His Highness, Eliza decided that maybe one's bloodline didn't matter so much: it was what one did with it. At least the Prince Regent was a famous sponsor of the arts. What had Abberly ever done? Take advantage of his estate tenants and ruin unsuspecting wallflowers, it seemed.

Abberly bowed deeply and welcomed His Royal Highness to Gordyn Manor. The Prince nodded graciously at Abberly, acknowledged the crowd, and then walked inside.

As one, the spectators breathed a sigh of relief.

'Fancy us being so close to His Highness,' whispered Aunt Mary as those closest to the doors slowly worked their way inside. 'I imagine we'll all go and get dressed for dinner as best as we can manage.'

'I'm glad we'll be at the other end of the table,' Eliza whispered back. 'Imagine trying to eat your soup across from the future King of England!'

'That's not for the likes of us, my girl,' said Aunt Mary, nudging Eliza's shoulder with her own. 'So let's simply enjoy being here.'

To Eliza's surprise, she and Aunt Mary were shown to rooms near the front of the house, with large hearths and reading nooks in the bow windows. She'd expected to be put somewhere quiet, near the back of the house. That was what their status merited, and Eliza honestly enjoyed having a bit of distance between herself and the higher echelons of Society.

She washed at the basin in her room, helped a very harried upstairs maid unpack her things, and was just pulling on her gloves when there was a knock at the door.

'Can you believe we have these rooms?' she asked, opening the door in expectation of Aunt Mary.

Gabriel barged his way inside.

'You might be seen!' Eliza hissed, more than two decades of habitual propriety taking her over.

'You can't go through with it,' said Gabriel abruptly. 'You can't do whatever it is that you've planned. The Prince, and my mother, and the whole better half of Polite Society are all here! You have to let it go. The stakes are too high.'

Eliza stiffened, disappointment and disbelief warring behind her breastbone. 'I thought you understood what this was about,' she said. What could possibly have changed since the night before? 'You know what this means to me.'

Gabriel paced in front of the fireplace and ran his fingers through his dark hair. 'I know—*I know*. And you're right. None of it is fair. But this…this can't be the answer, can it? You admitted yourself that it isn't equal to what Abberly did to you, so why don't we…? I don't know… Enjoy the party as well as we can and think of some other way to get your revenge?'

'Get out,' said Eliza, poking her nose into the air and blinking hard.

She abjectly refused to cry tears of frustration in front of this stupid, mercurial man. Maybe it was a good thing that she'd never be able to marry. Even the most seemingly intuitive men ended up being short-sighted boors.

'I didn't think this through,' said Gabriel, crossing the room to stand directly in front of Eliza once more.

He looked so handsome in his dark evening wear, and Eliza hated it that she'd noticed.

'There will be collateral damage if you take things too far—members of the ton who haven't done anything to you. It's selfish of you to prioritise your reasons for being here over theirs.'

'They didn't do anything to scold Abberly,' said Eliza. He knew this—he'd *been* there. 'Wasn't that selfish of them? To prioritise their standing in Society over mine?'

'That's not how Society works,' he argued. 'You can't expect people to change their minds on the rules of proper behaviour just like that.'

'I don't,' said Eliza. 'That would be unreasonable. I expect them to change based on consequences that inconvenience them!'

'Abberly won't realise that that's what this is,' said Gabriel. 'It's like punishing a puppy for chewing a rug two weeks after he's done it. He won't realise unless you tell him—and that would put your family's future in danger.'

He was right, but Eliza didn't want to hear it. 'Fine. It isn't about Society—it's about me. *I* want to see Abberly suffer because it will make *me* feel better.'

'Just don't include others,' said Gabriel. 'And don't include me. I didn't know what I was signing up for when I agreed to escort you north. You said this was about Abberly. But suddenly you think it's all right if other people are affected, too.'

'What has got into you?' Eliza asked, putting as much venom into her voice as she could.

She had to make her words sound biting, otherwise she'd be tempted to sob.

Gabriel ran his hand through his hair distractedly, not quite able to meet her eyes. It was a sharp contrast from the way he usually treated her, and it made Eliza feel cold.

'I'm just trying to protect my mother,' he gritted out.

'Maybe you can risk disappointing *your* family. I don't have that luxury.'

Eliza crossed the room and glared from Gabriel to the door. 'Out,' she said.

How dared he imply that he loved his mother more than she loved Aunt Mary? How dared he suggest that she was a disappointment at all?

'Don't include anyone else in your schemes,' he said as he turned the knob. 'Not even me.'

'I wouldn't dream of it,' said Eliza, and shut the door behind him.

And I won't, she thought as his footsteps faded away. *Not any more.*

Chapter Fourteen

Gabriel wasn't sure what he'd expected after he'd made his declaration to Eliza, but it hadn't involved catching her in the stables early the next morning, dressed in those benighted trousers. She even had a waistcoat on, and with her hair stuffed into a cap she might almost be mistaken for a groom...from a distance. If one squinted.

Or maybe he simply knew her too well to be able to ignore her arse in those trousers. Either way, he'd been unable to sleep well, and had spotted her marching across the grounds through the late-summer mist. Like Odysseus with the sirens, he'd felt helpless to resist. Out he'd gone, following her, slipping into the gloom of the stables behind her.

She'd poked her head into the stalls until she'd arrived at the tack room, which she'd crept into with all the stealth and cool panache of an amorous bullock.

'Why have you still got those trousers?' he asked, stepping into the darkness of the tack room and shutting the door behind him.

Eliza spun around with a gasp. The only light came from a small window high on the back wall, so all Gabriel could see of her were impressions: the gleam of her eyes, the shadowed outline of her shoulders, the occasional scuff of her little shoes across the floor.

'I bought them from the innkeeper,' she said, with a cautious and stubborn set to her chin. 'They're freeing.'

'They're indecent,' Gabriel groused. 'Three centuries ago you'd have been thrown in the Tower.'

'Lucky for me that I live in such a modern and enlightened time,' said Eliza, turning her back on him.

She was looking over the rack of bridles and squinting through the gloom to try and read the numbers above each hook.

'What are you planning to do?' Gabriel asked. He'd thought he saw the gleam of a knife in her hand.

'Why would I tell you?' Eliza asked. 'You're the one who told me to leave you out of my plans.'

'Eliza…' He knew he deserved that. But he couldn't take back what he'd said.

'I'm finding Abberly's riding equipment and I'm going to make a few adjustments,' she said, as though daring him to stop her.

Gabriel frowned harder. 'How do you know which is his?'

'These numbers correlate to the stall plates,' said Eliza. 'And Abberly rides that big white horse he won at Tattersalls last Season. He won't stop bragging about the horse, but he keeps refusing the race challenges he receives.'

'That does sound familiar,' said Gabriel.

Eliza made a satisfied little noise that travelled straight from his ears to the base of his…stomach.

He wanted to be the reason she made that noise.

'Here it is,' she said, and lifted a breastplate down from its hook. The T-shaped piece of leather was looped around a horse's chest and connected saddle to girth, but it wasn't crucial enough to be checked over frequently. Eliza picked away at it with her knife before replacing the piece of leather and crossing over to the saddles.

'Just a bit of work on the girth and we can leave,' she said. 'Unless you'd like to leave now? After all, "the stakes are too high".'

Gabriel grunted. Cheeky minx.

'This doesn't break any of your rules,' she said, taking down Abberly's girth and working away at the buckle. 'There's no collateral damage, and nobody will know that it was me. Unless you decide to tell,' she added as an afterthought.

The part of Gabriel that was still nine years old bristled at the implication. 'Of course I wouldn't tell.'

'Then there's nothing to worry about,' said Eliza, and with that she turned and marched out through the door.

Gabriel loitered, trying to give her time to get back into the house without the two of them being seen together. But he must have waited too long, because Abberly strolled into the stables not much later.

'Vane,' he said, stopping to greet Gabriel. 'Good morning. I'm afraid I didn't have a chance to welcome you yesterday, what with the arrival of my most esteemed guest. I'm pleased you decided to attend—you so rarely join our little entertainments.'

Gabriel shrugged, not feeling like playing games with Abberly so early in the morning. 'I needed a change of scenery, and everyone seemed to be coming north to your estate.'

Abberly scoffed and rolled his small pale eyes. 'Not that I'd call this *real* entertainment. Far too many proper ladies about for that. But I suppose they have their uses. Even if they are boring.'

It wasn't an unusual sentiment, but something about

the way Abberly said it made Gabriel's skin crawl.
Women were *people*—not draft horses too old to be
put to the plough. They were… Well, they were meant
to be cosseted and watched over and raised to be the
wives and mothers of the next generation of peers. They
weren't meant for Abberly's crass 'uses'.

Abberly continued on without missing a beat. 'Come
up to my spring solstice event. That's when we have
real fun.'

'I'll put it in my diary,' said Gabriel, vowing to do just
that. He'd write, *Come up with something to do other
than see Abberly, even if it means sailing for France.*

Thankfully Gabriel was saved from further socialising by the arrival of a few more of Abberly's guests,
and he was able to help the grooms get mounts ready
for himself and a few of the others. By the time he was
ready, nearly an hour later, the Prince Regent had come
down to claim his stallion, and the stables were too cha-
otic for any talking. Grooms bustled here and there, a
few hunting hounds were milling about, and the horses
were either half asleep or half mad from all the activity.

Gabriel wove his co-operative bay gelding through
the crowd, letting his muscles loosen and the horse adjust
to its new rider. The Prince Regent was astride an enormous black horse with refined features and shifty eyes,
and Abberly was up on his white thoroughbred, chatting with the Prince. Suddenly two of the dogs charged
through the crowd, barking and chasing each other, and
that was when Gabriel remembered Eliza's plan.

A few of the women had come out to see the riding
party off, and Gabriel scanned through them, looking
for Eliza. She was now properly clothed, in a pretty
pink day dress, and when he met her eyes she gave him
a crooked little smile.

On the other side of the yard, the dogs were still barking. Abberly's mount, beautifully bred but only half-heartedly trained, shied away from the commotion. The horse crow-hopped to one side, jolting Abberly out of his seat, and then kicked out a hind leg at something behind it.

The rest seemed to happen as if Gabriel was viewing it through a thick, glossy syrup. It was like watching time from the vantage point of a mayfly: each second seemed to stretch on, endless and clear.

One of the straps that crossed the chest of Abberly's horse snapped, dragging on the ground and flapping beneath the horse's front hooves. The horse went mad. It reared, pawing at the air, before launching itself forward in a series of wild bucks and twists. Abberly's hat flew off on the first leap, and he lost his stirrups on the second. When the girth began to slide, it was all over. Abberly was on the ground in a heap, and the horse had bolted for the horizon, trying to escape the saddle that had twisted awkwardly to one side.

For a moment the courtyard was silent. Even the other horses and dogs seemed stunned by what had just happened. And then someone rushed forward to dust off Abberly, and a few others rode out after the loose horse. Abberly himself was soon standing red-faced and dirt-covered in front of the Prince Regent.

Gabriel didn't turn back to look, but he could feel Eliza's smile.

Gabriel didn't see Eliza again until after dinner. He'd galloped along on the ride, then gone target shooting, and had participated in the brandy-drinking and cigar-smoking after luncheon. Dinner had been a lengthy affair, presided over by the Prince Regent, and now, finally, they were joining the ladies in the parlour for some after-dinner entertainment.

He could tell that something was off about the scene as soon as he stepped into the room. Oh, the air smelled of tea and ratafia, and one of the ladies was at the pianoforte, gamely playing Haydn. A group of ladies were playing spillikins in the corner, and the more senior matrons were gathered around the tea service with needlework or teacups held in their laps.

It was a scene of perfect domesticity, and Gabriel didn't trust it one whit. Not when Eliza was sitting off in the shadows beyond the fireplace and refusing to even look in the men's direction.

'Good evening, ladies,' said Abberly, leaning into a flourishing bow. 'We have missed you and hope we might prevail upon you for some gentle company.'

'Oh, of course,' said Lady Berkley. 'And may I compliment you again on the lovely dinner you served?'

Abberly waved away the compliment. 'Only the best for His Royal Highness, who has been so kind to honour us with his esteemed presence.'

The Prince lowered himself into a cushioned chair, and within seconds a footman had scrambled to provide him with a tufted stool on which to rest his puffed ankles.

'Only fools and the French think to lead those they do not know. Besides, a little entertainment is good for one's soul.'

Gabriel thought the state of the country might best be served with more leading and less indulgence. After more than a decade of war, His Royal Highness had decided that what the English really needed was a renewed focus on the arts, architecture and beauty. Gabriel, along with many in Parliament, had raised objections—but, then again, who was he to judge? He had vast landholdings and tenants of his own, and what was that if not a sort of tiny kingdom?

Of course he liked to think he ruled in a Kantian sort of way, with respect paid to the autonomy of his tenants, which conveniently left Gabriel free to go about life as he wished. It seemed to be serving all involved well thus far.

'Do any of these ladies know Schubert?' the Prince asked, which sent Lady Cecelia scurrying to the piano.

On the far side of the room the game of spillikins was reset as two of the women moved away and two young men took their places. Eliza, meanwhile, was still sitting quietly in the shadow of the hearth and picking at what looked like some embroidery.

Seeing her once more acting boring and meek was unsettling. But this was what he'd wanted, wasn't it? For her to act as her usual self until the house party was over and his mother and the Prince could no longer become collateral damage.

As if she were able to read Gabriel's mind, the Dowager Duchess called Eliza over and patted the seat next to her. 'I was just chatting with Mr Lewis, the local squire. Now, your aunt has mentioned that the two of you do most of your own gardening, and Mr Lewis tells me that he has been following the latest in agricultural sciences.'

'We met over dinner,' said Mr Lewis with a smile. 'It's been quite pleasant at our end of the dinner table, hasn't it?'

Gabriel decided right then and there that he didn't approve of Mr Lewis. It was bad enough that the man looked like a refined sort of Viking—all height and blond good looks—but he shouldn't be allowed to so obviously appeal to Eliza's radical nature. *'Our end of the dinner table'* indeed.

'Excellent!' said the Duchess. 'It is always a blessing to have good dinner companions.'

'You must visit London in the spring,' said Lady Joyce, tossing her head the better to show off her jewels. 'The Vauxhall Gardens make a wonderful sight.'

'Miss Hawkins has suggested that,' said Mr Lewis mildly. 'Though I'm afraid I don't come to London much. I'm better with plants than people.'

Lady Joyce leaned in and cast her voice down. 'Perhaps you've been speaking with the wrong people.'

She cut her eyes to Eliza and then took another sip of her drink, letting the comment stand on its own.

'Or perhaps he's simply met the right plants,' said Eliza. 'That's the benefit of talking to one's pets or flowers: they don't talk back.'

Lady Joyce flushed, and Gabriel was torn between admiring Eliza's clever mouth and wanting her to stop while she was still ahead.

'There are so many things in London that you could never do in the country,' said Lady Joyce. 'The grand balls, promenades in the park, visiting the Royal Gallery…it simply can't be topped.'

'Oh, yes, there are certainly no lanes gardens or ballrooms in the country,' said Eliza, stirring her tea. 'Whoever heard of such a thing?'

At this point Gabriel had completely abandoned his own conversation and was eavesdropping on Eliza. Lady Joyce was opening and shutting her mouth like an enraged goose, and the Duchess had to cover a startled laugh with the edge of her teacup. From her chair near a glass-shaded lamp, Mary merely shook her head.

'I believe you prefer the country as well, don't you, Your Grace?' Eliza asked his mother.

'Oh, yes. I come into London every spring, for a few events and to visit the Bond Street shops, but I have got into the habit of remaining in our country home since the death of His Grace.'

Gabriel remembered those days...that first Season. His mother would come out of his father's rooms during the day and ask after their lessons, and talk with them over supper. And then at night she would retreat to the Ducal suite and he would hear her crying on his father's side of the ancient four-poster bed.

Oblivious to Gabriel's trip into dark memories, his mother continued, 'Besides, there are so many things in the country one simply cannot enjoy in London. The fresh air, a good gallop without dodging carts and carriages, even a swim.'

Lady Joyce looked scandalised, but Mr Lewis and the others nodded sagely.

Eliza looked thoughtful. 'I've never been swimming. Perhaps I should add it to my list.'

Her Grace turned to Eliza. 'What list?'

'The list of things I'd like to try,' said Eliza. 'After—'

Aunt Mary coughed loudly, and then theatrically thumped herself in the chest. 'Sorry... A clove has been left in the ratafia by mistake.'

'Oh, I hate it when that happens,' said Lady Beatrice. 'Let me pour you some tea.'

'Thank you,' said Mary, shooting a look at Eliza.

Eliza continued smoothly. 'After another Season not yet married, I have decided to try new things and stop waiting for marriage to happen.'

'What a good idea!' said Gabriel's mother. 'What

do you think of that, Lady Joyce? Perhaps you two can compare notes.'

Gabriel had to admit that the Dowager had a nasty streak he'd never before noticed. He wasn't sure what to think about that—it didn't fit the image of his mother that he'd carried all these years. He'd never considered her weak, or a stickler for the rules…she'd simply always been there. And then suddenly a widow and Gabriel's responsibility as the head of the family.

'Yes, I'll certainly need to ask Miss Hawkins about her years on the shelf. Six, is it? But I think I'll take my turn at the pianoforte first,' said Lady Joyce, before stalking off in the direction of her own mother.

Eliza looked briefly triumphant before rising and excusing herself from the conversation. When he saw her slip out through the door to visit the ladies' retiring room, Gabriel counted to ninety before stepping out into the hall after her.

It was easy enough to lurk in one of the dark alcoves of the huge Elizabethan manor, and when she headed back down the hall he simply stepped out of the shadows and blocked her way.

She didn't even jump. 'What do you want this time?' she asked. 'Are you going to tell me my dress is too shabby? Or that my voice is too grating?'

'What are you talking about?' Gabriel asked. 'Why would I—? Never mind. We don't have the time. I want you to stop being…' he flapped his hand '…witty and daring. It isn't proper!'

Eliza's little jaw dropped, but Gabriel refused to spend any more time looking at her pert pink mouth than he absolutely had to.

'You don't decide what I can and cannot do!' said Eliza, her face flushing. 'And I'm not trying to be subversive, or whatever it is you'll accuse me of next. I was just being myself!'

'That's the problem!' said Gabriel—and wished he could take the words back immediately.

And maybe he wouldn't stop with just that sentence: maybe he wished he could take back this whole trip— no, the whole Season. Maybe the last few. Perhaps he should reach back through time and prevent himself being born at all, thereby saving him from having to face the next several excruciating minutes of his mortal existence.

'The problem,' said Eliza slowly, in crisp, monotone diction, 'is that I'm being myself?'

'No,' said Gabriel. 'That's not what I meant.'

'That's what you said,' said Eliza, her words clicking into place like beads on an abacus. 'You said that my problem is acting like myself.'

'I just don't want you to be such an…an original in front of my mother.'

This had all gone wrong. He had to explain.

'I need to start from the beginning. Since I arrived here with you, your behaviour reflects on me. In front of my mother. Who is already disappointed in me enough.'

Eliza's icy facade melted just a touch. 'You aren't making any sense tonight, Vane. Are you feeling all right?'

'Of course I feel all right,' said Gabriel. 'I just don't want you—'

'What? Embarrassing you in front of your mother?'

The question hung in the air like a noose, just waiting for Gabriel to step into its trap. He couldn't say yes, but he couldn't say no, either.

They stood for a long moment in silence, while Gabriel reassessed all his life choices.

'So I am right,' said Eliza, enunciating the 't' like the click of a coffin lid. 'Well, good luck, Your Grace. You'll simply have to manage your own life, because I shall be busy living mine.'

'Wait!' said Gabriel.

He was not even sure what he'd say next. He only knew he couldn't let her walk away with things so tense between them.

'I'm terrible at the diplomatic part of being the Duke. I don't know what I'm doing. Whenever I try to guess, I make mistakes. And I'm tired of my poor widowed mother suffering for them. All right? I just...' He trailed off.

He didn't know anything any more.

Eliza was right: Abberly deserved to be stopped, and she deserved better. She deserved a chance for revenge.

But Society was also right: people couldn't run around breaking the rules of propriety and expecting to get away without consequences. His mother, through patience and repetition, had taught him manners and the proper way of acting.

And now those two truths were in conflict with one another and he didn't know what to do.

'Fine,' said Eliza. 'I understand about your mother. But leave me alone in the future. You aren't going to change my mind.'

Just as she moved to step around him, they heard raised voices travelling out through the closed library doors.

'You said you would secure the deal,' said the first voice.

Eliza's eyes went round. 'That's the Prince!' she whispered.

Gabriel nodded mutely.

'I'm so sorry, Your Highness. I have traced the deed, but the current owner is dead, and the trustee is suspicious of me. If I pressure him too hard, he'll know he has something of value and raise the price. After all, the land has been effectively abandoned for decades—in his mind there's no rush to sell it now.'

It was Abberly who grovelled.

'I understand,' said the Prince. 'But I shan't wait much longer.'

The library doorknob rattled, which set both Eliza and Gabriel in motion. She sprinted down the hall to the parlour, with Gabriel hot on her heels. She smoothed her hair and let herself in. Gabriel counted to thirty and then slipped inside after her, hoping that nobody would notice that they'd returned so close together.

It appeared no one did. Eliza had returned to her seat by his mother and Mr Lewis. Lady Joyce had started a game of whist with Lady Berkley. Lady Stanley was sipping wine by the fire while some young dandy read to her from *The Swiss Family Robinson*.

He crossed the room and poured himself a brandy, then thought about it and splashed in some more. He should have known better than to get involved with a young lady. He hadn't been trained for this—had never learned how to talk to people and make them understand what he was trying to say. He'd been only fifteen, suddenly the Duke, left to comfort his grieving mother and run the duchy all at the same time.

Since then, his skills had not much improved.

Anyone could learn estate management and accounting from books—he was proof of that. But tact, comfort and emotional graces were skills that Gabriel didn't have. He'd learned that the hard way.

No, he thought, taking a long sip of his drink, this was an experiment that had failed. He'd taken Eliza for a test run at domesticity and he had failed.

It was a good thing he could live with disappointment.

Chapter Fifteen

The next morning Eliza decided to face the day with a stiff upper lip and dry eyes. So what if she felt as if she'd been betrayed by the one person who'd really seen her for who she was? And what did it matter if that one person seemed unable to make up his mind as to whether or not he liked her? That was his problem. If he wanted to try and protect his mother from Eliza's bad reputation, that was his prerogative.

Shoulders set and face washed, Eliza headed down the stairs for breakfast, which was being served out in the garden—of course it was. Eliza wouldn't be able to hide her puffy, dark-shadowed eyes in the more forgiving light of the morning room. No, she would have to sit at one of the pretty little tables outside in all the morning's supposed glory.

Thankfully the seat next to Aunt Mary was empty.

Each of the small tables was laid with a pressed embroidered cloth, pretty china, a tea and chocolate set, and an assortment of toast, fruits, jams and cakes.

Aunt Mary waited until Eliza had taken her first gulp of chocolate before greeting her. 'Are you all right?' she whispered, keeping a perfectly pleasant expression on her face.

Eliza grimaced and scooped some hothouse raspberries and a honey cake onto her plate. 'I'm quite well,' she said, enjoying the tartness of a raspberry. 'Don't I look it?'

'You look a bit tired,' said Mary in a hushed voice. 'And alarmingly ferocious.'

Eliza nodded, and cut her honey cake into six equal bites. 'Good.'

Aunt Mary patted Eliza's hand and topped up her cup of chocolate. 'You'll need it,' she explained. 'There's to be a scavenger hunt later this morning. Apparently it's an annual tradition, and last year Lord Abberly sent them haring all over the estate. His Highness is judging the entries this year, so tensions are high.'

Eliza grimaced, and plopped another little round honey cake onto her plate.

'It's so lucky that you can eat what you like, dear,' said Lady Joyce from the next table.

Her mother briefly looked up from the Society pages, glanced at Eliza, then returned to her reading.

'Oh?' asked Eliza, aggressively forking up a particularly large bite of cake. 'Why's that, Joyce?'

'*Lady* Joyce,' she said sharply.

This caught the attention of the ducal family, who were dining at a table on the other side of Lady Joyce. Both Her Grace and Gabriel were watching Eliza and Joyce over the rims of their teacups, and Gabriel was glaring darkly at Eliza.

He looked delicious in well-worn breeches and polished riding boots, and that somehow irritated Eliza even more.

She made a point of picking up her next bite of cake with her fingers. Eliza ate the sticky cake slowly, and licked the tip of her index finger when she was finished, maintaining eye contact with Lady Joyce the entire time.

Eat cakes in public—done.

Joyce had gone quite pink in the cheeks, and Eliza sent her a caramel-sweet smile. 'You've got half a year until the next Season, Joyce. Go ahead and eat a cake. It can only sweeten your disposition.'

Lady Joyce's face had bypassed pink and was sailing towards puce. 'At least it won't go to my hips!'

Beside Eliza, Mary loyally placed an orange water cake on her own plate. Eliza wanted to hug her. Instead, she made it a point of slowly looking over Joyce's willowy figure.

With an exaggerated shrug, she said, 'It's not as if thin hips have got you anywhere.'

It was no secret that Joyce had been left unmarried after three seasons—and, unlike Eliza, *she* had a dowry.

There was a snigger from the direction of Gabriel and Her Grace.

'How dare you—?' began Joyce's mother, but she was interrupted by the entrance of Mr Lewis.

He was in riding attire, and he looked attractively windblown. The morning sun shone off his blond hair and his beautifully polished riding boots.

'I see I've arrived just in time,' he said, gesturing to the chair across from Mary and Eliza. 'Is this seat taken?'

'Our table has a space,' said Joyce, with all the innocence of a hemlock flower.

'Good morning, Lady Huntbury... Lady Joyce.' Mr Lewis set his gloves down and took his seat across from Mary, sending both her and Eliza a bright white smile.

'Tea, Mr Lewis?' asked Aunt Mary, her excellent manners on full display.

'Please,' he said. 'A little milk, no sugar.'

Mary poured it out, all serene grace, and Eliza was momentarily soothed by the familiarity of the scene. She'd been living with Aunt Mary for most of her life, and had watched her preside over a tea service more times than she could count.

'Thank you,' said Mr Lewis, taking a sip. 'I was afraid I would arrive after the teams had been chosen for the scavenger hunt today.'

'You can assist us!' said Lady Joyce.

Mr Lewis smiled over at her, which crinkled the corners of his eyes in a charming sort of way. 'I believe I've now been added to a team, but good luck in the competition.'

'I'm surprised you're allowed to compete,' said Eliza, trying and failing to peel an orange daintily. There was no ladylike way to eviscerate something with one's fingers, was there? 'What with being a local and all. It could give you an unfair advantage.'

'Hush,' said Mr Lewis, pitching his voice low. 'Abberly hasn't caught on to that yet.'

Oh, Eliza did like anyone prepared to poke fun at Abberly in his own home. 'Have you won a scavenger hunt yet?'

'Only once,' said Mr Lewis. 'But I have a good feeling about this year.'

He gave her a flirtatious little glance, managing to imply that even if he didn't win the prize for the scavenger hunt, he'd consider the year a success because of Eliza's presence.

It was very sweet, and Eliza felt herself flush at his unspoken compliment, but he didn't give her the tingles the way Gabriel did. She sat up a little straighter in her seat and smiled back at Mr Lewis. It didn't matter if he didn't give her tingles yet—it might still happen. She hadn't taken to Vane from the beginning either.

The party ebbed and flowed as guests went inside to change into walking dresses and sturdy ankle boots. Eventually teams started to form, and it quickly became clear that Abberly was doing his best to arrange things so that he and Eliza would be on a team together—Mr Lewis had been partnered with the Dowager Duchess.

Eliza would sooner be on a team with Napoleon.

'I'm sure you want to play,' she said to Aunt Mary, trying not to make the comment too pointed. 'You love our walks around the park.'

Aunt Mary wrinkled her nose. 'It's dreadfully warm today, and the library here is so cool.'

'Oh, I'd love to spend some time with you, Miss Hawkins,' the Dowager Duchess said loudly, clearly having picked up on Eliza's dilemma. 'And I'm sure Gabriel would be happy to escort us—wouldn't you dear?'

'That would give your team an unfair advantage,' Abberly spluttered. 'I think—'

'Lady Joyce has four on her team,' said the Prince Regent. 'Let Her Grace have her choice.'

Eliza decided she was going to give the Prince Regent the benefit of the doubt the next time London's cartoonists decided to lampoon him. His Highness had earned a reprieve for today's help.

'Excellent,' said Her Grace, patting the seat next to her. 'I'm looking forward to spending the day with you, Miss Hawkins.'

'Likewise, Your Grace,' said Eliza with a bouncy little curtsey, before taking her seat.

Aunt Mary finished her tea before wandering back into the manor, content in the knowledge that one of the most powerful women in Society would be watching out for Eliza's best interests.

His plot foiled, Abberly was forced to read out the rules, pass out the list of items, and send the teams on their way.

It was a lovely day to be out of doors, and Eliza's sturdy half-boots thumped along the dusty footpath as Mr Lewis led their party out into the fields. He was tall and kind and handsome, and Eliza was determined to make the most of the day.

If only Gabriel wasn't looming along behind her...

'You could at least speak to me, since Mother has gone to the trouble of roping me into this silly game,' Gabriel said, offering his hand to Eliza to help her over a gnarled root that jutted through the footpath.

She ignored his hand and proceeded down the forest path on her own. He was being rebuked for his comments the night before, and he knew it. But what did she expect? That he would allow her to sully his mother's reputation? Just because *she* chose to face Society's ire, it didn't mean she could drag others down with her.

If she was waiting for an apology it would be a long time coming. It didn't matter how guilty he felt. He'd communicated his position to Eliza last night, and it was up to her how she reacted to that information. After everything his family had been through, Gabriel didn't want to invite any more drama into his mother's life than absolutely necessary—he had a younger sister for that...

'Have you seen a white mushroom?' the Dowager Duchess called back to them, reminding Gabriel why they were out here in the first place. 'I've only seen these little flat ones.'

'Not a spore!' Eliza called back, not even glancing his way. 'But I've been looking for birds' nests.

'It's certainly a beautiful day for it,' said James Lewis, rocking back on his heels and tipping his face up to the sun. 'Remember last year, Your Grace? So terribly windy...'

His mother gave a devious little laugh. 'Miss Blake lost her bonnet in the lake, and pouted when her escort declined to jump in after it.'

This was another little jab to Gabriel's familial pride. He knew he should be more involved with his mother—*he* should have little stories like this to share with his family.

But you have perfectly valid reasons for staying away, Gabriel reminded himself. *Things are just fine the way they are.*

'I can see one!' said Eliza.

'A mushroom?' Her Grace asked, folding the scavenger list and looking off to the side of the path.

'No, a bird's nest,' said Eliza, pointing up into the branches of a sturdy English oak.

She walked over to the tree and gave the lowest branch a speculative look that had Gabriel's senses tingling.

'Absolutely not,' he said, marching over and wrapping his hand around her arm.

Eliza shook him off, flung both arms into the air, and hopped a little.

'I can almost get it,' she said. 'Please, Gabriel. I wasn't allowed to climb trees when I was a child, and my cousins made it look like such fun.'

She'd used his given name in company. In front of his mother.

'It isn't done, Miss Hawkins.'

She glared. 'Are you planning to tattle, Your Grace?'

James Lewis walked over to join them beneath the oak, assessing the gap between Eliza's fingertips and the bottommost branch.

'I won't tell if you won't,' he told Eliza.

She smiled at him, and Gabriel found himself grinding his teeth.

James counted to three as Eliza bounced on her toes, and then, as she leapt, he boosted her into the air by the waist. She dangled for a moment, and then Gabriel got to her. If anyone was going to wrap their fingers around her pretty ankle to push her up into the tree, it was going to be him.

'Thank you, Mr Lewis,' said Eliza, as Gabriel put his palm to her foot and pushed her up properly.

'It's me,' he grunted, glancing back to make sure the groom assigned to carry their basket was standing far enough back that he wouldn't get a look up Eliza's skirts.

Except there was cloth beneath his hand…

'Miss Hawkins, are you wearing *trousers*?' Her Grace asked, sounding more fascinated than scandalised.

Eliza had pulled herself up into a standing position, balanced on the sturdy branch, and with a grin she smoothed her free hand over her hip. 'I thought they might come in useful today,' she said. 'I put them on when we all went inside to change into boots.'

'That would be handy under a riding costume…' said his mother thoughtfully. 'Made out of the same material as the skirts…so it blends in.'

'So this was premeditated?' Gabriel said, half tempted to climb up after her, all the better to scold her. 'That only worsens the offence.'

'What offence?' Eliza asked, yanking on the next

branch to test its weight-bearing capabilities. 'Tree-climbing has never been illegal in England.'

'She's got you there,' said James, grinning over at him.

Gabriel didn't know the man particularly well, and that lack of familiarity only made the man's teasing even harder to take. Eliza was working her way along the branch to the bird's nest, and for a lack of anything else he could do, Gabriel sent a glare towards their unlucky groom.

This story would be all over the servants' hall by dinner.

'What else is on the list?' Gabriel asked, glancing over at his mother.

She'd arranged herself on a tree stump, just as serene and prettily comfortable as if she was sitting on an overstuffed chintz parlour chair.

'A stone with no edges, a white horse hair, a breakfast mushroom, a vine with a purple flower, an egg, a piece of history and a fish.'

'I'm *not* kissing Abberly,' said Eliza from the tree.

She had reached the bird's nest and was trying to tease it from its perch without destroying the painstakingly built structure.

Gabriel closed his eyes, took a slow breath in through his nose, and counted to ten. *Again.* 'A fish,' he called. 'Not a kiss. Are you quite finished up there?'

'Yes,' said Eliza, hanging on to the branch as she triumphantly held up her prize. 'I'm trying to work out how to carry it down without breaking it.'

'Drop it,' said Gabriel. 'I'll catch it.'

She ignored him.

He was beginning to deeply dislike this new method of punishment.

Eliza scrambled down the first two branches easily

enough, cupping the nest against her in one hand and using the other for balance. The sticking point came when she reached the bottom branch and needed both hands to lower herself carefully into a sitting position.

'Just drop it,' Gabriel said, staring straight up at her.

Maybe the benighted trousers were a stroke of genius. Instead of being distracted by her pretty calves, he could be distracted by the fact they were dangling too far overhead for safety.

Eliza's pretty, clever eyes flicked from him to Mr Lewis, to the groom, and back again. Gabriel ground his teeth. Was she really so furious with him? So furious that she would not only continue to embarrass him, but that she'd wilfully endanger herself rather than accept his help?

'Fine,' she said at last, and lowered the bird's nest in the groom's direction.

He gamely trotted over with his basket, and carefully caught the nest in capable hands.

'An excellent specimen,' said John, cheerfully inspecting it.

'I'll be rather more pleased with it once Miss Hawkins is out of the tree,' Gabriel snapped.

Eliza lowered herself to the bottom branch and swung her legs back and forth, her battered half-boots flashing as she did so.

'Maybe I'm not ready to come down,' she said conversationally. 'It's quite nice up here.'

'You're being a detriment to your teammates,' said Gabriel, with his hands on his hips.

He was tempted to grab the insolent ankle that kept swinging past his head and give it a good tug—except that would pull her out of the tree and right down on top of him, and he'd been scolding her about scandal less than twenty-four hours previously.

'Oh, please don't come down on my account,' said Her Grace, who had been watching them both with interest. 'I have no interest in winning and no hope that we could even if we tried.'

Gabriel ignored his mother. God only knew what conclusions she was drawing from this little exchange.

'Will you please come down?' Gabriel asked. He was out of patience.

'Only because you have asked nicely, Your Grace.'

Gabriel decided to accept his victory graciously and not comment on her blatantly combative tone. She was running roughshod all over him—*in front of his mother.*

Eliza gripped the branch, shimmied nervously, then practically launched herself into the air.

She was a blur of skirts. Gabriel lunged forward, grabbing for her waist to try and help control her fall, but instead he ended up with a handful of muslin and Eliza more or less pressed against him, with her hair mussed and her skirts rucked up between them.

'See?' she said, balancing herself against his chest before stepping away. 'The trousers were an excellent decision.'

He hated them. Right then and there Gabriel resolved to send a maid into her room to steal the blasted things and burn them in the kitchen fire.

'Well done, Miss Hawkins,' said his mother, rising to her feet and brushing off her skirts. 'What shall we tackle next?'

Mr Lewis took the list from her and gave it a look. 'We can find a skipping stone in the trout stream where we'll set off to catch a fish. If we cut across the little wood now, we should be finished with the fishing by luncheon.'

'Excellent plan,' said Eliza, bouncing on the balls of her feet. 'Lead the way.'

Mr Lewis offered his arm to Her Grace, who took it with a smile. They set off at a stately pace, and Gabriel let them work their way down the path for a while before offering his own arm to Eliza.

'No,' she said, and trotted through the trees after the others.

'How long are you going to act like this?' Gabriel asked, striding after her.

'Until I feel you have been properly and thoroughly embarrassed,' said Eliza, without looking at him. 'Since apparently that's all I do to you.'

Gabriel resisted the urge to shout. It would probably be easiest simply to apologise, but he didn't have anything to regret. She shouldn't be tempting both fate and Society at this house party.

His mother had already survived the loss of her son and her husband, and his sister Caroline had yet to make a good match. They didn't need their good reputation besmirched through association. He hadn't been able to help them when tragedy had happened, but he would do his very best to prevent further problems.

No matter how ill-suited he was to the task, it was Gabriel's job to take care of his family. He wouldn't fail them again—not even for Eliza.

Chapter Sixteen

It might be petty, but Eliza was thoroughly enjoying discomfiting the high and mighty Duke of Vane.

She ignored him, or she answered his questions as if he was a small child. She flashed her trouser-clad ankles at him whenever the opportunity arose. She intentionally misunderstood his comments. And she directed all her good cheer towards Her Grace and Mr Lewis, who seemed to be enjoying her antics almost as much as she was.

As they trudged along the edge of a field, Eliza found she enjoyed chatting with Mr Lewis. He was agreeable, and polite, if a bit obsessed with grafting roses. He preferred music to reading, riding to walking, and savoury snacks to sweet.

'More for you—not that you need sweetening,' he'd added.

It was kind and flirtatious. She willed herself to feel the same sparks that flew when she so much as argued with Gabriel. But before she could come up with a way to ask him if he liked children, Her Grace hooked the toe of her boot on a tree root and very nearly fell on her face.

'Are you all right?' Eliza asked, picking up the silk-edged bonnet that had flown clear from the Dowager Duchess's head.

Her Grace gave a huffing sort of laugh and lay on her back for a moment, before pushing herself upright and sitting still. 'I think my pride is more affronted than anything else—though there's a terrible throb in my foot.'

'We'll rest for a moment,' said Mr Lewis. 'I'm afraid rabbit holes and tree roots are something that the pavements of London lack.'

'We should take you back to the house,' said Gabriel, crouching down at Her Grace's side.

As he rotated her ankle, they all saw her wince.

'Nonsense,' she said. 'I'm sure it will be fine. Now, help me up.'

Gabriel sighed, and hauled his mother to her feet. She took one long step that turned into an ungraceful hop.

'I'd be happy to escort Miss Hawkins to our next task while you walk your mother back to the manor,' said Mr Lewis.

Eliza's pulse jumped. She would be very nearly alone with Mr Lewis! The thought was both exciting and alarming. She liked him well enough, and a life with him would probably be better than a life spent as her cousins' charity case, but she wasn't ready to be alone with him.

He was a perfect stranger. Gabriel had been coming and going from Uncle Francis's house for years.

That was what made Gabriel different, she told herself. Simply his proximity.

'Absolutely not,' said Vane.

And Her Grace said, 'I'm not sure Gabriel knows the way.'

Eliza shot Her Grace a look, which the Duchess serenely smiled away. The manor was no more than half a mile away, and all of them knew it.

Was Her Grace…? No. Why would she?

'Of course,' said Mr Lewis, placing his arm around the Dowager Duchess's waist and pulling her towards him. 'We'll have you back in no time, and I can pick up a pair of fishing rods while I'm at the house. I should have brought some of my own lures with me—I tie my own. Do you do much fishing, Your Grace…?'

And off they slowly walked, with Mr Lewis still discussing fishing.

Eliza would need to send Her Grace some flowers the next time the woman came down to London. She'd just saved Eliza from a long conversation about lure-tying. Perhaps Mr Lewis really was too much of a country gentleman for his own good.

It was a quarter-hour's walk to a secluded section of the stream, and Gabriel and Eliza marched there in a tense but non-aggressive silence as the groom followed along behind. She was surprised Gabriel had agreed to them going off on their own, considering that he was suddenly the keeper of all things virtuous. But maybe having her by himself meant there would be no one else around to witness her embarrassing behaviour.

The idea stung, and Eliza resolved not to think about it any more. The morning was giving way to a perfect late-summer afternoon, and she was determined to enjoy it while she could.

'You look for the stone,' said Gabriel, peeling off his beautifully fitted coat and laying it neatly over a dry tree stump. 'I'll scout for duck eggs.'

'Ducks nest in the spring,' said Eliza absently, scanning the riverbank for worn smooth stones.

'Usually. But if they don't successfully hatch a brood then, sometimes they'll nest again in late summer,' he said, carefully separating the reeds along the edge of the stream with the toe of his boot.

'Where do you learn that sort of thing?' Eliza asked, picking up one possible stone and then discarding it again.

Gabriel shrugged, his shoulders moving the fine material of his shirt in a very interesting way. The perfect fit of his white waistcoat emphasised the narrowness of his hips and the flat expanse of his stomach.

Eliza abruptly felt as though wading in the cool stream was the finest idea she'd ever had. She would freeze these feelings right out of herself.

'Books, mostly,' Gabriel answered, unaware of the turn Eliza's thoughts had taken. 'When my father and brother died so unexpectedly I ordered all the latest books on estate management and agricultural sciences. They were somewhat helpful,' he added, stooping as he investigated something in the tall grass. 'Though I only remember the useless bits.'

Eliza nodded, trying unsuccessfully to unlace her boots and watch the play of his trousers over his behind at the same time. Finally she had both the trousers and her boots off. She toyed with the idea of removing her freshly laundered walking dress, but decided that wasn't necessary for a peaceful wade in the stream.

'What do you think you're doing?' Gabriel asked, his voice strangled and anger-roughened. He glanced over at the groom, who sat several hundred feet away under a tree, whittling a stick.

'I'm going to wade in the stream.'

'You are going—?'

'Oh, surely even *you* can't scold a woman for getting her feet wet,' said Eliza, rounding on the source of her hurt and irritation. 'Every child who ever spent time in the country understands the joy of cool water during the heat of summer.'

His anger was so frustrating. She'd thought that he understood her, that he'd seen her for what she was, but now that she wasn't funny and daring any more, he was trying to shove her back into the box in which he'd found her.

It hurt so much more than she'd expected.

'I'm not scolding you. I'm trying to protect you from yourself, you stubborn little termagant,' said Gabriel, glaring at her bared feet. 'You're the one who black-mailed me into this position in the first place. Blame yourself.'

Eliza took a step back from him and poked her nose into the air. 'I didn't blackmail you. I only attempted to. There's nobody out here to see us, and I thought you wanted to complete the scavenger hunt as soon as pos-sible. I'll find the stone, you find the egg, and when Mr Lewis returns you can set off to find a piece of history. If none presents itself you can show the Prince Regent your sudden attack of morals—because they are abso-lutely *medieval*. So much for your reputation as a rake!'

Gabriel didn't say anything. His eyes glittered in the sun and a muscle ticked in his jaw, and Eliza re-alised that perhaps she had finally pushed this tall, well-muscled and influential man too far.

'Medieval?' he repeated, his eyes dark and hot, flick-ing from her trousers to her breasts, to her face and back again.

Eliza took another step back, feeling the ground soft and damp under her feet.

'Would you lock me in a tower, Your Grace? Would you have me wear a veil, so that no other man could look upon me? Perhaps you would send me to a nunnery, where I could take a vow of silence and embarrass you no more.'

His expression, which had started out full of ire, had taken on an entirely different cast. He slowly stalked towards Eliza, his eyes dark and his features hungry.

'Locked in a tower? Oh, no, minx. I don't think so. If I was going to lock you anywhere it would be in my chambers, where nobody else could see you in those damned breeches.'

'Oh?' Eliza asked, not willing to show him the effect his words were having on her. 'I didn't realise such an innocent article of clothing could have such a terrible effect on a grown man's equilibrium. Perhaps I'll wear them to dinner tonight! Or, better yet, to church. Do you think the vicar knows that women have legs under all those skirts? Or does the church assume we can float?'

'I hate those stupid trousers,' said Gabriel, his eyes fixed on her as he paced closer and closer, like a great predator preparing to leap. 'I hate the way I can't stop looking at the way they fit over your arse. The way you walk in them and stand up straighter. I hate the idea of other men seeing you in them because I found you first. Even when you pretended to be a wallflower. Those other men can't have you.'

Eliza had turned so that her back was to Gabriel. Looking over her shoulder, she asked, 'Are you sure I wouldn't embarrass "those other men"?' She smoothed a palm over the curve of her behind, where the fabric pulled just slightly too tight. 'After all, you're one of London's most infamous rakes, and I make you… uncomfortable…'

'Put your boots back on,' said Gabriel, his voice low, 'and we'll go back to the house. Then I'll show you just how uncomfortable you make me.'

She still hadn't forgiven him for the things he'd said last night, but she wanted him anyway.

'This is a bad idea,' she said, pulling on her trousers and her worn left boot.

'No argument here,' said Vane, tossing over her other boot.

As she did up her laces Eliza knew that getting any more involved with Vane was a terrible idea. He would only hurt her feelings again, and eventually this house party would end, and he would be in her life no longer.

She shouldn't do it. And yet she wanted him so badly. He was the only person who'd ever made her feel so alive, so confident, so free. And after a fortnight of bad ideas…what was one more?

'You're dragging me around like a kite!' Eliza protested as Gabriel ducked into the servants' staircase.

He ignored her. He'd been like this since that scene in the woods, walking with single-minded purpose as he towed Eliza through the woods, losing the groom along the way, herding her up the hill to the house, and now hustling her up the back stairs.

Had anyone ever wanted her this badly before?

Would anyone want her this badly again?

Gabriel's room was near the end of the long corridor and was noticeably smaller than Eliza's. She was having some kind of thought about that—what possible reason could Abberly have for putting a duke in a worse room than an untitled spinster?—when she heard the lock tumble in the door.

Eliza turned to look back at Gabriel, and then…

She wasn't sure which of them leaned in for a kiss first. It might have been her, clinging to his shoulders as he scooped her up, big palms under her arse, and held her against him. It might have been him, with his dark eyes glittering and his fingers kneading into her flesh.

Ultimately it didn't matter who instigated that first kiss, because it bled into the next, and then another… Soft, gentle kisses and messy, wet, deep ones, all strung together with soft words and panted breaths like pearls on a necklace, shining and beautiful.

Eliza's legs were around Gabriel's waist, and she could feel his muscles bunching and shifting as he carried her across the room to the bed.

'This doesn't mean I forgive you,' she gasped as he dropped her onto her feet, sucking in the air their kisses had denied her. 'You're still a rude, idiot man.'

'And you still can't embarrass me in front of my mother,' said Gabriel, scraping his teeth along the curve of Eliza's throat. 'Doesn't mean anything, this. First rule of raking. Rutting can be just that.'

'Fine,' said Eliza, fumbling at the buttons of his waistcoat.

He batted her hands away and kissed her again. Eliza fell into the kiss, into the clever softness of his mouth, while between them she could feel him yanking at his waistcoat and loosening his cravat. He went after her dress next, pulling it off over her head with the same efficiency he'd displayed by the stream.

'Trousers,' he barked, taking his cravat and shirt off entirely, leaving himself naked from the waist up.

'What about them?' Eliza asked. 'Is it that they're divine? That I've discovered the source of men's power?'

She was taunting him and they both knew it.

'That they're *mine*,' said Gabriel, lunging at Eliza and knocking her down to the ground.

The fall was almost dizzying: the tilting landscape, the sense of weightlessness. And then his strong arms banded around her, keeping her tight to the bare skin of his chest even as he controlled their descent.

They landed on the carpet beside the bed. His mouth found the hinge of her jaw and pressed hot kisses there as his hands scrabbled between them, tearing at the button fall of her trousers.

'What—?' she asked, glancing down at her body when Gabriel gave her trousers his first great tug.

His head snapped up, his eyes met hers, and he did it again: he held on to the open flap of the and tugged again. It pulled Eliza's hips up into the air, and—

And she was furious with him for destroying these things that were now hers, that gave her independence and joy.

But she was aroused, almost embarrassingly so. His chest and shoulders were bulging with the exertion. His jaw was working and his eyes were still locked on hers, hot and dark and wicked. *This* was the rake she'd heard so much about.

The seam of her trousers began to rip. Cool air rushed in where fabric had once been, baring her sensitive core to the sunshine-filled room. Eliza didn't know if she should wriggle away or press in closer, so she fisted her fingers in his mussed hair and pulled him up to kiss her, all teeth and heat and pent-up emotions she would rather die than name.

He didn't let go of her ruined trousers. With his lips still on hers, nibbling and licking and sucking, he continued to tug and rend the material, pulling the fraying scraps down her thighs, over her calves and off, then taking her stockings and boots off in one fell swoop.

'What are you doing?' Eliza asked, her voice high as Gabriel bent forward and scraped his teeth along the crest of her thigh.

'Hush,' he told her, turning his head and running his tongue along the soft inside of her opposite leg.

His hands were on her hips and his fingers were swiping back and forth along the crease where her thigh and her body met, slowly sensitising the skin there.

'But—'

His face was so close to the heat of her. This couldn't be proper. But then again…where exactly had propriety got her?

'But what?' Gabriel asked, rubbing his cheek against her again. 'But you're so soft here? But I'm the only man to have seen this part of you? But you smell like summer…like warmth and life and salt?'

Eliza was panting now. Her nipples had drawn tight beneath her stays and she couldn't—

With his eyes still locked on hers, Gabriel lowered his head, parted her sex with his thumbs, and pressed a hot, open-mouthed kiss to her hidden, sensitive nub.

It was all heat and wetness and gut-clenching tension. Eliza had never felt anything like it. But it was nearly too much too quickly, and she couldn't decide if she wanted to press closer or wriggle away. The sight of it was obscene: the breadth of Gabriel's shoulders wedging her thighs open, the pink of his mouth and tongue, and the shine of her arousal over his jaw and cheeks.

Gabriel tilted his head and did something with his tongue, and Eliza found her hips rocking up into his face with desperate little tilts she couldn't have stopped for anything.

'You were saying…?' he asked, resting his chin on her belly and giving her an arch, smug expression.

Eliza shoved at his face, aroused beyond words.

Gabriel laughed, his eyes crinkling at the corners, and settled back to the task before him. When he slid two fingers into her wet heat she moaned, and her thighs trembled. He seemed content just to stroke her. She held a fistful of his hair, and could feel each time he tilted his head to one side or the other, methodically driving her higher and higher.

Eliza had never known it could be like this between a man and a woman. She'd come close with Gabriel that night after the fair, but now…? Now it felt as if her body was an instrument, strung high and tight, and Gabriel was the virtuoso playing her. Her thighs were trembling, her stomach muscles were clenched, and nonsense words mingled with Eliza's gasps and moans as her arousal reached almost painful levels.

His mouth had to be getting tired, but still he gave her no quarter. It was all luxurious swipes of his tongue and the hot suck of his lips, and Eliza didn't know if she could survive any more, or if she would shake apart at the seams, thoroughly wrecked by Gabriel's attentions.

Then, finally, she came. For the space of one long, endless moment it felt as though she couldn't breathe, as if she was suspended in a hot, soft, honey-coloured place where the only thing in the world was Gabriel's mouth at her sex and the pleasure sizzling in her veins.

And then the world came roaring back. Eliza's limbs were still shaking and her heart was racing and Gabriel was braced above her, his face shiny with her wetness and one hand fumbling at the buttons of his own trousers.

'We can't— We can't!' she said as his cock sprang free, swollen and flushed and larger than she remembered.

She would not go home with a bastard in her belly. She would live her own scandal, but she wouldn't wish it on a babe that could never outlive the reputation of its mother.

'We won't,' said Gabriel, and his voice sounded hoarse, sex-rough and dark. 'Just let me… We won't, but I just need—'

'Yes, please,' said Eliza, rolling her hips against him.

He fitted his cock to her cleft and slid through her arousal-soaked lips, a nearly frictionless glide of flesh against flesh. The thick root of him pressed into Eliza's over-sensitive nub and made her squirm, all without him ever dipping inside of her.

'Hell,' said Gabriel.

And Eliza looked up into his beautiful face as he clenched his eyes shut and began moving in earnest. His weight against her increased as he ground his cock through her wet folds, and Eliza craned her neck down to watch the pink, flared head of his arousal appear and glide along her belly before retreating again.

She should have felt trapped, boxed in against the carpet by his heavy body. The hanging bed curtains gave them the illusion of privacy, but the bright sunbeams coming through the windows caught on the sweat beaded across Gabriel's brow and Eliza's chest. The whole scene should have felt naughty and oppressive and wrong, but Eliza only wanted more.

She reached between them to tentatively touch his cock—hard and slick within her—and he jerked when she did it.

'No,' he said, gritting out the word as if he was barely clinging to the concept of a spoken language.

'Yes,' she said, undulating against him.

Gabriel dropped his forehead to the curve of her throat and Eliza kept her hand on his cock, flat now, keeping pressure on it as it slid through her wet sex. Gabriel groaned, loud and low, and began to thrust more quickly against her, so she concluded she was doing something right.

Gabriel came all at once, in a hot spatter of seed that landed on her belly and her hand. His big body went limp over hers. Eliza smiled to herself, and kissed the sweaty skin of his shoulders. She decided that maybe he was wrong about his first rule of raking: it didn't have to be only about the act.

He'd declared that bed games could be meaningless, and Eliza supposed that maybe they could. But this game certainly hadn't been. There had been passion between them, but it had been a passion that went beyond the physical. He'd wanted her *because* she was stubborn and outspoken and daring enough to wear trousers. Regardless of whether or not he thought she was a scandal, he clearly desired her just the way she was.

With a contented sigh, Eliza pressed a kiss to Gabriel's hair. At the moment they weren't bickering. Whatever other meaning there was in this encounter was something she would worry about later.

When he rolled off Eliza, she took a moment to admire the way his body was constructed; all smooth planes and hard lines. It was so different from her own, in highly intriguing ways.

'We probably shouldn't have done that,' he said, smiling over at her. 'But damn if I don't feel better.'

'More arguments should be resolved thusly,' said Eliza. 'Although I really am annoyed about my trousers.'

'I'm not,' said Gabriel, rising to his feet and doing up his falls.

Eliza stole one last look at his bum before getting up herself.

'Will you tell me what set all this off?' Eliza asked,

as she smoothed her chemise down and looked for her second stocking.

'Those damned trousers,' said Gabriel, washing his face at the basin.

'No, not that—or not *just* that, I suppose. Your whole…change of heart. Wanting me to act like a proper lady.'

He made a face at her in the shaving mirror. 'Must we?'

'We really must,' said Eliza. 'And then we can declare this little truce over and you can go back to glowering at me.'

It hurt to think about that, but not knowing was worse.

Gabriel shrugged—which did very interesting things to his unclothed shoulders.

'I publicly escorted you here. My reputation affects my mother's. I'm a rather poor substitute duke, and I try to leave all the…' he waved his hand through the air as though he could catch the words '…all the *people* business to my stewards. I'm no good at dealing with tenants or helping with my mother's problems, but I can try to stop problems before they occur. And you, minx, are a lovely little problem.'

Chapter Seventeen

The next morning, Eliza loitered outside Aunt Mary's room, waiting for her to be ready to go downstairs for the day's games. Unlike yesterday, she did not intend to lose spectacularly, publicly claiming fatigue. She'd never live down the ignominy of pretending that a country scavenger hunt was too tiring for her.

'Miss Hawkins!' said Abberly, coming around the corner in what smelled like a cloud of heavy floral cologne.

It was all Eliza could do not to take a step back from the man.

'I'm so glad I found you! How have you been enjoying your stay at Gordyn Manor?'

'Your home is lovely,' said Eliza, trying to be polite while also providing as little positive affirmation as possible.

'I'm very proud of it. The only thing it's missing is a mistress,' he said, taking a step towards her and sending Eliza stepping away out of instinct.

'Aunt Mary would love to hear more about the manor, I'm sure,' she said, hoping that Aunt Mary would hear her. If she didn't show up soon, Eliza might just attempt to push Abberly out of a window.

'I'd hoped that you'd reconsider my suit,' said Abberly, his little eyes fixed on Eliza's face. 'You'd have everything. A title, the estate, a place in Society. As my countess, you would—'

'There you are, Miss Hawkins. I'm terribly sorry to be late,' a familiar voice called.

Without needing to turn and look, Eliza could feel Gabriel approaching her from behind. It was a change in the air pressure. And when he looped her arm through his own, she felt fully justified in clinging. It was hang on to Vane, or hit Abberly in the nose.

'Vane,' said Abberly, with a nod shallower than a puddle. 'Miss Hawkins and I were having a private discussion.'

Gabriel blustered on. 'Can't have been terribly private out here in the corridor. Thank you for keeping her company,' he called back over his shoulder as he walked Eliza away.

It was all Eliza could do not to giggle nervously. 'Oh, he'll be furious about this, for sure. You interrupted his proposal.'

'Out in the corridor like that? The bastard—the blighter—has no sense of style.'

'I don't know about that,' said Eliza. 'He was wearing a velvet waistcoat.'

'In August? Then he's a fool.'

Gabriel walked them out through the front door and onto the neatly clipped lawn, navigating them around the house to the gardens.

After a moment of tense perambulation, he asked, 'What did you tell him?'

Eliza gave him a sour look. 'What do you think? Honestly, I thought you were cleverer than that.'

Gabriel winked at her, and Eliza realised he was teasing. 'You never know, minx. You might have taken one look at his estate and decided that this place was exactly what you deserved. Marry the man, survive the honeymoon, and then put arsenic in his decanter. The way the man drinks, no one would have cause to suspect you.'

Eliza gasped theatrically. 'Your Grace! You scolded me for wanting to duel him, but you endorse the hypothetical murder of my not-husband?'

'Poison is traditional,' said Gabriel. 'Just ask anyone.'

'I'll keep that in mind if he asks again,' said Eliza. 'Though I cannot determine why he's so adamant that I marry him. Lady Joyce would fall over herself to take up the role of countess, even if it does mean tolerating a creature like Abberly.'

'And she has a cash dowry,' Gabriel reminded her helpfully.

'True. His obsession doesn't make any sense.'

He patted her hand before releasing her into the custody of Aunt Mary. 'Just a few more days and you'll be free of him for the autumn.'

'Free of whom?' asked Aunt Mary, who had beaten Eliza downstairs and was lounging in one of the chairs that had been brought outside and arranged under the trees.

'You know who,' said Eliza darkly.

Gabriel whispered, 'It rhymes with Shabberly.'

Mary rolled her eyes in an affectionate sort of way. 'I should have known.'

'He has proposed again,' said Eliza, slumping down on the arm of Mary's chair.

Aunt Mary poked her in the side. 'Don't slouch, dear.'

'Why not?' Eliza asked, but she straightened up.

'It will spoil your pall-mall form,' said her aunt,

watching a handful of liveried servants setting a course for the game.

It was only one of the garden activities planned for the day. There was to be a rowing race on the lake, an egg-toss, and battledore in the afternoon. It sounded like good fun, but Eliza couldn't ignore her rising frustration with Abberly. The man was still pursuing her, despite everything he'd done to harm her reputation. And none of these silly games *mattered.*

The other women were still ignoring her at best, or being hostile at worst. Aunt Mary was enjoying herself, which did please Eliza, but she knew she was enjoying her holiday before returning to Town and a Society that might or might not judge her for Eliza's actions.

It was so stupid and unnecessary. Just like Abberly. Eliza had let Gabriel and her heartache distract her from her purpose, but there was a reason she was at this event: to besmirch Abberly's reputation the way he'd muddied her own. After her stunt with the saddle, Eliza had been lax in looking for more opportunities to embarrass him. She knew there would be dancing later on—perhaps she could untune the pianoforte…

The Prince Regent had been stationed in a miniature Royal Pavilion, which provided him with shade and a place to rest. He was still tolerating Abberly's fawning, and the Earl had asked him for permission to open the day's activities, before announcing that it was time to select partners.

As the co-winners of the scavenger hunt, Lady Joyce and Lady Berkley had first choice.

Lady Joyce milked the moment, looking around in flirtatious debate. 'Would you agree to partner me for the games, Your Grace?' she asked, looking at Gabriel.

Before he could reply Joyce locked eyes with Eliza, letting her know that this time *she* had won.

Eliza shrugged. Spending time in Gabriel's company was…tolerable—and invigorating, arousing, irritating and confusing—but she didn't own him. If Joyce wanted to spend the afternoon hanging on Vane's arm, it was none of Eliza's business.

Lady Berkley went for the old Marquess of Merlon, in a surprise move, considering the man was very nearly old enough to remember the invention of the wheel, let alone the pall-mall mallet.

'Excellent choices, ladies,' said Abberly, giving his audience a well-practised smile. 'As for the rest of us, I suggest we choose by rank. Lord Brockelmore, you're first.'

And then…surprise, surprise…it was Abberly's turn. He sent Lady Beatrice a sly smile, before turning to Eliza and bowing in her direction. 'Miss Hawkins, I'd be honoured to partner you for our games.'

The women tittered, and Gabriel shifted his weight uneasily. Aunt Mary, in anticipation of Eliza's fit of blinding rage, grabbed a handful of Eliza's dress, unsubtly reminding her that beating a titled peer over the head with a pall-mall mallet would result in a fate worse than death: a sentence to Bedlam.

'Of course,' said Eliza, trying to sound cool and unaffected, but probably sounding short and slightly constipated. 'Thank you.'

The partner-picking continued, and then it was time for the first event.

'What excellent form you have,' said Abberly as Eliza stepped up to take her first turn on the pall-mall green.

'Thank you,' said Eliza. 'We unpopular ladies have to entertain ourselves somehow, and I spend quite a lot of time in the garden with the pall-mall set.'

She drew back her mallet as if she was going to pick-axe her way to freedom and hit the ball firmly, sending it launching down the course, where it landed several feet beyond Abberly's ball.

'Stroke one,' she said.

'That can't be allowed,' said Lady Joyce from the side-lines. 'Her ball is very nearly at the post!'

The Prince Regent set down his wine glass and peered out at the course. 'I believe that is the point of the game,' he called out. 'Well played.'

Eliza curtsied to the Prince, deciding that maybe the day wouldn't be so bad after all. She was surrounded by people, so Abberly was unlikely to try anything, and it was a beautiful day. Besides, all the time she was spending sitting around waiting to take her turn would provide plenty of time for her to plot.

The pall-mall tournament resulted in Abberly and Eliza taking second place, and in Eliza deciding that inventing ways that would sabotage Abberly's reputation without being immediately traced back to her was going to be more difficult than she'd expected.

Maybe the brandy... she thought as Abberly led her down to the ornamental lake and its little white boats.

She could get water easily enough, and it shouldn't be too hard to water down the decanters in the library and the parlour. Serving mid-level liquor was shameful enough, but having to water that liquor down halfway through a house party was absolutely mortifying. It would signify that Abberly had been entirely cut off from sources of credit and hadn't been able to purchase an adequate amount of liquor.

Serving watered-down brandy to the Prince Regent? He'd never live it down.

Drops of water flicked into Eliza's face and she

blinked at Abberly, who had rowed them a few yards out to the unofficial starting line.

'Are you reconsidering my offer?' he asked, perspiration beading on his brow.

Eliza shook her head, reconnecting to reality. 'I cannot think of anything that could possibly convince me to reconsider,' she said bluntly.

A gun was fired into the air and Abberly dug the oars into the water, huffing out his breath. 'What will it take?'

'Take?' asked Eliza, taking a perverse sort of joy in the man's physical suffering.

'For you to marry me?' he asked, clearly knowing that the splashing of the oars and the cheers of the bystanders would drown out his question.

'Why in the world are you so determined to marry me?' Eliza asked. 'It makes no sense. I have no real dowry—just a piece of pointless land somewhere, I'm not a beauty... I'm not particularly talented or well-connected. It couldn't possibly benefit you.'

'Have you never,' he wheezed, 'heard of...falling in...love?'

Eliza sniggered. 'You're not in love with me.'

Abberly was glaring now, and red in the face. Gabriel, with his long arms and strong back, was at least a boat length ahead of them, and Lord Hurley was passing Abberly even as he spoke. Even without words, his discomfort was clear.

'You've spent no time with me,' she said. 'You don't look at me at balls. You spend all your time with dandies or fawning women. And yet now, this Season, you've suddenly decided that nothing will do but to marry me. You have to be up to something.'

'Family...' Abberly gasped out as cheers went up for Gabriel's win. 'Heir...'

'You won't get one from me,' said Eliza.

Abberly leaned on the oars, panting heavily as the boat drifted. 'Bitch,' he said.

Eliza shook her head. 'Better a bitch than a wife,' she said. 'A bitch can still make her own decisions.'

That was true—though she'd never thought about it in quite those terms before. After a woman had married and taken her husband's name, he made all her decisions for her. He could send her to the country, commit her to an asylum, take her children, sell her property— and make use of her body with or without her consent.

In a system like that, why did *any* woman agree to be married?

Abberly picked up the oars and slowly began rowing them back to the shore. 'I'd hoped you would see reason, but it's clear that you're just as contrary now as you were in Hyde Park. Your aunt and uncle will see reason, though. I'm sure of it. They'll save so much without your care and feeding.'

This time Eliza did think her actions through. It was as if the world slowed down, and everything was so clear.

Abberly's oar struck something just below the surface of the water, knocking him off balance and sending the boat rocking from side to side. All Eliza had to do was bump the opposite oar and lean into the tipping of the boat and Abberly lost his balance completely, landing among the muddy reeds with a splash.

'Are you all right?' Eliza asked, making sure her voice would carry. 'Lord Abberly, you must be exhausted after that race. Here, get back into the boat and I'll paddle over to the dock.'

Abberly was spluttering out a string of swear words Eliza had never heard before. Two footmen waded in and got Abberly back on his feet, and while he sloshed his way to shore they towed Eliza and the boat a few feet forward so that the little craft was quite firmly beached.

'Thank you so much,' said Eliza prettily as she was helped onto dry land.

Abberly stalked away, heading towards the manor, where he would presumably wash and change his clothes.

Yes, Eliza thought to herself. *My revenge is off to a good start.*

Chapter Eighteen

There was only so much Society-approved fun a house full of people could get up to with their clothes on. To release a little of the pent-up pressure, the following day was mostly unplanned, although a group of guests was travelling down to the local village for a little shopping and reconnaissance.

Abberly had deployed both his carriages, and a group of more dedicated riders wove in and out of the little parade trundling down from the manor to the village of Dimford.

Abberly and his ilk were riding ahead of the carriages, in an attempt to keep the dust off their pretty riding clothes. Gabriel's ennui with Society had returned with additional interest, so he was content to ride behind and sulk in his happily solo cloud of dust.

Spending an afternoon on the arm of Lady Joyce had felt very much like swimming in shark infested waters: he had been in close proximity to a cold-blooded predator, and while he had known she *probably* wouldn't bite him, the chance had been too far from zero for Gabriel's liking. It had been even worse after having been in such close proximity to Eliza. Having her close had discomfited him. Being away from her was even worse.

Lady Joyce didn't laugh because she thought Gabriel was funny, or foolish, or even amusing. She laughed with a practised little head tilt that told him she thought she *had* to laugh. She agreed to everything he said without challenging him, stared longingly at food she wanted but didn't dare eat, and acted as if being in his company was some kind of accomplishment.

Eliza would never have done that. She'd have told him off, stolen strawberries from his plate, and acted like...well, like a friend. Someone who actually liked him because he was Gabriel Livingston, not because he was the Duke of Vane.

'You're brooding over something,' said his mother, dropping her horse down to a brisk walk beside Gabriel's mount. 'I still have a sense for such things, you know. Some silences are peaceful, while others mean you're up to something. This is not a peaceful silence.'

'I'm not up to anything,' said Gabriel, dismayed at how quickly she could make him feel twelve years old. 'I'm riding along and minding my own business.'

His mother gave him a long look, and then puffed her fashionable ostrich feathers out of her face. 'I wanted to congratulate you on your discovery of Miss Hawkins. She is such a refreshing character.'

'That she is,' said Gabriel.

Eliza even got on with his mother—something his future wife needed to do as well. The women in his family tended to live for somewhere between eighty years and a geological age.

Not that he should be too worried about it. He had no plans to take a wife.

'You've made a fine choice,' said his mother, shortening her reins to prevent her horse from snatching mouthfuls of grass from the verge. 'When will you propose?'

Oh, no. No, no. That could not be where she was taking the conversation.

'I'm not going to propose!' said Gabriel, horrified. 'She isn't... Oh.'

His mother was laughing, and not even bothering to hide it. 'You're not still determined to leave the title to your brother, are you?'

Gabriel was tempted to urge his horse into a gallop and ride well away from his mother. He would make it to the village and then... What? Why stop there? He could ride to Scotland and become a shepherd, or catch a boat for Australia, or sail to the West Indies and see waters clearer than a window.

This didn't have to be his life!

But it was, and part of that meant, apparently, seeing to the succession.

'I quite like Lady Beatrice. You know...the young lady with red hair,' said his mother companionably. 'This was only her second Season, so she's on the younger side, but not completely green. Her mother has a level head: an important consideration in a future mother-in-law that many men fail to take into account.'

This was why he never went home to visit. He'd been having such an enjoyable time this week that he'd very nearly forgotten. Between his mother's nagging and his own crushing guilt, there wasn't much comfort to be had in homecoming.

'I'm not marrying Beatrice,' said Gabriel, trying not to sulk.

'You should be grateful I'm not suggesting Joyce,' she said. 'But it's discomfiting to see someone looking at one's own son with such open hunger.'

Gabriel wrinkled his nose. 'You don't need to find me a wife,' he said.

'Good. Then choose one of your own.'

His mother rode on, leaving Gabriel stewing with only himself for company. He'd originally taken on Eliza and Lady Stanley as a sort of experiment, to see if perhaps he was wrong and he *would* be able to handle the emotional and logistical responsibilities of fatherhood and husbanding. He'd had high hopes while they were on their own, but now he'd mucked up his friendship with Eliza. It might be beyond repairing.

What kind of a dolt told a woman that he found her embarrassing? His kind, apparently.

Nothing made sense any more.

Gabriel couldn't help but look at the village through Eliza's eyes. There were empty cottages, which seemed unusual for a village of this size. The roads were in good condition, but there were only a few people gathered in the square or wandering along the pavements.

This was ridiculous. It wasn't as if Eliza had ever even said anything to him about villages or estate management or marriage—she wasn't the cause of anything that was on his mind. She was simply the catalyst: the change that had come rocketing into his life and from which he couldn't look away.

Gabriel watched as a group of women swarmed into a little shop, while another group drifted over to peer inside the bakery. Gabriel loitered by his horse until most of the group had dispersed. He wondered what Eliza would do in this situation. And he wondered why the answer mattered so much to him.

Well, he thought, *Eliza would make a decision and stick with it.*

She'd do something she enjoyed and she wouldn't second-guess it.

Spirits renewed, Gabriel headed straight into the pub.

The inside was dark and cool, and Gabriel felt himself relaxing immediately. The air smelled of ale, sausages and baking bread. There were two men in the corner, wearing sturdy canvas trousers, and Gabriel was pleased to see the familiar jar of pickled eggs on the corner of the bar.

If he left here smelling like ale, vinegar and sulphurous egg, all the gently bred ladies were guaranteed to avoid him.

He ordered a pint and a snack, slid over the requisite coin, and then wandered back outside to enjoy the last of this fine weather. The vicar was sitting on a bench beneath the pub window, and Gabriel walked over to him, taking a seat but leaving a comfortable amount of space between them.

'Mind the company?' he asked.

'Not at all,' said the vicar, giving Gabriel a salute with his own pint.

They sat in companionable silence for a moment. Flowers gently waved from upstairs window boxes, the air smelled of sunshine and roast meat, and the tidy stone walls echoed with the distant sound of women laughing.

It was lovely, and Gabriel felt he could finally breathe all the way out.

Eliza had been so angry with him over the past two days, and it was becoming more and more clear that she'd been in the right.

'It's a lovely village,' he said, breaking the companionable silence that had fallen between himself and the vicar.

'That it is,' said the vicar. 'We're very proud of it.'

'I noticed a few empty cottages on my way in. Is that usual?'

The vicar made a noise of disapproval. 'It's becoming usual under the new Earl. Those stewards of his think the village is nothing but an income-generator for the great house.'

Ahh, there it was—the feeling he'd momentarily sidestepped. Guilt. The old version of Gabriel would have changed the topic or fled this conversation entirely. This new version that regretted scolding Eliza and was attempting to open himself to change made him stick it out.

'The old Earl, he'd come down to the pub once or twice a year to have a chat with the villagers around harvest time,' said the vicar, leaning forward as if he was sharing state secrets. 'A bit old-fashioned, a bit formal, but a decent old man all the same. He sent baskets round to the hungrier families at Christmas, and he was known to forgive a new widow her rent after her husband died.'

'The new Earl doesn't follow his father's example?' Gabriel asked.

He couldn't remember his own father drinking with their tenants. Then again, Gabriel hadn't been of an age for pub-going, and it was Matthew who'd been in training to inherit.

'Not a bit,' said the vicar. 'He sends his pompous stewards round when the rents are due, and they doesn't wait around to hear if there are things that need fixing, either. Those empty cottages you passed on your way into the village…? One of them, the roof could be used to strain cheese. Leaks like a sieve. It's a wonder there's still a roof on it at all. The widow woman who rented it has moved to Birmingham to live with her sister.'

'But the stewards?' Gabriel asked, concerned and confused. 'Isn't it their job to have these things repaired?'

The vicar gave him a canny look that lasted several seconds too long.

'Oh, it is, and they should, right enough, but they work for the Earl, you see? They're paid by him, and it's in their best interests to save him money and make sure he's pleased with their work. Who's to speak for the tenants?'

Now that Gabriel had heard the answer it seemed horribly obvious: the Earl's stewards were middle men, whose livelihood depended on the satisfaction of their titled employer. There seemed very nearly no space in that equation for human welfare at all.

'So…the Earl needs to instruct his stewards to ask about the cottages, repairs needed, and the state of each household. And he needs to take their reports seriously.'

He was mostly talking to himself, but the vicar nodded along with him. 'That would be a good start, I'm sure.'

The conversation wandered to other things: the ale—yeasty and fresh, a wonderful northern brew—the weather, and the recent news.

A wandering dog nosed up to them, hoping for scraps, and the vicar set his empty pint aside.

'This is Vixen, old Mr Taylor's companion. She's always slipping out as he's coming in the door. I'll walk her back on my way home. Thank you for the conversation,' said the vicar, and then he was off, herding the squat, rotund dog back through the winding lanes of the village.

Gabriel tipped his head back and thought. At this moment he was uncomfortably like Abberly—which was entirely unacceptable. At least he *read* his stewards' reports…but still… If he wanted to give being a proper duke another go, he needed to be more involved.

Across the street, some of the high-born ladies from the house party exited the village shop and headed into the bakery, chatting and laughing as they went. Gabriel wondered what mischief Eliza was getting up to. He hoped the other women were being kind…

He did not, however, have to wonder what Eliza would do about his ducal situation. If there was a problem, she'd take care of it herself. She'd gone on a five-day coach journey just for the tantalising possibility of revenge. If an entire village full of people needed setting to rights, she'd be on a horse within minutes.

He wasn't a teenager any more. Even if talking with his tenants was awkward, he'd get through it. And if they judged him for it… Well, that would be his cross to bear. It had to be better than the guilt.

Before he could brood himself into a proper state, Eliza exited the village shop with a bounce in her step. She spotted him on the opposite side of the road and headed in his direction, all glowing skin and general good cheer.

Just looking at her brightened Gabriel's mood—and that was a warning bell all on its own. When this week was over, and he'd taken her safely back to London, they wouldn't be able to talk like this any longer.

'I see you've found your own entertainment,' she said, nodding towards his pint and empty plate.

She sat down on the bench beside him and surveyed the little village square. The blacksmith's was across the way, and the rhythmic fall of his hammer whiled away the time just as surely as the ticking of a clock. It was a peaceful village, and Gabriel found himself soothed by Eliza's company.

'I have,' said Gabriel, finishing the last of his ale and setting the tankard aside. 'I needed a bit of quiet.'

'I know just what you mean,' said Eliza. 'Your mother and I crept out early to walk down to the inn, where we posted some letters. Aunt Mary and I have written to Uncle Francis, and it looked as though Her Grace has written to half of England.'

A pang of guilt shot through Gabriel. Perhaps his mother was merely socialising, as mothers were wont to do, or maybe she'd been taking on more of the work for the duchy than Gabriel had realised.

The carriages that had ferried the party down to Dimford were waiting by the corner, and a small group of partygoers had already begun to gather.

'I suppose that's my cue,' said Eliza ruefully. 'At least it's only a few miles this time.'

'Walk with me,' said Gabriel, the words blurting out of his mouth before he could consult his brain. 'My mother is riding as well. She'll chaperone.'

Together they glanced down at her slippers. They were made of worn fawn leather. The toes were pointed. The sturdy material of Eliza's everyday stockings showed over the top of her foot. Walking shoes they were not.

It was the perfect excuse to send her off in the carriage without openly rescinding his offer. He didn't even know why he'd made it—just a quarter-hour ago he'd been enjoying his solitude, and yet now he was requesting the chance to spend more time in Eliza's company.

'You ride and I'll walk,' he said, gesturing to his dozing horse, which was loosely tied at the side of the pub.

'All right,' said Eliza, as if sensing something in his mood. 'If your mother is agreeable.'

'She will be,' said Gabriel grimly, remembering her unsubtle hints about proposing. 'Trust me.'

When Her Grace was suitably mounted, and had sent her horse walking down the road towards home, Gabriel boosted Eliza into his saddle. It wasn't a lady's side-saddle, so she was forced to keep one hand gripping the pommel while her feet rested against the horse's barrel.

Gabriel held the reins, and they began their walk towards the manor.

'I had an interesting talk with the vicar,' he said, breaking the comfortable silence that had fallen between them.

'That's unusual,' said Eliza. 'In my experience vicars either gossip, talk about sin, or try to force more coin out of us.'

'He told me that Abberly has been a poor landlord to much of the village,' said Gabriel.

He felt as if he was following breadcrumbs towards some sort of discovery, and the conversation with Eliza was helping the path unwind.

'Yes,' said Eliza gravely, looking down at Gabriel with a straight face. 'But there's simply too much for him to do. Such carousing to be done, such schemes to plot. His diary is full. It's hard work, being a peer of the realm.'

Gabriel frowned. 'It is. Well, sort of…'

'I thought the rules of Society had made it very clear that those of good breeding don't sully their hands with work,' she pointed out. 'So, by definition, being a peer can't be work.'

She had a point. 'All right. Being a good landlord and an involved Parliamentarian is work,' he said. 'Those things take effort.'

'I suppose… Though if we take this much further we'll enter into philosophical territory. Is "goodness" defined by the measurable amount of aid one gives, or by the effort and persistence one expends?'

'I'm not sure,' said Gabriel. 'But I think that by either definition I'm not measuring up.'

Eliza frowned down at him, and Gabriel had to stop himself from taking her hand in response. It was simply so easy to talk with her, and she was one of the very few people outside his immediate family whom he trusted to give him an honest opinion with the minimum of flattery.

That was friendship. Strange that it had taken him so long to work that out.

'Anyone can see that you're a loving son—and you and I only know each other because of your involvement with Uncle Francis in Parliament,' she said. 'As for the rest of it…your dukedom doesn't seem to be suffering.'

'Yes, well, I have to assume so,' said Gabriel. 'And that assumption is the problem.'

'Oh. Well, fix it. Write some letters, pay some calls and put things to rights. It can't be too hard.'

'You think it's that easy?' Gabriel asked. 'Just appear in the village and call around?'

But as he talked with her, it did sound easy.

'Isn't that what you did today?' Eliza asked. 'When you chatted with the vicar?'

She had yet another point.

'Remember what I told you at Burton's Hotel,' she added. 'You always know what to say. Just don't second-guess yourself and everything will be fine. You aren't fifteen any more, Gabriel.'

This was why he'd wanted to talk it over with her— because she knew his entire story and didn't judge him for it. Eliza had all the relevant information, and she was able to give him an opinion unbiased by time and familiarity.

He simply couldn't stop himself from giving her ankle a gentle squeeze in thanks. He'd miss this when they were back in London. God help him, he'd miss *her*.

'You're right,' he said. 'I've got to face up to it on my own.'

'You can always let Uncle Francis know how it goes,' said Eliza, unaware of Gabriel's inner turmoil. 'He'd be happy to pass a message on to me, I'm sure.'

That sent a pang through his chest so sharp that his breath hitched. He wasn't sure if he was deeply touched by her casual faith in him or hurt at the casual way she referenced a time when they wouldn't be able to talk like this.

'I will,' said Gabriel, keeping his eyes focused on the road ahead of him. 'Thank you.'

It was always going to end this way, Gabriel reminded himself. And, unlike his usual short-term arrangements, this one just might leave him a better man for it. He wanted to send Eliza that report—and he wanted to make her proud.

Chapter Nineteen

When Gabriel walked into the library that evening, he didn't expect to find Eliza standing behind the desk with a water pitcher in her hand. It had a lovely lavender pattern embossed on the porcelain, and seemed entirely out of place with the dark wood and leather-bound tomes of the library. A candlestick would have fitted right in. A wine glass would have been beneath notice. But a pitcher?

It must have come from her bedroom basin.

She was up to something. Dread and anticipation leapt in Gabriel's chest.

'All right, minx,' said Gabriel, leaning his shoulder against the nearest shelf and crossing his legs at the ankles. 'Tell me what you're up to.'

Eliza shrugged, managing to look nonchalant despite the circumstances. 'Checking the flower arrangements,' she said. 'The one in the upstairs hall was looking peaky.'

'There is no flower arrangement in here,' said Gabriel.

'How was I supposed to know that until I looked?' Eliza asked. 'Now that I've determined that there are no flowers, I'll head back upstairs.'

'I don't think so,' said Gabriel, finally noticing that

the decanters on the sideboard looked suspiciously full, given the lateness in both the day and the duration of so many guests' stays. 'Good Lord, you were the one who watered down the brandy in the sitting room last night.'

'I'm sure I wouldn't know anything about that,' said Eliza, showing him wide, innocent-looking eyes. 'Brandy and whisky aren't for ladies, Your Grace.'

She was back to Your Gracing him—and, heaven help Gabriel, he was starting to find even her starchiness erotic.

'Did the servants realise?' he asked. 'Did they replace the ruined drink with fresh? So now you have to water down the decanters to keep up the ruse? Lord Merlon was muttering about cheap brandy for half the evening yesterday.'

The look of pure, unadulterated satisfaction on Eliza's face was very nearly obscene. It looked as though she'd eaten an indulgent cake, taken a swallow of the finest wine, and then had an orgasm all in a row.

Pull yourself together, he told himself. *There are people just down the corridor, and the two of us are not supposed to be alone!*

'The Prince Regent and Abberly keep on slipping into the library to scheme about whatever purchase Abberly is brokering for His Highness,' said Eliza. 'Tonight, or maybe tomorrow, Abberly will come in here and serve diluted brandy to the Regent with his own hand.'

Gabriel had to hand it to her: this piece of sabotage was simple and effective. It undermined everything Abberly had done so far, and if she managed to keep the ruse afloat Abberly's finances would be whispered about through all of London.

'If Abberly finds out he'll want your head.'

She made a face. 'He wants more than my head. In fact, he'd probably prefer me without it. Aunt Mary says he has approached her about marrying me. As though I'm some kind of expensive pet she no longer wishes to care for!'

Gabriel very wisely kept his mouth shut, despite the fact that unmarried female relations often *were* seen like animal companions that needed to be put out to pasture. No longer useful, and incapable of earning their keep.

'Aunt Mary turned him down as best she could, but it appears I will have to stop him myself,' said Eliza. 'I found saltpetre in the gardening shed. If I can slip some to Abberly he'll be useless to his mistress—and she is *not* known for her subtlety.'

Gabriel crossed the room to stand on the other side of the large, ornate desk like a penitent schoolboy. 'Eliza, you have to let this go. The brandy and the dunking in the lake—that's all in good fun. But that's enough. Poisoning the man? You're risking everything.'

'It isn't poison,' said Eliza. 'I'm not *that* desperate. Yet. It's just something to keep him from…enjoying himself.'

Her little chin was set stubbornly, but for the first time Gabriel recognised something new in Eliza's brown eyes: fear.

'This isn't how it needs to end for you,' said Gabriel, desperately wishing he believed that. 'You're staring the scandal down. My mother has been spending time with you…and a few of the other ladies. Next Season might be uncomfortable, but you aren't going to be banished. You aren't going to end up in a cottage somewhere with no one to write to.'

He could promise her that much. He'd write to her

himself, even if he had to employ an army of spies and private couriers to make it happen.

Eliza crossed her arms over her chest, leaving the empty pitcher sitting on the edge of the desk. 'You can't know that,' she said. 'This Season is over. Everyone has gone off to their estates, and their hunt parties, and all they remember is me striking a belted earl in the face while standing in the middle of Hyde Park. Lady Beatrice and Lady Cecelia and your mother are all lovely, but… Well, you and I both know that talking to me while in close proximity is less awkward than ignoring me. It will all go back to the way it was next spring.'

She might be right. But, then again, he might be right, too.

'Why are you so determined to do this?' he asked, leaning his weight on the desktop. 'There are other options. My mother is so fond of you that you could easily ask her to sponsor invitations for you. Nobody refuses the Dowager Duchess of Vane. You could continue to attend Society events and smile your way through them. You could flirt with the men and befriend the less snobbish ladies.'

'Why do you want me to play along with all this?' Eliza asked, answering his question with one of her own. 'I see the way you look at Abberly, and how little interest you have in being chased by debutantes and the wandering wives of the ton. You're the only other person I know who can look at Society and see how frivolous it all is—and yet you want me to play along anyway.'

'Because there has never been a revolution of one!' said Gabriel, finally losing the control he always tried to cling to when he was around her. 'Nobody changes a society all by themselves, and the people who try are, at best, remembered as martyrs! The only person you can possibly hurt is yourself, and I like you too damn much to stand by and watch it happen!'

To emphasise this last point—a deeply unfortunate truth—Gabriel slapped his hand down on the desktop. As he did so, two things happened: the pitcher toppled off the desk and crashed to the floor, and a small hidden drawer popped open along the front of the desk.

It was about two feet wide and four inches deep, and the seams were perfectly hidden along the carved scrollwork. A handful of papers had been tucked into the drawer, each tightly rolled in order to fit in the space.

Eliza and Gabriel stood in silence, eyes locked on each other.

He wondered if he'd got through to her.

He wondered if anyone else had heard the crash of breaking porcelain.

He wondered if Eliza would stop him if he tried to kiss her.

'I'm not trying to start a revolution,' said Eliza quietly.

Her face was expressionless, and those eyes that had always sparkled up at him were once more keeping her thoughts and feelings hidden away.

'I'm not ambitious enough to think I can make any real change. All I want to do is look back at this summer and be able to live with it. Because if you're wrong, this is all that I will have. This one chance to stick up for myself—even if I'm the only one who knows it. If I can sully Abberly's social reputation the way he ruined mine, so much the better. That was the goal. But if I can't, I have to know that I tried. Because I'm the one who will have to live with it.'

It wasn't the first time she'd said something like that to him, but it was the first time that everything had come together in a way that Gabriel could not only understand but *feel*. Eliza didn't think that all this was going to change her world. She didn't even think it would particularly affect Abberly. For her it was about embracing the possibility of success against the probability of failure. It was about owning the decisions she made.

Gabriel hadn't done that. The only thing in his life at which he had truly failed was being the Duke, with all the duties that encompassed: caring for his family, tending to his landholdings and seeing to the needs of those who had depended on him. Instead of working towards the chance of success, he'd passively accepted his own failure. He'd had too much responsibility thrust upon him too quickly, and he had internalised his own guilt and his mother's grief as some kind of immutable stain upon his character.

Gabriel had given up, and had been content to accept that he didn't have the skills that it took to be the sort of duke his father had been.

He'd spent every year since his father had died running from the knowledge that *he* was the one who had made that choice. Nobody had forced him into it. And if he didn't carry on with his life and have a son, he'd be forcing the same situation onto his brother.

'We should see what those documents are,' said Eliza, nodding towards the drawer. 'They might be useful.'

Gabriel had to remind himself that the axis of the planet hadn't tilted for anyone but him. 'It isn't a good idea,' he said.

He knew it wouldn't stop Eliza, but he felt as though someone needed to say it.

Eliza rounded the desk and smoothed the first document open. It was a map of Brighton, showing carefully

plotted parcels of land. The second was a letter written
to Abberly from a solicitor in Kemptown.

Abberly had apparently enquired as to the history of
a piece of property on the edge of the developed part
of the city. The solicitor had replied that, yes, he could
trace the property rights, and it had last been deeded
to one Thomas Hawkins, Esquire.

'That's my father's name,' said Eliza, looking up at
Gabriel with a frown.

He had a bad feeling that he knew where the rest of
these documents would lead.

'Hurry,' he said, urging her on.

This involved Eliza, somehow, and they'd already
lingered in the library for far too long. Gabriel had simply walked in to look for paper, so he could write to his
stewards, but God knew what excuse Eliza could give.

She pulled out a sheet of figures. 'I'm not sure what
these are,' she said, passing over the folded parchment
and continuing to investigate further.

The numbers were neatly plotted on the back of a bill
sent to Abberly from a Bond Street tailor. Abberly had
added several thousand pounds to the amount he owed
the tailor, and Gabriel assumed that those figures represented more of his debts. Another calculation seemed
to show potential interest, and…

'This is a letter from someone at the offices of Mr
John Nash, Architect,' said Eliza. 'It says the Prince
Regent intends to expand the Brighton Pavilion… Oh,
my God.'

The penny dropped.

'Bloody hell,' said Eliza. Then, more loudly, 'That
bastard!'

'He was going to take your dowry when he married
you—that piece of property in Brighton—and then sell

it to the Prince for an exorbitant amount. And it would have been pinned on the non-existent owner of the property, whom Abberly is supposedly dealing with!' said Gabriel. 'Wellington's hairy ball-sack…'

The sheer shamelessness of Abberly's plan was terrific, in the original meaning of the word.

'He intends to fix his solvency problems via the Royal Exchequer.'

'He was going to use me to defraud the Crown,' said Eliza. 'That's why he was so dead set on marrying me. He could have picked any girl with a dowry, but only mine would solve all his problems in one fell swoop.'

'You need to put the documents back,' said Gabriel.

'We have to tell the Prince,' said Eliza, clutching the papers to her breast as if Gabriel was trying to take away her firstborn child. 'This is the proof!' she said. 'If we put them back now, Abberly might realise that somebody knows and destroy them! Don't you realise what this means? We can ruin Abberly once and for all!'

Gabriel went cold, and the hair on the back of his neck prickled. 'We have to take this information to His Highness privately. We'll let him know what has happened, and then we'll bow out until he makes a decision as to what happens next. It isn't our place!'

'Yes, it is,' said Eliza, her eyes shining. 'This is *exactly* our place.'

'You're talking about publicly revealing that the Prince Regent is being swindled! Do you know what happens to people who embarrass royalty?'

'No…' said Eliza, blinking.

'Exactly! Because nobody is stupid enough to try it!'

Eliza shrugged off his warning and began tucking the papers into her stays. 'I'll do what seems best at the time. Besides, it's not as though I'll be able to request a private audience with the Prince Regent. And for the full story to get out there needs to be at least one witness.'

'How are you being so calm?' Gabriel demanded. 'You were almost going to be married to a traitor—one who was willing to ruin you as part of his scheme—and now you're coolly discussing revealing the plot to the future King of England!'

'I've never had the advantage before,' said Eliza. 'I've never had any real power. And now I have. You'd feel calm, too.'

Gabriel was feeling anything but calm. He was feeling annoyed, awed and helpless in one churning, confusing mix. God only knew what consequences Eliza would face for these actions—and they were consequences he'd be helpless to prevent.

'Marry me,' he said, not even aware of the thought until it had come out of his own mouth. 'They can't hang a duchess. They wouldn't even try to banish you.'

She was funny and clever and resilient and beautiful. He couldn't leave her on her own to face whatever happened next. He took a few steps forward, pulled towards her the way a meteor was pulled in by the earth's atmosphere, ready to burn up in the glory of proximity.

'Marry me,' he repeated.

He hadn't thought about the sentiment the first time he'd said it. Now he could picture it—life with Eliza. Now he said it with conviction, with the knowledge that he could keep this stubborn woman safe.

'Don't do this alone.'

Chapter Twenty

Marry me. It was what every spinster longed to hear. The words that would supposedly solve all her life problems. She'd be a wife, and then a mother, secure in the properly formatted family unit that had been ordained by both God and King.

Even worse… This demanding proposal was from a man she actually *liked*.

'Why?' Eliza asked over the ringing in her ears.

She hadn't realised that she'd drifted so close to him—close enough to smell his cologne on the air and feel the warmth of his body on her skin.

Why would he do such a thing? His lack of interest in marriage was one of the reasons Eliza had targeted Vane to escort her on this trip. He was an inveterate bachelor, he had shown absolutely no interest in the young and marriageable women of the ton, and they were *friends*.

Or… Well, perhaps they weren't friends. Maybe too much had happened between them… There had been too much honesty and passion for them to remain friends. But he didn't love her, and Gabriel deserved some wife who wouldn't embarrass him or put him in an unstable position with the Crown.

'Why should you marry me?' he asked, taking a step towards her. 'Because I could keep you safe. They'd never be able to banish a duchess.'

He was such a good man. She'd thought him useless and vain once. Just another aimless, spoiled peer, with no cares and no worries, who couldn't see further than the end of his own nose. But he doted on his mother, and worried about failing at his duties, and he wanted to keep her safe at the cost of the entirety of his future.

Eliza gave herself a second or two to mourn the things that might have been: the snuggling mornings and cosy nights, the laughter and adventure and the arguments that turned into kisses. It was everything she'd ever wanted—and nothing she could reasonably expect.

If he married her he would come to resent her. It was as sure a thing as the sun setting in the west.

'I can't do that to you,' she said. She swallowed hard. She would *not* cry. 'But thank you for asking.'

Thank you for seeing me. Thank you for treating me as though I'm special.

'I'll see you at dinner.'

She took one last look at him, wanting to commit him to memory. His handsomeness was still absurd, but somehow the symmetrical features and fine form had faded into the background of what Eliza saw when she looked at him now. His warm brown eyes were wide and hurt, his brows slightly furrowed between them. His lips were parted, and although the light was too low to see it, Eliza would have been able to find that maddening little scar with her eyes closed.

Gabriel's back was straight and his shoulders were braced, as though her problems were a physical burden he could take on. He was leaning towards her, every part of his body focused on hers. Every part of him made her feel as though she mattered. Every part of his stubborn, attractive, perceptive self made her want to say *yes*.

Before she could second-guess her decision and beg him to take her as his wife, Eliza turned her face away and fled the library.

She kept a hand pressed to her breastbone all the way back to her room, blinking hard and barely seeing the house she was moving through. She could feel the papers moving inside her clothes, rustling like angel feathers.

Be not afraid.

Power was a strange sensation. And even as her heart broke for Gabriel, and everything she couldn't have, there was a sort of inner resilience buoying her up. She felt strangely impervious, as though nothing could truly harm her—not even the shattering of her most dearly held dreams.

For the first time in her life Miss Eliza Hawkins had a major social advantage. It was a heady and foreign sensation. She'd never had beauty to trade upon, nor wealth to give her clout, nor any social influence that she could bring to bear. She'd gone through life being kind because it was the right thing to do, acting like a polite and proper young lady because it was the clever thing to do.

And now…? Now she had *insurance*.

Revenge wouldn't give her everything she wanted— nothing could do that now, not after Gabriel's proposal. And revenge might not even solve her problems. Even if Abberly was shunned by Polite Society for the rest of his days, Eliza's own reputation might not be rein-stated. She would still be the girl who'd been dragged off the path by an earl, had struck him in the face, and refused to play along with Society's expectations for the situation.

Eliza understood that.

The papers she had tucked inside her dress weren't revenge. They were *justice*.

But even as Eliza flopped back on her bed and held the papers to her breast she knew it wasn't justice that would comfort her. No, only time would be able to do that. Time and distance from Gabriel, the man it would be so easy for her to love...

Gabriel stormed up to his room and began roughly packing his trunk. He couldn't stay here and watch Eliza go through with whatever mad plan she decided to enact. He couldn't watch her being scorned or cut down by the Prince, entirely banished from Society altogether. He wouldn't do it, damn her stubborn hide.

'Serves me right,' he muttered to himself, scooping up his shaving kit and dropping it into the trunk. 'After a dozen years of avoiding marriage at all costs, the moment I finally propose the woman turns me down flat.'

She hadn't even thought about it! She'd simply looked surprised and then said no, before fleeing the room.

Gabriel's throat went tight at the memory. He'd been left standing in the library surrounded by a broken water pitcher and air that smelled like lemon and Eliza: all soap and stubbornness and warm brown eyes. He'd been left standing in the rubble of his first—and definitely last—marriage proposal.

Gabriel stood in the middle of the room with his shirt untucked and ran his fingers through his hair. What did she think he was going to do? Stand around to watch her go after Abberly, ending up on the wrong side of the Crown, and pretend he hadn't offered for her? This entire trip had been a mistake. He couldn't be responsible for women, and Eliza was right to have turned him down. He was merely—

Wait.

Gabriel kicked the trunk lid closed and then sat down on top of it, bracing his elbows on his knees and letting his head hang. He had accused her of not thinking logically, but was he? Or were his feelings hurt, making him run from them and everything else?

He'd gone down to the library to get paper for letters. Letters he planned to write to his estate stewards, instructing them to send him comprehensive reports about his landholdings, tenants and income. While there he'd found Eliza, discovered the documents, and proposed.

And now… Now what? He was going to leave. But he'd only be giving up again—walking away from a situation at which he hadn't even tried to succeed.

He'd actually done a rather good job of escorting Lady Stanley and Eliza to the house party. He'd even been able to comfort Eliza that night in Burton's Hotel. And, while he'd taught Eliza to drink and to play cards, those weren't particularly harmful pastimes. They also fitted *her*, as an individual. He'd never have taught his younger sister such things because she'd shown no interest in learning them.

When he didn't worry about what to say and merely said what he was thinking or feeling, he did very well for himself. The rest would take practice. The idea of having to live with a woman for the rest of his natural life did still set his nerves on edge, but he wasn't entirely worthless. He'd managed to untangle the Royal Tax Regulations and their relevance to the income of the Vane duchy, so he was certainly capable of learning.

Unlike Abberly. That fool had followed Eliza around

for an entire Season and seen her only as a walking investment.

'So what do I do?' Gabriel asked aloud, focusing his attention on the stern portrait hanging over the mantel. A grey-haired man in the last century's fashions looked down at him silently.

He had two options: leave, and understand that he'd be undoing all the progress he'd made. Or stay, and support his friend the way he should, all the while hoping Eliza would make good choices.

He no longer needed to ride the coattails of her sense of purpose. He had found his own. And in the end there was no choice at all—of course he was going to stay. Being a more attentive man and a better duke started that night.

Chapter Twenty-One

Eliza walked into the dining room of Gordyn Manor with a heavy sense of destiny hanging over her. Whatever happened that night would change the course of her life for ever. Tonight she would not only dine with the Prince Regent; she'd dine with fate. The letters detailing Abberly's scheme were safely tucked away in her dress—all Eliza needed to do was gather the courage to expose him.

The room glittered with candles and crystal, and that light was reflected tenfold in the jewellery of the women. It was the final night of the house party, and the occasion was being marked with splendour. For Eliza, it was the very reason she'd headed north in the first place—but now, in the face of success, she was losing her nerve.

They were once more sitting in order of precedence: the Prince Regent at the head of the table with Vane, the Marquess and Abberly, while Eliza occupied the opposite end. The air smelled like roasting meat and long-aged wine, and Eliza was once more seated with Mr Lewis as her dinner companion.

'It's been quite a nice gathering this year,' he said, nudging Eliza beneath the table. 'I, for one, deeply hope you'll grace us with your presence again next year.'

'Thank you,' said Eliza, watching as a small army of servants began serving a soft green pea and mint soup to the guests.

She'd give Abberly this: the food at his party had been beyond reproach, having taken full advantage of the season's fresh produce.

'What of your plans?' Eliza asked. 'Will you be coming to London for the Little Season?'

Even Eliza loved the Christmas gatherings of those families who chose to return to London once the first snow had fallen. They were cheerful and more relaxed, and most Town houses were cheaper and easier to heat than their larger country homes.

'I just might,' said Mr Lewis, neatly scooping a small amount of soup onto his spoon.

Eliza toyed with hers, too nervous to eat. She needed to reveal Abberly's plot, and had told Gabriel she would do it, but now…

'The Christmas season is lonely up here, with only the snow for company,' Mr Lewis concluded.

'I do wish London got more snow,' said Eliza. 'We have so much fun in the park.'

'Ah, but in the country we have sleigh rides,' said Mr Lewis. 'Perhaps I can tempt you to come back before next summer?'

Eliza smiled politely and changed the topic, vaguely dissatisfied by Mr Lewis's flirting. It was too general, too polite, too clichéd. It didn't have anything to do with Eliza as an individual. Having been really *seen* by Gabriel—even just for a moment—Eliza doubted she could ever settle for anything less.

'Are you all right, dear?' Aunt Mary asked as the soup was cleared from the table.

'Of course,' said Eliza, smiling brightly.

Aunt Mary frowned. But further conversation was prevented by the arrival of the next course: trout, sweetmeats and a roast beef tongue were beautifully displayed over roast carrots and artichokes with a herbed dressing. A dish of more vegetables accompanied the meats, along with a beautifully moulded salad of spinach and eggs.

What was she waiting for? Her victory was assured. Yet Gabriel's words haunted her... She shouldn't risk the ire of the Prince Regent, but in order for justice to be done at least one witness needed to be in attendance, to spread the gossip of Abberly's perfidy.

Maybe after dinner, when the men joined the womenfolk in the parlour, she would send Vane to the Prince to beg a moment of his time. It would be public, but not...not among this glittering spectacle.

It would be safer, so that was her decision: an after-dinner audience with the Prince.

Ease temporarily regained, Eliza tucked into her meal, enjoying the salt of the fish against the brightness of the vegetables. Mr Lewis was recounting a story about the pony upon which he'd learned to ride, and the little creature sounded halfway to legendary already.

'That little beast lived feral in the woods for more than a month,' he was saying. On the other side of the table, Aunt Mary hid a laugh behind her napkin. 'We finally told the village children that anyone who could catch him could keep him. I believe a series of rope snares were deployed, but somehow they never managed to hold old Mephistopheles down for long.'

'Well, that was your mistake,' said Eliza, debating whether she should risk the spinach and egg salad, or save room for the next remove. 'Names are destiny. If you name a pony after a biblical demon, that's exactly what you're going to get.'

'We had puppies named Lady and Rake when I was growing up,' said the lady on Mr Lewis's other side. 'I believe Miss Hawkins is on to something.'

And then in came the next course: chicken crusted in crushed nuts, beef in aspic, mashed beets and boiled potatoes, along with mince and apple pies. A pork tenderloin with seared mushrooms was placed in front of the Prince Regent, and Eliza risked looking down the table.

The Prince was flushed and pink-cheeked, though he seemed to be paying more attention to the victuals and the cleavage of the Dowager Duchess than to Abberly. For his part, Abberly seemed to be attempting some kind of light-hearted conversation with his neighbour, who had entirely abandoned him for Gabriel.

Just before Eliza looked away Gabriel turned his head and their eyes met. It was inexplicable that the moment remained unremarked upon by the other diners—it seemed so searingly intimate, a flash of understanding that lit up the room like lightning. Understanding, empathy, acceptance and regret flashed like the muzzle flare of a gunshot. And then it was over, with only a lingering flush of *something* working its way down from Eliza's cheeks to her decolletage.

Gabriel wasn't furious with her. He understood.

As the third course was removed Abberly stood up at the head of the table and a hush fell over the room. Picking up his wine glass, the Earl turned towards the Prince Regent and bowed deeply as he prepared to start the toasts.

As he was the guest of honour, it was both expected and traditional that the host would first toast the future King.

'To the Prince of Wales, who symbolises the very best of this age: discipline and mercy, beauty and truth, tradition and innovation and generosity of spirit—why else would he choose to grace our humble party with his enlightening presence? To His Royal Highness!'

With the exception of Prince George, England's acting Regent, all the party members stood, echoed the sentiment, and took a sip from their glass. As the rather nice red wine washed over Eliza's tongue, she had to admit that it was a better toast than she'd expected from Abberly...he'd definitely been practising it in the mirror.

The Prince nodded beneficently at Abberly. In the normal course of events Gabriel, Duke of Vane, would be the next to propose a toast, and so on and so forth, until all of the guests had been toasted. Unusually Abberly, still standing, began to speak again.

'Your Royal Highness, if I could have a moment of leniency for a small announcement?'

As Abberly's gaze turned to Eliza the night began to feel very much like a delicate chandelier: crystalline, brilliantly lit, and precariously balanced over a long and devastating drop.

He wouldn't, she thought, unconsciously touching her bodice, beneath which lay the papers proving his intention to defraud the Prince. *He wouldn't announce—*

'I am so very pleased to tell you all, my dearest friends, that this party has not only been a social success, it is a personal triumph as well. Our very own Miss Hawkins has finally agreed to become my wife.'

Chapter Twenty-Two

Fifteen minutes earlier

Gabriel couldn't wait to go home. And yet at the same time, he dreaded it.

He was sick of Abberly, and formal dinners, and making polite conversation with talk so small one needed a magnifying glass to see it.

Yet once he was back in London he'd only have other issues to face: reviewing the work of his stewards, socialising with his sister, taking up the work that came with being the Duchy of Vane...

Most of all, back at home, he'd miss Eliza terribly.

He wished he'd had a moment to catch her before dinner. He wanted to tell her... What? That he hadn't meant the things he'd said in the library?

He had meant them. It was foolish to risk publicly antagonising the Crown, but it was also incredibly brave. *She* was brave—and it was one of his favourite things about her. She was willing to do scary and improper things for what she thought was right.

Eliza was an inspiration. She'd travelled all the way to Abberly's estate to rectify a wrong that she knew nobody else would take seriously. She'd even embarrassed higher-status society harpies—Lady Joyce had had it coming to her.

Eliza was wonderful.

If only she didn't cause him so much worry.

'Once more I must congratulate you, Abberly, upon your cook,' said the Prince Regent, serving himself another plateful of chicken crusted in walnuts. 'The food has been excellent.'

'Thank you,' said Abberly. 'He's French…quite temperamental.'

'A good cook is worth the fuss,' said Prinny. 'One or two of the Privy Council used to joke that Napoleon would win the war because everyone knows an army marches on its stomach. They had camp followers, laundresses and cooks and such, following old Bonaparte from battlefield to battlefield. Quite bad for morale, for our lads to smell their campfires.'

'We beat him in the end,' said Abberly. 'Thanks to you and the Duke of Wellington.'

Gabriel nudged his food around his plate. The Dowager was the highest-ranking woman in attendance, and Gabriel was supposed to be dinner partners with his mother…but she was busily engaged in conversation with the Marquess next to her. That left Gabriel trapped with Abberly and the Prince Regent when talk turned to politics.

'I like Lord Liverpool. He's already lasted longer as Prime Minister than I expected. And he has a canny way about him,' said Prince George. 'He chooses his battles carefully.'

'He's putting Britain first,' said Abberly, punctuating the statement by enthusiastically stabbing a piece of beef with his fork. 'The Corn Laws will keep those cheap competitors out of the country. British grain, first and foremost.'

'It's affecting the economic welfare of the working class,' said Gabriel. 'Bread prices are up, and half of London turned out for the riots.'

'A short-term blip,' said Abberly, waving away Gabriel's comment.

Gabriel tuned out the rest of the conversation and went back to brooding about Eliza.

If he could, he'd tell her that he still thought publicly exposing Abberly's plot was a dangerous idea, but he'd support her if she decided to go through with it. That was what it meant to be a good friend—accepting someone's bad qualities along with the good. Running away from her wouldn't make her plan less dangerous: it would only abandon her without allies.

Gabriel was done with running away from what scared him.

When he looked down the table Eliza was engaged in conversation with Mr Lewis. She looked wonderful. Her skin was flushed and glowing, her glossy curls were piled on the crown of her head, and her pretty blue gown emphasised her breasts without calling overt attention to them. She looked beautiful, and happy, and in that moment Gabriel realised that that was all he wanted for her.

Eliza deserved to be happy and content, in whatever form that took. Even if it was with Mr Lewis. Even if Gabriel would never see her again.

The thought was too painful to be borne, so Gabriel signalled to one of the footmen to refill his wine glass. He couldn't even contemplate the fact that, after being turned down for marriage, he'd still have to escort Eliza back home.

Another week in the carriage…with nothing else to do but look at her. And all because he hadn't said, *I disagree, but I will support you either way.*

That was one mistake he'd never make again. If Gabriel ever did have children he would be prepared: that line was locked, loaded and ready to fire.

'Cheer up,' said Abberly, breaking through Gabriel's morose inner monologue. 'It's time for the toasts.'

'Excellent,' said Gabriel, not thinking any such thing.

He only half paid attention to Abberly's toast to Prince George, idly wondering how long Abberly had needed to practise it. Gabriel was watching the doors to dining room, wondering when the servants would come in with the pudding. Toasts could go on for hours at these things, and all Gabriel wanted was a stiff drink, a hot bath and his bed. At least there he could brood in peace.

Abberly had started speaking again. 'I'm so very pleased to tell you all, my dearest friends, that this party has not only been a social success, it is a personal triumph as well.'

How could it be 'a triumph'? Gabriel wondered. The only thing Abberly wanted, other than the Prince's attention, was—

Oh, no. He wouldn't…

Gabriel's head snapped around and he looked down the table, locking eyes with Eliza just as Abberly turned in her direction, raising his glass one more time.

'Our very own Miss Hawkins has finally agreed to become my wife.'

At that moment Gabriel only had one thought in his mind: *absolutely not.*

Eliza sent him a desperate look, and Gabriel had never felt so helpless in his life.

He nodded at her, slowly and subtly.

Do it. I believe in you. You've already come so far!

Every head had turned to look at Eliza, and suddenly the table seemed longer than the River Thames. It was a physical representation of the gulf that lay between Eliza and Abberly: their personalities, their goals and their status were irreconcilable.

Even as the room broke into subdued but polite applause, whispers started.

Aunt Mary leaned across the table, throwing propriety to the wind. 'Is this true?' she asked, her face pale. 'Did you…?'

'Of course I didn't,' Eliza hissed.

Next to her. Mr Lewis shifted uncomfortably.

Eliza pushed to her feet, causing the volume of the whispers to triple briefly before dying away. As she faced Abberly, Eliza couldn't help but risk a glance at Gabriel. His jaw was set and tense. But their gazes connected and he gave her a slight nod.

Despite his worries, she had Gabriel's support.

With a mouth suddenly gone dry, Eliza tried to find words. 'Your Royal Highness, my friends, I am so sorry, but I cannot let Lord Abberly's words stand. I have not agreed to marry him—as I have told him repeatedly.'

The whispers returned.

'I must also beg your mercy and your ear, Your Highness, for I have something that I must tell you as soon as possible.'

Because she was watching for it, Eliza saw Abberly's eyes momentarily widen, before his jaw set stubbornly. The murmurs around them were increasing in volume, and Abberly had to raise his voice to be heard.

'Anything you need to say can be said in front of all

of our friends,' said Abberly. 'Especially if it has to do with our happy news.'

'I am honoured to have spent time in such close proximity to our kind Regent,' said Eliza, sweating profusely and hoping that it wasn't yet showing through her gown. She curtsied deeply and then continued, 'But, other than being in his presence, I have no happy news. Please, Your Highness, just a moment of your time.'

'I forbid it!' said Abberly, his face flushing more and more red. 'As your future husband—'

'You cannot forbid or allow anything on my behalf, and I will not remind you again,' said the Prince sharply. 'Miss Hawkins?'

Eliza decided that in her next life she was going to be even *more* of a wallflower. She'd positively cling to those potted ferns with both hands. Standing under the direct attention of the next monarch was like being in the centre of a pyre: scorching hot, and quite likely to be fatal.

'As Lord Abberly has assured us that whatever it is you need to say can be said in the presence of your friends, you may continue.'

'Um...'

Eliza looked desperately at Gabriel. He had a muscle ticking in his jaw, and the expression in his warm brown eyes was bleak. He wanted to help her but he couldn't.

Eliza was stuck between two impossible choices: publicly embarrass the Prince Regent in the way Gabriel most feared, or refuse a direct order from the future King of England.

'Well?' said Abberly.

That prompted Eliza into action. Blushing crimson, and once again wishing that she'd been born willowy and fashionable, she turned her back as much as she dared and extracted the papers from her gown.

There was a muffled laugh, and then she turned back to face the guests.

'Your Highness, I am sorry to inform you that I have discovered a plot, authored by Lord Abberly, to defraud you of nearly thirty thousand pounds.'

As one, the room gasped. Eliza was shocked that her ears didn't pop the way they did before a terrible storm.

'That's a lie!' said Abberly. 'My Prince, you know I would never—'

Eliza pressed on before she lost control of the situation entirely.

'My father, Thomas Hawkins, Esquire, bought a piece of property in Brighton some years ago. Upon his death the deed passed to me, as his last direct relation, to be held in trust in place of a dowry. I was aware of it only in the abstract sense.'

She held the papers up to the room.

'Somehow Abberly found out about this landholding and has been attempting to take it from me through marriage ever since. I believe… I believe he intended to sell it to you for an exorbitant price in order to pay off his debts and live off the interest of the remainder of the sum paid.'

The Prince's face had gone darker than Abberly's, and Eliza wondered momentarily if she would be held responsible for the fatal apoplexy of the Prince of Wales.

They can only hang me once! she told herself manically. *Nothing to worry about!*

'Your Highness, if I may?'

Gabriel stood up. His posture was relaxed and open, but Eliza could see the tension in his jaw and the narrowing of his eyes.

Prince George nodded.

'Lord Stanley, Eliza's guardian, tasked me with acting as escort for Lady Stanley and Miss Hawkins on their travels. Since our arrival, Abberly has pestered both Miss Hawkins and Lady Stanley for Miss Hawkins' hand, without once consulting me or sending a letter to Lord Stanley in London. It is behaviour most unbecoming.'

'Men often behave thus when emotionally affected,' said the Prince.

Gabriel gave the Regent his best charming rake smile. 'That we do, Your Highness—which means that we can also tell the difference between sincerity and something more sinister.'

Eliza couldn't believe what was happening. After everything—after calling her an embarrassment and telling her that she was a fool for wanting to confront Abberly and Prince George publicly—Gabriel was aligning himself with her in front of all Polite Society. He was standing up for her, just as he had that night at the Crofton Fair, and it was all she could do not to burst into tears.

'I think we should hear Miss Hawkins out,' said Gabriel, turning the warmth of his gaze upon her. 'After so many Seasons of good behaviour, she deserves that.'

Eliza wanted to hug him. She wanted to kiss him. To beg him to marry her and to ride off with him into the sunset, where they'd never have to deal with the rules of Polite Society again. He'd managed to put Abberly on the back foot, even while reminding everyone of Eliza's preciously good name. And he'd done it for *her*.

'Miss Hawkins? Do you have any evidence to support these allegations?' the Prince bit out.

Eliza resisted the impulse to clutch the papers to her chest. 'I do, Your Highness.'

'Fakes! Forgeries!' cried Abberly.

The Prince snapped his fingers and a footman cautiously approached Eliza, holding a silver tray. As Eliza laid the sheets of paper down she felt vulnerable and exposed. The entire party tracked the footman's progress around the table with wide eyes, waiting for the Prince to pass judgement on this drama of all dramas.

He picked up the first sheet of paper and held it close, then at arm's length, scanning the letter from the office of John Nash. He then perused the figures, and the map—the sum of Eliza's hopes and fears.

Without saying anything, the Prince folded the papers, tucked them into his pocket, and rose from his seat. The room erupted as everyone else followed suit.

'Your Highness! You cannot believe this...this nobody!' said Abberly, turning to the Prince to plead.

With devastating coolness, Prince George's blue eyes wandered sightlessly over Abberly, before he turned his face away and began walking towards the door. Abberly had been given the direct cut by none other than the Prince Regent. Everyone watched in stunned silence as a footman wrenched open the door—and then the Prince was gone.

Chaos erupted.

Women were calling for their maids and ordering them to pack.

A group of men rounded on Abberly and demanded to know if the accusations were true.

Someone screamed that Eliza was a demon who had ruined everything.

Two confused footmen walked in with trays of iced

cream and ginger biscuits, and then milled around to add to the sense of a claustrophobic stampede.

Eliza, still standing behind her place setting, reached for her wine, stunned and feeling slightly numbed to everything that had happened.

Abberly had claimed that he was going to marry her. Eliza had told the Prince of Abberly's plan. And the Prince Regent had apparently believed her.

She took a sip of wine and risked a glance at Aunt Mary, who was pale-faced but vehemently defending Eliza's actions to Lady Huntbury.

'It is quite proper for one to expose a plan to defraud the Crown!' she said, clinging to her dinner knife in a slightly worrying way. 'If my niece were a man, she'd probably be knighted!'

Eliza didn't want a knighthood. She wanted this to be over. To be back in her own bedroom, with her familiar books and her comfortable little life. She wanted her ruination in the park not to have happened. She wanted the world to be a different place.

Letting her gaze sweep over the crowd, Eliza found Abberly. He was red-faced, surrounded by the group of men, who were now edging closer and closer to his person. The sheer loathing that emanated from him was palpable.

With a wry smile, Eliza raised her wine glass in a silent toast.

To Lord Abberly, she thought. *Ruiner of women and defrauder of princes. The most popular fellow that English masculinity has to offer. To Lord Abberly, defeated by a duke and a wallflower.*

Abberly bared his teeth, but his view of Eliza was blocked by Gabriel's broad back as he loomed over him, aggression writ in every line of his body.

One of the confused footmen passed Eliza, holding a tray of rapidly melting iced creams in tiny crystal dishes. Eliza snatched one off the tray and plopped unceremoniously into her seat.

'I'd appreciate a little warning next time,' said Aunt Mary, returning from the sideboard with a bottle of wine and pouring it into her glass.

'There is not going to be a next time,' said Eliza darkly, spooning a bite of dessert into her mouth. The cream was smooth and cool, and the tang of fresh raspberries went perfectly with the sweet, expensive confection. 'I've had enough of public scandal to last several lifetimes.'

'It's your own fault,' said Lady Joyce to Eliza, as her mother towed her out of the room. 'You shouldn't have invited scandal in the first place.'

Eliza toasted Joyce with her crystal ice cream dish, smiling at the pinched-faced blonde with as much genuine pleasure as she could manage.

'Nobody is going to marry that girl with a mouth a like that,' said Aunt Mary, reading the label on the wine bottle approvingly. 'Her poor father is going to have to add to her dowry *again*—I hear it's already up to six thousand pounds.'

'Abberly is looking for a countess,' said Eliza, finishing her ice cream and looking around in case a perplexed servant happened to come wandering by with another. 'Maybe the Tower of London has a honeymoon suite.'

Chapter Twenty-Three

Since the death of Eliza's parents, her life had been blissfully free of chaos. She hadn't known the exact details of her coming days—nobody had—but the general shape of them had been predictable and familiar—like a well-worn pair of shoes.

That sense of security had fled when Abberly had pulled her off the path, and the events tonight at dinner had demolished whatever sense of self-determinism that Eliza had retained.

Was she still ruined? Or was she worse than ruined?

It seemed reasonable that if the man who had non-consensually besmirched her had later proved to be a nefarious villain, it would cancel out the ruination. That was practically mathematical.

Then again… Polite Society wasn't known for functioning on logic.

And underlying all of it—the anxiety, the tossing and turning, the uncomfortable night sweats—was her niggling instinct that Gabriel would be able to make sense of it. Even if he couldn't, he would certainly be able to make her feel better.

The curtains fluttered, and somewhere out in the darkness a hunting dog bayed.

What did Eliza have to lose?

She tossed a light shawl over her shift, stuffed her feet into slippers, and peered out into the corridor. This late, even the harried maids had gone to bed, and the coast was clear.

Eliza had a moment of panic when she reached for the knob at the door to Gabriel's room—what if he'd locked it?—but the door opened smoothly and Eliza quietly stepped inside.

His room was dark, with only slivers of moonlight slipping in through a crack in the curtains. The air was still, and she could hear the soft, even breaths of deep sleep emanating from the bed. The air smelled like soap, and just the simple act of breathing Gabriel in made some of Eliza's tension unwind.

'Gabriel?' she whispered, not wanting to reach out and touch him. 'Gabriel…'

Nothing. Keeping her distance, Eliza carefully smoothed her hand over the crest of his shoulder.

'Your Grace!' He hated it when she called him that. Surely that would get his attention.

Sure enough, his breathing changed, and he rolled over onto his back and squinted into the darkness.

'Eliza?'

'Yes.'

He sighed and raised the covers, wordless inviting her into his bed.

It was, quite possibly, the moment Eliza fell in love with him. Or it would have been, Eliza told herself, if she allowed that sort of thing. No, she was Gabriel's friend. They couldn't have a future together, and that was that. She had gone to a friend for some comfort— no more and no less. She rounded the bed and clambered under the light sheet, immediately relaxing into a pillow that smelled like Gabriel.

'That was certainly a scene at dinner, minx.'

His voice was rumbly and raspy with sleep, and Eliza thought maybe her intentions weren't so pure after all.

'I was going to ask you to get the Prince alone after dinner,' she said. 'I wanted to talk to him in the drawing room.'

'Then Abberly forced your hand and came out the worst for it,' said Gabriel. 'I think Edmonton and Hartley are keeping him under house arrest until further instructions come from the Prince.'

'I'm glad *I'm* not under house arrest,' said Eliza.

Gabriel laughed, and his warm hand cupped her hip. 'You won't be. You didn't do anything wrong.'

Neither of them commented on the fact that when it came to women and their reputations they didn't need to have actually done anything wrong.

'What do you think is going to happen next?' Eliza whispered.

Gabriel rolled onto his side and spooned himself behind her. That was when Eliza realised that if Gabriel wore any clothing to bed, she couldn't feel it.

'I don't know,' he said, stroking his fingertips up and down the dip of her waist. 'We go home. We do our best. That's all we can do.'

Eliza bit her lip to the point of pain. She wouldn't ask him if they would see each other again. She knew better than to ask questions she didn't want to know the answer to.

She was a veteran wallflower and a newly minted rakess.

She'd be fine. Just fine.

'When did you get so good at this?' Eliza asked. 'Knowing what to say.'

Gabriel froze. She couldn't even feel his chest rising and falling against her back. And then he sighed, and traced his fingers up and down her side once more.

'You're the only one who thinks so.'

'Well, you are,' said Eliza stubbornly. 'Except for that time you called me embarrassing. That definitely wasn't the right thing to say.'

'I am profoundly sorry,' said Gabriel.

He'd shifted, and Eliza could feel his breath ruffling the little baby hairs that curled at the nape of her neck.

'I forgive you.'

'Thank you,' said Gabriel, before pressing an impossibly soft kiss on the back of her neck. 'You deserve better, minx.'

There isn't anyone better.

Hopefully he meant that she deserved to be *treated* better, and that he saw the error of his ways. That had to be what he meant. Because there was no better man than Gabriel. Some things a woman just *knew*.

Once again, Eliza had the sense that everything hinged on this moment—that she was standing with one foot in the past and one in the future. It was irritating and terrifying: humanity hadn't been built to make sense of the randomness and opaqueness of the universe.

To hell with it. *This* would be their goodbye—not whatever awkward and proper thing they'd say to each other when he returned them to Uncle Francis's townhouse. Here in the dark, with the humid summer air around them, they were Eliza and Gabriel: friends, partners in argument and allies. Out there they were a duke and a possibly ruined nobody.

'Kiss me,' said Eliza, leaning back against Gabriel's bare chest and looking at him over her shoulder.

He didn't hesitate.

But it wasn't the kiss Eliza had expected.

He'd kissed her hotly in the alley at the Crofton Fair. He'd kissed her angrily by the stream, and he had kissed her senseless on the floor by this very bed, after he'd ripped the trousers off her.

Now, in the soft summer dark, he kissed her as if he wanted to remember it for the next fifty years—kissed her the way a blind man traced the features of his beloved.

He worked his way from her mouth to her cheeks, pressing wet kisses to her jaw while gently scraping his prickly cheek against her own. He rested his nose in the divot of her temple and breathed her in, before cradling her face and pressing a series of featherlight kisses across the bridge of her nose.

He traced his thumb along her eyebrow while he kissed the opposite eyelid. He rubbed the tip of his nose against hers. And he nearly made her cry when he finally took her mouth again. He kissed her slowly, thoroughly, taking her bottom lip between his, and then her upper lip, flicking his tongue in to taste her before lazily withdrawing and allowing her only the most taunting sort of friction as he gently dragged his mouth against hers.

Eliza had spent her life thinking of herself as sturdy. She was plump, round, cushioned... Rubenesque. What she *wasn't* were any of the words that the romantics used to describe their heroines: delicate, ethereal, fae or willowy. She had shapely strong legs that marched her body wherever she wished it to go. She had a soft stomach that made an excellent cushion for cats. She had breasts that would have been very, *very* much in fashion during virtually any other era in Western history. She had a symmetrical face, excellent skin, and beautiful hair.

Men in romantic novels treated their heroines as if… Well, as if they were special. Fragile, delicate beings, whose feelings and physical bodies were something beyond the everyday. When men danced with Eliza, or partnered her in games, they touched her respectfully and politely, but with an expected amount of thoughtlessness.

Fat girls didn't require gentleness: they were insulated from it.

She was plump, easy-going Miss Hawkins, who had never, ever seen herself in a romantic novel.

Not until now. Not until she found herself on her back, with Gabriel hovering over her in the dark, touching her as if she was made of spun sugar and magic. He didn't kiss her tentatively, or touch her as if he was concerned for her safety. No, he touched her with a deliberate tenderness that showed that he *cared*. That he thought she was beautiful. That her body and feelings were worth lingering over.

It was almost as though he knew this was Eliza's last chance for intimacy and romance, and he wanted to give her enough to last her a lifetime.

Eliza shoved that thought away and pressed her face into the shadowed hollow of Gabriel's throat, kissing his warm skin and feeling his pulse flutter against her lips.

'Eliza…' he purred, catching her mouth again and pressing her down into the mattress. 'Eliza, please…'

He said her name like a prayer…a hope given voice in the darkness.

'Yes,' she whispered, running her hand down the

smooth skin of his back to the place where the sheet pooled around his waist. *'Yes.'*

He slipped her shift over her head before turning her onto her side again. She felt a moment of loss—she couldn't see him—before he spooned up behind her and guided her leg back, hooking it over his own. She was vulnerable, but she wasn't. She was open to the exploration of his clever fingers, and bared to room, but safely curled in the lee of Gabriel's long body.

One of his hands was under her head, and the other was gently playing with her nipples, moving from one to the other before sliding down her body. He tickled her waist, let his fingers trace patterns over her belly, and drew shivers from her when he gently stroked the crease where her torso met her thigh.

Maybe it was good that Gabriel couldn't see her face. Eliza was sure she looked devastated. This was a kind of intimacy she'd never anticipated. She hadn't braced herself for such kindness.

There was no flirtatious banter as he parted her folds with his fingers and rubbed circles around her nub. There was no scandalously dirty talk. Only the sounds of their breathing and the gentle slide and press of their bodies.

When Gabriel lowered Eliza's leg from his hip and fitted his cock between her thighs, the moment almost felt holy—as if something sacred was happening. A sacrament for two…a ritual heavy with time and meaning. He rocked into her, sliding his cock along the outside of her damp folds while his arm hooked over her waist and played with her most pleasurable parts.

They moved together by inches, undulating like the tide, neither of them chasing pleasure with any hurry. This wasn't about the destination; it wasn't for the physical catharsis of completion. They were revelling in their closeness, mirroring each other's breathing and heartbeat and pleasure.

In Gabriel's arms, with his breath in her ear and his fingers playing at her mons, it didn't matter what the next day would bring. She had this. And with Gabriel Eliza was enough.

Eventually they couldn't hold out any longer. Gabriel's thrusts became choppier and his arms banded around Eliza more tightly. She hitched her hips back against his when he removed his fingers from between her thighs, catching her wrist with his damp hand. He drew her fingers down to replace his, and then his big hand was braced against her breastbone, right over her traitorously pounding heart.

It was that feeling that tipped Eliza over the edge. The sensation that Gabriel was holding her in the palm of his hand. He was holding her against him so tightly, and Eliza turned her face into his arm as she trembled through her climax. He pressed a hurried kiss against her throat before grinding himself against her. It was only another moment or two before she felt the wet heat of his spend on her thighs.

Neither of them moved, still twined together on the sweat-damp sheets. To move would be to break the spell…to move would acknowledge that this moment had to end.

In the end, Gabriel was the brave one. He pressed his face into Eliza's hair, kissed the crown of her head, and then slid from the bed, leaving her inexplicably chilled. There was the sound of water being poured from the pitcher and then he was back, still nude, holding a damp cloth.

She didn't know what came over her, but when Gabriel's cupped her knee with his broad hand and guided her thighs apart she let him. He was tender and thorough as he tidied her thighs and her womanhood, leaving cool water drying on Eliza's warm skin.

What was letting him see her body in its most honest form when it felt as if he'd already looked inside her soul?

He stepped behind the screen, and Eliza pulled her shift on.

'I should go,' she whispered as Gabriel padded back to the bed.

He took her hand in hers. 'Stay,' he said, lying on his back and curling Eliza into him, guiding her thigh to rest over his. 'Please.'

Eliza stayed.

It was only when the deep gloom of the night began to pale with the coming of the dawn that she returned to her room. And as she began to pack her trunk Eliza realised that she'd never said goodbye.

Chapter Twenty-Four

The carriage ride home was gruelling.

Without the righteous fury that had carried her north, and the simmering attraction between herself and Gabriel, Eliza was so much more aware of the heat, and the discomfort, and the sheer length of each day.

Gabriel did his best to provide what little comforts he could: he purchased flasks of cooled tea and cold luncheons from the inns where they stopped to change horses, and he played round after round of cards with them as best the carriage allowed. He even taught Aunt Mary to play Vingt-et-Un, and she took to the game as if she'd been born to it.

Mostly, though, Gabriel and Eliza took turns watching each other whenever the other wasn't looking. Gabriel would let his fingertips brush over the bare skin of Eliza's wrist whenever he helped her in and out of the carriage, and each night Eliza had to stop herself from going to him when they were settled in their rooms.

It wasn't fair to take comfort from a man after you'd turned down his proposal of marriage—even if he hadn't really meant it at the time. If she went back to him now, she didn't think she'd be able to stop herself begging him to reconsider.

Marriage to Gabriel would make her so happy.

Marriage to her would make Gabriel miserable.

Finally, five days later, temptation was removed: they were home.

Gabriel spoke with Uncle Francis while the footmen unloaded Eliza and Aunt Mary's trunks, and then the Duke of Vane was gone, out of Eliza's life in every meaningful way.

'How was the trip?' asked Uncle Francis, following Aunt Mary into the parlour, where she called for a tea tray.

Aunt Mary and Eliza looked at each other.

'Fun?' Eliza suggested.

Aunt Mary giggled. 'Eventful?'

Uncle Francis looked confused. The man could predict political decisions down to one or two votes, and could do sums that went into the millions of pounds, but banter had always eluded him.

'We drank champagne in beautiful grounds, stayed in an Elizabethan manor, and ate raspberry ice cream,' said Eliza. 'There was a scavenger hunt and garden games.'

'It sounds as if you had a good time,' said Francis, accepting his just-so cup of tea as Mary passed it to him.

'We also dined with the Prince Regent, and Eliza uncovered a plot to cheat the Crown out of tens of thousands of pounds,' said Aunt Mary, pouring Eliza's tea.

Uncle Francis spluttered.

They explained everything that had happened.

'What do you think we should do now?' Eliza asked.

Her tea was strong and sweet. No matter how well she emulated her aunt, a cup of tea prepared by her always tasted that little bit better.

'I don't think there's anything we can do,' said Francis. 'We'll have to wait and see what happens.'

As it turned out, what happened was mostly nothing. For the next few days Eliza woke, dressed, and sat with Aunt Mary in the parlour, just in case callers came. In the afternoons Mary spent time with her sons, and Eliza practised her pall-mall shots in the back garden. In the evenings they read together, practised the pianoforte, watched the boys' skits and daydreamed about the weather finally turning cool.

And then the invitation came.

It was morning, and all five members of Lord Stanley's household were seated around the table for breakfast. Lord Stanley was on his third cup of tea, the boys and Eliza had emptied the chocolate pot, and Eliza was trying to decide if she should go for another egg.

'Post, Your Ladyship,' said the head footman.

'Thank you, Noah,' said Aunt Mary, absently setting the small tray of mail beside her plate.

'Anything interesting? Uncle Francis asked, not looking up from his paper.

Her aunt opened the first envelope. 'A charity luncheon and—' Aunt Mary blanched.

She was holding a heavy linen envelope, and the brilliant scarlet seal was unmistakable.

'It's from Carlton House,' she whispered.

She set the letter on the tablecloth and they all stared at it.

'What is it?' asked nine-year-old Thomas, craning his neck to see.

'Isn't Carlton House where the Prince lives?' asked his brother Luke.

'Yes…' said Eliza hoarsely.

'What do you think it is?'

'I bet he's going to make Father the Prime Minister. Wouldn't that make sense, Mama?'

Uncle Francis stifled a laugh. 'I'm not nearly influential enough to be made PM, but I appreciate your vote of confidence.'

They all looked at the letter once more.

'We should read it,' said Aunt Mary. 'Eliza, you open it.'

'Generally what one does with letters,' said Uncle Francis.

Eliza straightened her spine, took a deep breath, and picked up the envelope. Her fingers only trembled slightly. The overall effect of her bravado was slightly tarnished when her breakfast knife left a smudge of butter on the wax seal, but a quick swipe of her thumb soon set that to rights.

'Read it out loud,' said Aunt Mary, who was holding her serviette in a death grip.

'"Lord and Lady Stanley and Miss Eliza Hawkins. Your presence has been requested for a private audience with His Royal Highness the Prince of Wales at Carlton House at three in the afternoon on the twenty-fifth of August. A coach will be sent to collect you." It's signed "Colonel Sir John McMahon, Baronet."'

'That's all?' asked Aunt Mary.

'A private audience?' said Uncle Francis. 'Seems a bit unusual.'

'It must be about Abberly's scheme—which isn't something the Regent would want getting out,' said Eliza.

At first her spine had gone nearly liquid with relief: she wasn't being arrested or summoned before a judge—hooray! But she *was* being summoned before the acting monarch. *Oh, no.*

For a few seconds they all sat in stunned silence.

Then Aunt Mary gasped. 'What am I going to wear?'

Uncle Francis shook his head. It was amusing, in a dark sort of way, that after everything that had happened, appropriate clothing was the matter that Mary's mind went to.

'We'll come up with something,' said Eliza. 'We have a week. We can alter our promenade dresses.'

'They're from two seasons ago,' said Mary. 'And I don't know why I ordered yellow. It makes me look insipid.'

That Eliza didn't have an answer to.

Uncle Francis, however, did. 'Ladies, I believe it's time to dip into the Christmas fund.'

Two hours later, Mary and Eliza were standing outside Madame Badeaux's shop, waiting for the current crush of people inside to clear.

The afternoon was warm, but mellow, and the air carried the scent of soap, warm sugar and working horses. London felt busier than it generally did after the conclusion of the social Season—perhaps it wasn't only Eliza who felt a general air of anticipation.

Eliza was peering through the glass, trying to determine which bolts of cloth were still available, when a shadow fell over her. It seemed as though there was a change in the air pressure, and she knew who she would see before turning around.

Gabriel, Duke of Vane.

'Lady Stanley, Miss Hawkins…what a lovely surprise. Caroline, these are the ladies I escorted to the house party last week. Lady Stanley, Miss Hawkins, this is my sister, Lady Caroline.'

Eliza studied the girl as everyone bobbed curtsies. She was several inches taller than Eliza, and possessed the type of hourglass figure that never went out of fashion. Her hair was nearly blonde—a sort of a tawny colour—and she had the same intelligent brown eyes as Gabriel. With her perfect skin and curious expression, it was hard to determine her age, though she would put her as at least ten years behind her brother.

'I am so glad we have bumped into each other,' said Lady Caroline. 'Now I don't have to orchestrate some ridiculous excuse to invite you for tea. Mother has told me all about you, and I couldn't wait to meet the woman who turned an entire house party on its head. Were there really ladies' maids weeping in the corridors?'

'Um…' said Eliza eloquently.

'No,' said Gabriel. 'I believe there was only one incidence of tears—and that was because Lady Huntbury wouldn't know kindness and understanding if she sat on them.'

Lady Caroline wrinkled her delicate freckled nose. 'I'm glad I have talked Mother into spending the spring in Italy. English Society doesn't have terribly much going for it.'

Gabriel gave Eliza a look that seemed to say, *How did I end up with two of you?*

It was all Eliza could do not to giggle. Looking at his familiar face, smiling and handsome and exasperated, she felt a surge of affection and longing. He deserved this…to be happy with his family.

Before she could decide what to say, there was a flurried exit of chattering, laughing women from the modiste's shop. They were loose acquaintances, in the way most of Polite Society were acquainted, and they raised their eyebrows at the sight of Eliza chatting with the Duke and his young sister.

'Ladies…' said Gabriel with a nod.

They tittered, and then went on their way as the door to the modiste's shop opened again.

'Good afternoon. Your Grace... Lady Caroline,' purred Madame Badeaux.

Eliza and Aunt Mary suspected that she wasn't really a Frenchwoman, and had donned the persona in order to justify charging high prices for her clothing. Eliza hadn't seen enough of her to study the woman's accent, as she and Aunt Mary could rarely afford her services. But whatever the woman's story, one thing was certain: her clothing was truly worth the money. You didn't choose a pattern at Madame Badeaux's. She chose for you.

'Good afternoon, *madame*,' said Lady Caroline, curtseying beautifully. 'Thank you for finding an appointment for us.'

'For you I will move all the other appointments,' said Madame Badeaux, her 'S' sounds slipping into 'Z's.

Eliza tugged subtly on Aunt Mary's sleeve. The shop had clearly been booked for a private fitting, and they would need to come back another time.

They had bobbed curtsies and turned to slip away when Lady Caroline asked, 'But, Miss Hawkins, where are you going?'

Eliza looked over her shoulder, confused. Caroline and Gabriel were looking at them with the same brown eyes and open expressions, while Madame Badeaux watched with a calculating look.

'We didn't know the shop had been booked,' she said. 'But it was lovely running into you. Do let me know if you wish me to call.'

At some point Gabriel had suggested that perhaps she should put more effort into making friends. She would start here—no matter how much it would hurt to look into eyes that so reminded her of Gabriel's. Having met Caroline's mother and older brother, Eliza knew the girl couldn't be anything but lovely.

Caroline pouted. 'But why don't you come in with us? I'd be happy to share my appointment. I only need a few things for the winter season.'

Eliza glanced at Gabriel, who nodded.

'We would very much appreciate it. We're only looking for one dress each.'

They all entered the shop, and soon Caroline and Aunt Mary were cooing over bolts of silk and velvet. Eliza allowed her fingers to trail over muslin, silk, sprigged cotton and brocade with an increasing sense of panic.

'We can't do this,' she mumbled into the wall of fabric. 'Promenade dresses? What were we thinking. We should be wearing court dresses—and they take months!'

'Court dresses?' Gabriel hissed. 'What's going on?'

Elia jumped—she hadn't realised he'd wandered so close to her.

She pretended to consider a deep chocolate-coloured velvet. 'We've been summoned to Carlton House,' she said. 'I didn't think a short-sleeved ball gown would be appropriate for the afternoon, but I'd completely forgotten that court dresses require hoops. Hoops! In this day and age!'

When she turned away from the bolts of fabric, she found all those in the shop watching her with wide eyes. Her voice had been getting progressively higher-pitched as she worked herself into a proper tizzy.

'Um…' said Lady Caroline.

'You have been summoned to court?' asked Madame Badeaux, with interest.

'No. Not court. Just Carlton House,' said Eliza. As

if it could ever be 'just' Carlton House…'just' a private audience with the Prince.

'Yes… I can see the difficulty,' said Madame Badeaux with a frown. 'The Prince, 'e supports the Queen, with her hoops and plumes, but in private 'e is very conscious of the fashion of the day. You cannot attend in a plain day dress,' she continued, eyeing Eliza's current dress with clear distaste. 'You are in need of something new. Something better.'

'You don't think we need hoops?' asked Eliza, with relief. 'I was thinking that maybe I could wear one of my own dresses and put panniers over that. Like a sort of temporary skirt arrangement.'

Madame Badeaux looked horrified. 'No, you will not!'

Eliza held up her hands in surrender. 'But this is Lady Caroline's appointment,' she said. 'Let her go first.'

'Have you lost your mind?' Caroline demanded. 'All I need are some winter walking dresses and morning dresses. You're going to see the Prince Regent! Please say you'll let me help you choose the fabric.'

Over Caroline's shoulder, Aunt Mary was nodding enthusiastically. If it wouldn't have hurt Caroline's feelings, Eliza would have rolled her eyes. But she didn't need prompting: of course she would welcome Lady Caroline's input.

'I'll gratefully take any help I can get,' she said, and surrendered herself to Caroline and Madame Badeaux.

Chapter Twenty-Five

Two of Gabriel's realities were colliding, and he didn't know how to feel about it.

His fortnight with Eliza had been wonderful, irritating, terrifying and enlightening. He'd learned about himself, about Eliza, and about the ways he could choose to interact with the rules of Society. He'd had one of the most profound sexual experiences of his life, and he'd been refused in a proposal of marriage.

And since this had all happened far from London, it didn't feel totally…real. It was as though it had happened in a particularly vivid dream, or in a book he'd read over and over, until pieces of the prose became a part of his everyday vocabulary.

He hadn't taken Caroline on an outing in at least four years, and most of his memories of her involved a stubborn little blonde with the face of an angel and the mind of a court barrister. Now Eliza and Caroline were side by side, bent over a shortlist of materials for Eliza and Mary's new dresses, and everything was getting confused.

'You must wear your hair up, upon the top of your head,' Madame Badeaux was telling Lady Stanley. 'It is imperative for the neckline I shall create.'

'My maid will practise,' said Aunt Mary.

Meanwhile Caroline and Eliza were trying to decide between three bolts of silk: a shimmery pink, a light blue, and a red the colour of dark, expensive wine.

'That one isn't appropriate,' Eliza was whispering.

'Now I've heard it all,' he said, joining the ladies at the side table. 'Miss Eliza Hawkins, clinging to propriety?'

'Even *you* can't think I'm stupid enough to antagonise Prince George,' said Eliza.

'Not stupid,' said Gabriel, rubbing the pink silk between his thumb and forefinger. 'Brave enough, yes.'

'Well, it wouldn't gain me anything, so I have no reason to be brave. Besides, I've never seen a fabric like this. It changes colour as the light moves.'

'Very unusual,' said Madame Badeaux, setting Mary's fabric selection aside. 'But not right for you.'

Eliza pouted.

Gabriel had to drop his body into one of the undersized, overstuffed chairs set in the little sitting area to hide his groin from the others. Eliza's pout made him want to do things to her mouth that would see both of them barred from the kingdom of heaven.

'It's lovely, and I will absolutely be ordering an evening gown in that material,' said Caroline, with more authority in her voice than Gabriel had expected. 'But Madame Badeaux is right, as always. You need to wear the red.'

'This material is not meant for a lovely Grecian column dress,' said *madame*, draping the burgundy silk over Eliza's shoulder. 'You were not meant for such fashion either. This will be better. A highlight of the current shelf bosom, but with a waistline like the Queen's court dresses. You will see.'

Eliza shrugged, clearly helpless against the united front of *madame* and Caroline.

'It's a once-in-a-lifetime-dress, dear,' said Aunt Mary. 'We should take *madame*'s advice.'

Gabriel wondered how he could arrange matters so that he would be able to see Eliza and Mary in their court dresses. Perhaps he could drop by to chat with Lord Stanley that morning…but that would be too transparent, and he'd already been seen in Eliza's presence for long enough. He had Caroline's reputation to think of as well, now.

Speaking of Caroline—it was his sister's turn as the centre of attention. She'd gone straight for brushed cotton and velvet, warm and cosy materials for her winter wardrobe.

'It needs to be loose enough for me to go skating,' she said, her words floating to the top of the feminine chatter like a trout leaping out of a stream.

Of course. Skating. Gabriel had announced that after the early December socials he'd like to spend some time at the family seat with his mother, sister and younger brother—though no one seemed to know where Hugh had gone to. He'd spent time in Italy with Mother and Caroline earlier in the summer, and had apparently travelled on from there to Greece.

For just a moment Gabriel envied him. He'd been a younger brother once, able to imagine a life in which he could take up a gentleman's career, or travel the Continent, or do whatever damn well suited him. But that pattern of thinking was simply habit. Gabriel didn't really want to flounce around Europe or study law. He wanted to be exactly where he was: working with his land stewards and getting to know the person his baby sister had become.

As it turned out, she had developed into a confident, self-assured young woman.

'Gabriel,' Caroline said now, demanding his attention. 'For the brown velvet, don't you agree that bronze epaulettes make more sense than silver?'

'Wouldn't silver be brighter?' he asked.

Caroline rolled her eyes and turned back to the other ladies. 'I like the silver threading and buttons on the riding and walking ensemble, but I must insist on the bronze for my skating dress.'

'On this I will compromise,' declared *madame*. 'Now: measurements.'

And that was Gabriel's cue to leave.

He walked briskly down one side of Bond Street before turning and walking back up the other. He loitered outside his bootmaker's, wondering if he should order another pair of Hessians in anticipation of a slushy winter. He'd step inside just in case…

And that was when inspiration struck.

A quarter-hour later, he expected to find the ladies in wrath with him for being late. Instead he found Eliza's Aunt Mary sipping tea and watching the shop girl wrap dress trimmings, while Caroline was at the back, still being measured. Eliza was on one of the undersized chairs, apparently brooding.

'Well?' Gabriel said, dropping into the opposite seat and resisting the urge to drag her into his lap. 'What are you pouting about this time?'

He wanted to laugh, and then kiss her, and then swear a blue streak about the injustice of the universe as he watched Eliza's head snap up and her expression change from morose to annoyed.

'I do not pout,' she said.

'You do,' said Gabriel. 'So, come on. Tell a friendly duke your problems.'

'I'm worried,' said Eliza flatly. 'I don't know what's going to happen next.'

None of them did. Gabriel was still resisting the urge to somehow tag along on Mary and Eliza's expedition to see the Prince.

'You'll get through it,' said Gabriel. 'You always do. That's a perfect, one hundred percent record—you can't do much better than that.'

'Are you saying my success is a matter of mathematical certainty?' Eliza asked, with a little smile.

God, how had Gabriel ever found her plain?

Her skin was perfect, her smile made him feel warm, and it was all he could do not to touch her.

'Well…not your *success*, per se,' said Gabriel, forcing himself to look away from the most perfect woman he'd ever met. 'But you could take the fact that you'll endure it as gospel.'

When it came to sheer, single-minded persistence, Eliza rivalled the pyramids of Egypt.

They sat in silence for a moment, and then Eliza looked at him through her lashes. 'You never did tell me what went wrong between you and your mother. In Yorkshire she acted as if she hadn't seen you in years. But you must know that she adores you? That there's no way you could disappoint her?'

How did he explain that he'd used his mother as a stand-in for his own sense of inadequacy? Of course she didn't wish he'd died in his older brother's place. She loved all her children too much. It had taken one conversation with a strange vicar and a week in Eliza's presence for him to realise it.

'When my brother and father were killed, I didn't

know what I was doing. I couldn't take care of the dukedom, and I couldn't comfort my mother. I messed up the
few ducal duties I did attempt. And all of those things
got…confused.'

Eliza gave him a stern look. 'Really? Avoiding your
mother and then worrying about her reputation could all
have been solved by her telling you that you're a good
duke and a good son?'

'Well…no,' said Gabriel. 'I'm sure she's told me that.
But I didn't believe it. I wasn't a good duke.'

Eliza shook her head.

'Besides,' he continued, 'worrying about her reputation is true! I can't have you giving her or Caroline any
ideas…'

'Ideas about what?' asked Caroline, snapping the
curtains back.

Gabriel wondered how much she'd overheard.

'I do believe our business here is done,' said Caroline,
with a brisk nod to Madame Badeaux. '*Madame*, thank
you for your time and your brilliant insight, as always.'

'And thank you, Lady Caroline, for sharing your
appointment with us,' said Eliza. 'I do hope you'll call
soon.'

'Oh, we most certainly will,' said Caroline, looping
her arm through Gabriel's. 'I'm quite sure my brother
knows where to find you, and I'll be dying to hear how
your audience with Prince George goes.'

Moments later Gabriel found himself out on the
pavement, watching Eliza walk away from him again.
He'd hoped spending some properly chaperoned time
with her in the shop would provide…what? A sense of
closure? The realisation that she wasn't as beautiful and
compelling as he remembered?

Well, neither of those had happened. And now his

sister was looking at him with an insight that Gabriel did not find at all comfortable.

'Did you mean those things you said?' she asked. 'That you can't be a good duke or son?'

Blast. She *had* been listening.

'Yes,' said Gabriel glumly, dreading whatever it was she'd say next.

Caroline paused to think. 'Well,' she declared, 'that is absolutely ludicrous. You've always been an excellent brother. I haven't seen much of your duking, but the estate is doing well, and the villagers never gripe to Mother or myself in the churchyard.'

'Thank you,' said Gabriel, not sure what he should say.

Caroline wasn't finished. 'I should have known it would be something masculine and foolish like guilt. I had started to wonder if you preferred the company of gentlemen, until I heard all those rumours about you and half the married women in London. Honestly, Gabriel, what were you thinking?'

'You're not supposed to know about such things!' he spluttered. 'Besides, it's none of your business.'

Wonderful. Now he sounded as if he was all of fourteen and telling his baby sister to stop touching his things.

Caroline rolled her eyes. 'Gabe, nuns in cloisters have heard about your exploits. You were not as discreet as you'd like to think. The only reason the husbands of your mistresses didn't challenge you is because you outrank them and they were too busy spending time with their own mistresses. It does give one a rather bleak outlook on married life, doesn't it?'

'You won't have to worry about that,' said Gabriel, engaging his mouth before his brain.

Caroline patted his hand. 'No, I don't think I *will*

have to worry about that,' she said. 'I'm much more choosy than you have been…at least historically. However, I *do* quite like Miss Hawkins.'

'She turned me down,' said Gabriel as he handed Caroline up into their waiting carriage.

'Did she? Hmm… I hadn't considered that. Did she give you a reason?'

Gabriel could remember it vividly. The scent of beeswax candles and old books, the way dust motes had floated through the glow of the sconces, and the flush on Eliza's face as she told him that she couldn't do that to him. As if marrying her would be some kind of punishment for him.

Maybe he would have considered it a punishment once. But now that she'd been set free Eliza was well and truly herself. She was charming and witty and fair-minded and stubborn as a mule. She'd ruffle feathers and make friends wherever she went—Gabriel could see that now. But for every stiff-necked matron Eliza offended, there would be another who appreciated her charms.

'She said, "I can't do that to you." And then fled the room,' said Gabriel.

Caroline's eyes narrowed on him, and in that moment she bore an uncanny likeness to their mother. Gabriel felt the urge to adjust his cravat and sit up straight.

'I'm beginning to suspect that flowers and poetic language were not involved,' his sister said crisply.

He really shouldn't get Caroline involved in this. It was embarrassing to admit having been turned down, and he didn't want to burden his sister with his problems. At the same time she was possibly the only neutral party to whom he could talk with no fear of gossip.

With a sigh, Gabriel gave her the summary of that night's events.

When he had finished, he saw Caroline was eyeing him with crossed arms and a disbelieving expression.

'Of course she didn't want to marry you under those circumstances,' she said. 'You framed it as a favour you would be doing her.'

Oh. Well, put like that…

'And with her reputation in such a…a delicate state,' Caroline continued, with all the diplomatic finesse of a seasoned politician, 'I can understand why she was hesitant to saddle you with her problems. The woman is clearly mad about you.'

'No, she isn't,' said Gabriel, directing his words mostly at the hope stupidly ballooning in his chest.

'Oh, come on!' said Caroline, bouncing a little as the carriage took a turn too quickly. 'She looks at you as if you're a Christmas pudding, a thousand pounds and a cure for all ills rolled into one. But only when you aren't paying attention. Would you like to know the way you look at *her*, when *she* isn't paying attention?' Caroline asked, with all the sugary sweetness of an arsenic-laced tart.

'Absolutely not, pest,' said Gabriel through a grin. 'I think I can work it out from here.'

'Good—brute,' said Caroline.

She was smiling too, and had returned fire with the tongue-in-cheek insults and names they'd called each other during Caroline's pre-teen years.

'Let me know if you need me to draw you a diagram.'

'I'm glad you aren't holding my poor behaviour against me,' said Gabriel impulsively, as the carriage rolled to a stop outside their Town house.

'I'm glad you finally came to your senses,' said Caroline.

Chapter Twenty-Six

Time moved in strange ways in the week between the Prince's invitation and the day of their audience. It would crawl during the morning hours, when no callers came and no letters arrived, and then Eliza would blink and it was time for bed, and her candle had burned down to nearly nothing as she tried to read her nerves away.

She returned to Madame Badeaux's shop once more, to have her gown fitted, but even that didn't make the Prince's invitation feel any more real. It was as though Eliza had an appointment to speak with selkies, or view the second coming of King Arthur: it felt equally impossible.

And then suddenly the day arrived. The boys were subdued at breakfast, and it was all Eliza could do to nibble on a piece of buttered toast. Her stomach felt as if it was full of acid, and her mouth was so dry that she kept having to take sips of lukewarm tea to get the toast down.

'It's going to be fine,' said Uncle Francis for the third time. 'He's such a busy man that the audience will be over before you know it. Just tell the truth and be respectful.'

'And we'll make sure to thank him for his grace and

understanding,' said Aunt Mary, as though speaking lines for a play. 'And we've been practising our curtsies. Goodness, it feels a little bit as though I'm about to be presented to the Queen all over again. And that was almost thirty years ago!'

Eliza had never been presented to Queen Charlotte, being of too low a rank. If it felt like this, she was quite grateful not to have had the opportunity.

'What time is it?' Aunt Mary asked, craning her head to look at the little clock on the sideboard.

'It is ten minutes after nine, Lady Stanley,' said Noah the footman.

'Only ten minutes past the last time you asked,' said Eliza.

'Oh, hush,' said Aunt Mary, nervously buttering another piece of toast for Thomas, who already had three uneaten slices balanced on his plate. 'We're all nervous.'

'I'm not,' said Luke. 'This doesn't have anything to do with me.'

'He could have Mama and Eliza hanged,' said Thomas.

'That's stupid—and Prince George isn't stupid,' said Luke. 'He helped defeat Napoleon.'

'That was Wellington,' said Uncle Francis decisively.

Finally, when the tension could no longer be tolerated, Eliza went upstairs to take a bath and prepare for the day. So what if the carriage wouldn't arrive for another five and a half hours? It would probably take her that long to do her hair the way Madame Badeaux had insisted it must be done.

It was worth it, however, when her maid, Susan, put down the curling tongs and stepped back to admire Eliza in the mirror.

'You look lovely, miss,' she said. 'This ought to become the fashion for everyone, I reckon. Those high waistlines are only flattering on wispy girls that couldn't last for a single lap of Hyde Park.'

Susan had a point when it came to empire waistlines. On everyone but the very thin, they had a tendency to make the wearer look with child. They were the fashion, however, and Eliza had never particularly minded because, unlike the costumes of yesteryear, Grecian column dresses were quite comfortable.

'Thank you for all the work you have put into this,' said Eliza, turning to get a better look at herself in the mirror. 'I just hope Prince George shares your opinion.'

'He's a great lover of fashion,' Susan insisted. 'He'll know it when he sees it.'

The gown was gorgeous. The wine-red silk had been turned into something Eliza would never have been able to imagine. The waist was much lower than the current fashion, but somehow it brought to mind the natural waistlines and pannier-emphasised hips of the seventeen-eighties. Instead of hoops, there was an extra layer of petticoats under the skirt, which balanced out the modern shelf-style bust. The neckline revealed only her collarbones, as this was a daytime appointment, and the sleeves were tight, closing with little black buttons at the wrist.

Clothed in the magic of her new dress, Eliza's natural hourglass figure was revealed. And with her hair looped into curls and pinned to the crown of her head she had a smooth, elegant neck. The dress didn't hide any of the features over which Eliza had long despaired, but it highlighted features that only Madame Badeaux had been able to see beneath the voluminous, empire-waisted gowns of whimsical popular fashion.

The door to Eliza's room opened and Mary stepped

inside. She gasped, and held a handkerchief to her mouth. 'Oh, dearest, you look stunning.'

'So do you,' said Eliza, turning to admire Mary's sapphire-blue gown.

It created a similar silhouette, merging modern styles with those favoured for court dresses, but it had a different neckline. Mary's was square, and at the hem and wrists were edges of cream-coloured lace.

'I hope you will wear that to a ball next Season.'

'It wouldn't be suitable,' said Mary, turning to look down at her skirts. 'But I intend to anyway.'

They both looked in the mirror for a moment, admiring their costumes, before Mary cleared her throat.

'I have something for you,' she said. 'They're quite small, but they were your mother's. I'd thought to save them for your wedding, but… Well,' she said briskly, 'I think this might be an even bigger fuss.'

'Meeting the Prince is certainly a bigger to-do than a wedding,' said Eliza.

She really meant it. She'd had her time with Gabriel. She'd come to respect and know the man, and she knew what it was to be respected and known in turn. She wouldn't settle for less simply for the sake of being married. She would meet the Prince, and then she would get on with her life to the very best of her abilities.

'Here they are,' said Mary. 'A bit old fashioned, but in lovely condition, I think.'

In her palm, wrapped in a scrap of cloth, were some pearl earbobs. A round, cream-coloured pearl adorned the stud from which a teardrop-shaped pearl dangled, catching the light with a pretty, silvery sheen.

'Oh, Aunt Mary,' said Eliza, touching one with the tip of her finger. 'They're lovely.'

'I was going to save them for your wedding, but…

well. Every girl should have something pretty of her own,' said Aunt Mary, who'd always encouraged Eliza to share in the jewellery she owned. 'Now, I do believe we're ready to go.'

'Absolutely,' said Eliza. 'Because if we stay up here another minute we might do something silly...like cry.'

They went down the stairs, where Uncle Francis and Noah the footman were waiting with their shawls and plume-adorned headpieces—another nod to current court tradition.

'You ladies are looking just lovely,' said Uncle Francis, pushing his wig back up onto his forehead.

'Thank you,' said Aunt Mary, adjusting the tilt of her plumes in the mirror. 'We feel lovely.'

And now the carriage was arriving, all sleek and black with the royal seal, and Eliza and Mary were off to meet the Prince.

Carlton House, off St James's Square, was a sprawling Greco-Roman construction that appeared to be part temple and part palace. A portico of Corinthian columns fronted the house, and it was difficult to tell just how deep the house extended from the road.

For one crazed moment, Eliza considered turning around and walking herself back home. This monstrous, glittering stone palace was not a place where people like Eliza were welcome.

Unfortunately, elaborately liveried footmen were already opening doors and ushering Eliza, Aunt Mary and Uncle Francis inside. Out of sheer, childish intimidation, Eliza reached out and caught Aunt Mary's gloved hand in her own while they waited in the enormous, domed hall of the great house. Black and white tiles echoed under their footsteps, more columns stretched up to the ceiling, and carved frescoes arched over each of the doorways.

Eliza was gratified when Aunt Mary, looking wide-eyed at the splendour around them, squeezed Eliza's hand back.

A butler—or a secretary, or an aide, or *someone*—dressed in an immaculate black suit of clothes announced, 'His Highness will see you now.'

Eliza reminded herself that the most likely outcome of this audience was that she'd have her property seized by the Prince and be sent away with a scolding. That was absolutely fine with her. She didn't need that land anyway, and she'd been scolded by the best of them.

Her life wouldn't change, and she'd always be able to remember the time she had an audience with royalty. He definitely wouldn't have sent the carriage if he wanted to have her hanged. Not that she'd given him reason! *She* wasn't the one who'd tried to take tens of thousands of pounds from him.

Eliza decided that this was very good practice for standing before St Peter at the gates of heaven. They followed the servant into the famed Circular Room. It could have comfortably held five dozen people, and a complement of serving staff besides. The domed ceiling had been painted to look like the sky, and heavy blue-and-silver-tasselled curtains framed each of the floor-to-ceiling windows. Afternoon light streamed in from the gardens, catching on the five crystal chandeliers and sending tiny rainbows whirling around the room.

The Prince Regent was seated in the centre of one of the many cosy seating arrangements, reclining back in a plushly upholstered chair of French design. Eliza's little party approached slowly, and curtsied deeply when they were a few feet from him.

'Lord and Lady Stanley,' said the Prince, nodding to Uncle Francis and Aunt Mary. 'And Miss Hawkins.'

'Your Highness…' they murmured.

'Thank you for accepting my invitation to Carlton House,' he said.

'It is truly as magnificent as the papers have reported,' said Uncle Francis, letting his eyes trail over the works of Old Masters and current painters.

'It serves its purpose,' said Prince George.

Eliza wondered how anyone could become used to living in such splendour. It was like standing inside the Royal College of Art, the French Court and Buckingham House all at once.

'May I congratulate the two of you ladies on your fashion choices for the day?' said the Prince.

Oh, heavens. Maybe they should have worn their promenade dresses. He had to know they weren't high in the instep, didn't he? They'd risked too much…

'You've combined my mother's courtly fashions with the modernity and sleekness of today's silhouette. Well done.'

Eliza blushed and murmured her thanks.

'Now,' said the Prince, his attention squarely on Eliza, 'tell me about Lord Abberly.'

In the modiste's shop, Eliza had told Gabriel that when she met the Prince Regent she would have no need to be brave: the worst was behind her. Now she knew that Gabriel had been exactly right, and she would need all the courage she could screw to the sticking place.

She wished Gabriel were here now.

'Of course, Your Highness,' said Eliza, dry-mouthed. 'Where would you like me to begin?'

He raised a greying eyebrow. 'At the beginning, of course.'

'The Earl and I have moved in similar circles for many Seasons now, but soon after the most recent Season began, Lord Abberly began to take an unusual interest in me…although not in public. He asked me to marry him at a musicale in June, and I turned him down. Events…um…escalated, until the events in Hyde Park the second week in August. He tugged me from the path and tried to kiss me behind a tree.'

'You were unharmed?' Prince George asked.

'She was unharmed, Your Highness,' said Aunt Mary.

'I struck him, you see, which drew attention to us,' said Eliza. 'And I refused to apologise for it.' She'd also scolded the onlookers—but he probably already knew that.

'Was this when you began to suspect that Lord Abberly was up to something untoward?' asked the Prince. 'So you decided to attend his house party?'

'Er…no, Your Highness,' said Eliza, wondering what would happen if she decided to lie to the Prince about her real motives.

When she cleared her throat, a servant stepped forward with a tray bearing four small cordial glasses.

'Do have a drink,' said the Prince. When they took their glasses, he showed a rare hint of charm and added, 'Much finer than the stuff Abberly was serving.'

Eliza hoped he'd write off her blush as a lack of familiarity with the drink. She sipped her cordial and continued, 'Your Highness, I admit that I attended Abberly's house party hoping that I would discover a chance to take revenge.'

The Prince barked out a laugh, startling Eliza and Aunt Mary, but quickly recovered. 'Young lady, you were hoping to take *revenge* upon a peer of the realm?'

'Yes, Your Highness,' said Eliza.

She wondered if old St George had felt this much anxiety when facing the dragon.

'Well, that was inadvisable, but it looks as though you were successful, wouldn't you say?'

'It looks that way, Your Highness.'

'How did you discover his plot?' the Prince asked.

Eliza shot a sideways look at Aunt Mary. 'Um… I was in the library, arguing with the Duke of Vane. He hit the top of Lord Abberly's desk and a hidden drawer popped out.'

'I see. Did you know that His Grace the Duke of Vane has written to me this week, corroborating your story?'

Gabriel was worried about her.

'No, Your Highness. We ran into each other at the modiste's last week, but I haven't heard from him since.'

'Yes, at Madame Badeaux's,' said Prince George.

Goodness. He really did have spies everywhere.

'Do you have any further designs upon Lord Abberly? I could force him to marry you,' said the Prince.

Eliza gasped, and next to her Aunt Mary stiffened. While George was known for womanising, and all manner of insalubrious pastimes, he was a stickler for proper behaviour in Society. She shouldn't be surprised that after having admitted to being ruined he would want her to marry the man responsible.

'I have no further designs upon Lord Abberly,' said Eliza stiffly, deciding to ignore the last part of the Prince's statement. In this case, discretion truly was the better part of valour.

'Hmm… I cannot say the same,' said Prince George. 'In which case, Miss Hawkins, in exchange for having your guardian sign over the Brighton property to me,

I would like to dower you. Twelve thousand pounds should be more than adequate.'

In lieu of fainting, or doing something even more stupid, like trying to hug the man, Eliza sank into a deep curtsey, murmuring her thanks.

'In addition, I would like it if you would consider accepting my future invitations to salons and openings at the Pavilion,' said the Prince Regent. 'Some of our peers could do with your moral fibre.'

'We would be most honoured, Your Highness,' said Aunt Mary, pink-cheeked, and bobbed another low curtsey.

If they didn't leave soon, Eliza was going to get a cramp in her legs.

'One last thing, Miss Hawkins. If you ever uncover another plot involving the Royal Family, or Parliament, or perhaps an invasion of the French, it would be in your best interests to deliver the information to me *privately*.'

He said this sternly, all the while looking down his royal nose at her. But under his fringe, his eyes were twinkling.

'I understand, Your Highness,' said Eliza.

This couldn't be happening. Not only had he not done anything nasty to her—like force her to marry Abberly—the Prince had dowered her like a princess and invited her to his broader court gatherings.

This was…whatever the opposite of being ruined was.

She could afford to send the boys away to school and to marry if she found someone to take her on. And if she didn't marry—why would she? No one could match Gabriel—she would no longer have to worry about being destitute or a burden on her young cousins in the future.

'Your Highness, thank you for the favour and grace you've shown me this afternoon,' she said, curtseying once more as she backed towards the door with Mary and Francis hot on her heels. 'I will always be grateful.'

Prince George nodded, and then they were back in the hall, staring at each other with wide eyes.

'Did he really…?' Eliza asked in a low voice.

Mary shook her head, and they walked, trance-like, to the front doors and out to where the coach awaited. A footman handed them up, the reins snapped, and then they were off, rolling away in a carriage bearing the Prince's seal.

For a moment, nobody spoke. There was only the sound of the horse's hooves on the cobbles, the buzz of London, and the heavy thumping of their hearts. And then maybe Mary caught Eliza's eye, or Eliza caught Mary's, but she started to giggle.

Soon they were both belly laughing, holding handkerchiefs to their eyes as the carriage rolled on towards home. Uncle Francis was smiling and shaking his head, and everything was right with the world.

'I can't believe it,' said Eliza, dabbing at her eyes. 'I just can't believe it.'

'Did you hear that?' Aunt Mary beamed. '*Moral fibre.* That's you, my girl!'

'I have wasted all these years behaving myself,' said Eliza. 'I should have started being obstinate years ago.'

'Started?' said Aunt Mary. 'I didn't think you'd ever stopped.'

And then they were laughing again—two women who adored each other overcome by joy, and relief, and happiness.

'Now, then,' said Aunt Mary. 'I should have told you this earlier, but I've been talking with Francis since we arrived home. He keeps postponing all the trips I want to take—he's busy with Parliament, or the tutor is away, or something is going to keep him here…'

'I have been busy!' Francis protested.

Aunt Mary ploughed on. 'So, after such an entertaining time with His Grace, I put my foot down. The boys will be away to school, and Francis and I are going to go to France to see his brother.'

'Aunt Mary, that's wonderful!' said Eliza. 'It's about time.'

'You're welcome to come with us,' said Mary. 'I have a feeling the Frenchmen will enjoy you.'

Eliza smiled. 'We'll see…'

She did want to see France—but not for the men. There was only one man in which she was interested, and he'd written to the Prince Regent on her behalf.

The softie…

Chapter Twenty-Seven

Word about the royal carriage had clearly got out.

'Welcome home,' said the footman with a straight face as Francis, Mary and Eliza arrived in the hall.

There were two bouquets on the sideboard, a teetering stack of calling cards, and many voices emanating from the parlour.

'Things have been a bit busy in your absence.'

'I can see that,' said Aunt Mary. 'Have you had Beth bring a tea tray?'

'Two,' said Noah. 'We're going to have to send to the shops for more soon.'

A nasal voice emanated from the parlour—one Eliza had never wanted to hear at home.

'Oh, Miss Hawkins, you've returned! We are so excited for you,' said Lady Joyce, leaning through the doorway while holding one of Aunt Mary's best teacups. 'Come and tell us all about it. And look at your dress! Daring, aren't we?'

Eliza smiled at Joyce. She had a feeling her expression heavily featured her teeth. 'Just a minute, Joyce. I'll be right down.'

'Go on,' said Aunt Mary, pulling Eliza in for a hug. 'I'll deal with them.'

Eliza hoped that she would. It was the height of rudeness to overstay a morning call, let alone stay as if she were angling for a supper invitation. All Eliza wanted was dinner alone with her family and to act as if everything was normal. It wasn't that she was ungrateful for the Prince's generosity—it was simply…overwhelming.

None of these people had been interested in her when she'd acted like a wallflower. Now, after one invitation from Prince George, everything had changed. Suddenly she was 'someone', for all the wrong reasons.

There was a package lying on her bed when Eliza closed herself in her room. She almost tossed it to one side, to be ignored until later, but the weight of the box and the writing on the card immediately changed her mind.

On a piece of paper bearing his crest and his title, Gabriel had written:

> *Hello, minx,*
> *Congratulations on your victory today—Prince George has too much taste not to admire you.*
> *Every rakess or budding Society smash needs a signature look. You've already discovered yours. Besides, I owed you.*
> *Yours,*
> *Gabriel*

Eliza carefully folded the letter, tucked it away in her bedside table, and then tore into the package.

Inside were beautiful knee-high Hessian boots and a pair of soft doeskin breeches. They were much better than the trousers Gabriel had destroyed during their scavenger hunt tryst.

She smoothed her index finger along the rounded toe of the heavy leather boots. They looked as if they were just her size—and to have had them made so soon he must have ordered them immediately after returning to London.

Surely that meant something. He hadn't sent her a gift purely because she'd been acknowledged by royalty. He hadn't sent her something generic.

Did this mean she didn't really embarrass him with her scandalous ways? Or was he approving her breeches and boots because he knew he no longer had to deal with her?

With hope growing in her chest like ivy along a brick wall, Eliza knew there was only one way to find out.

She hiked up her skirts, yanked on the breeches, and paused to admire her rear end in the mirror. Then on went the boots, bringing with them her next problem: how was she going to get out of the house?

Mary, Francis, Joyce and the rest of the company were all downstairs. If she made it to the kitchens, Beth and the scullery maid would never let her go.

That left one option.

The leap onto the clematis trellis winded her, but it was the feeling of two broad hands gripping her waist that made Eliza yelp.

'It's me!' said a familiar voice, and the hands released her immediately. 'Sorry!'

Once her feet were firmly planted on the ground, Eliza turned to glare at him. 'What were you thinking?' she asked. 'I could have fallen!'

Gabriel's shoulders shook as he laughed. 'I waited until you were only three feet from the ground. Even you have to admit that isn't much of a fall.'

Eliza attempted to maintain her glare, but she was simply too happy to see him. The light was low and golden, catching on his dark hair and highlighting the smile that was beginning to form crinkles at the corners of his eyes. He was still irritatingly handsome, and Eliza was even more enamoured of the way he seemed to *see* her—all of her, not just the trousers or the scandal or the generous breasts.

Wait...

'Why are you here?' she asked. 'Have you been lurking in the garden the whole time?'

Gabriel gave her an indulgent look before taking a handful of her skirt and sliding the material up the outside of her thigh. Eliza felt her skin break out into goose pimples. Even like this, fully clothed in her aunt's garden, she wanted him.

Finally Gabriel stopped, when the hem of her skirt was halfway up her calves and his fist rested on Eliza's hip. He let her skirts drop, but pulled her in closer. 'I knew you wouldn't be able to resist taking your new clothes for a stroll.'

'Oh?' said Eliza. She wanted to sound arch, but knew she mostly sounded breathless.

'Mmm...' Gabriel purred. 'I know you, minx. You've had your reprieve from Prinny, so why not court an entirely new scandal?'

'I was going to bring a footman this time,' said Eliza, resting the palm of her hand on Gabriel's chest. She had to crane her head back to look him in the eye, and beneath her fingers she could feel his heart thumping almost as wildly as hers. 'I wanted to come and thank you for my new boots.'

'You're very welcome,' said Gabriel. 'They look wonderful on you.'

'You have not told me why you were waiting in the garden,' said Eliza. 'Trying to avert a scandal?'

'Oh, no,' said Gabriel. 'I'm here with a message. You see, your revenge isn't quite over.'

'What?' asked Eliza. That wasn't what she'd been expecting. 'Abberly is finished. Nobody will socialise with him now, and he may yet have to face Prince George before the courts. I have a dowry, and I will be able to live off the interest. And Aunt Mary is probably inside planning her future travels right now.'

Gabriel leaned forward, very nearly resting his forehead against hers. He smelled like soap and cinnamon, as if he'd eaten a spice biscuit before washing his face and walking across town to keep vigil beneath her bedroom window.

Eliza brushed her fingers over his jaw, hoping beyond hope that he would kiss her…want her…marry her…

'That's all well and good,' he said, his voice low. 'But now you need to finish it off. Marriage and romance and children, Eliza. The whole package—a full life. That's how you complete your revenge.'

She felt as though the world had stopped spinning. She couldn't hear anything above the rush of blood in her ears or feel anything other than Gabriel's warm breath against her cheek. This couldn't be real. Things like this happened to other women, not to Eliza. Nobody had ever known her so well—nobody had ever taken her dreams so seriously.

'I don't understand…' she whispered.

What he said had nothing to do with vengeance.

'That's what you want, isn't it?' asked Gabriel, cupping her cheek. 'Adventure, and a family, someone who loves you?'

'Yes, but—'

'Then please marry me,' said Gabriel, kissing one

cheek. 'Let me give all that to you.' He kissed her other cheek and rested his forehead against hers. 'Because, Eliza, haven't you heard? Living well is the very best revenge.'

And then he kissed her, properly, right on the lips.

The air smelled like sun-warmed flowers and Gabriel's cologne. He tasted like biscuit and all she could feel was love. Love overflowing, spilling out of her in great bubbles of thankfulness and joy.

She fisted her hands in his coat and pulled him in closer, not wanting to forget a single second, not wanting the moment to end.

'Of course,' she said, when they pulled back for air.

She saw Gabriel's eyes widen and a smile stretch over his face. 'Yes?'

'Yes. I will absolutely marry you. I love you. And I'm keeping the trousers.'

He laughed and kissed her again, backing her up until her shoulders were against the brickwork of the house and they were standing in her aunt's hydrangeas.

Eliza hoped that the rest of her life would be filled with moments like this: with flowers, and laughter, and kisses.

'What do we do now?' she asked.

Moments, one after the other, mundane and important both. Moments strung together to form a life.

Gabriel took her hand. 'We go inside and tell your aunt and uncle. And then, traditionally, we live happily ever after.'

'Your Grace,' said Eliza, bobbing a little curtsey. 'You have yourself a deal.'

Epilogue

The April air was soft and cool, though the inside of the ballroom was warm. An orchestra played in the corner, the room was filled with the soft glow of a hundred beeswax candles, and around them Society buzzed. It was the first ball of the Season, and the air smelled like spring flowers and hope.

'I was wondering if this dance had been spoken for, Your Grace,' Gabriel asked, even as he snaked his arm around Eliza's waist.

Her dance card was no longer relegated to the potted ferns, and she'd saved the supper waltz for Gabriel—they both knew it.

Eliza gave him a bright smile as she placed her gloved hand in his. 'But you never dance with wallflowers,' she quipped, remembering another ball, in another time—one that felt so distant now.

'I believe I told you that we should all try new things,' said Gabriel with a wink, leading her out onto the dance floor as the musicians started to play. 'And I was right.'

'You occasionally are,' said Eliza, falling easily into step with her husband. Her *husband*.

'I'm always right,' said Gabriel, and Eliza trod on his foot.

Gabriel only pulled her closer. 'You know…' he said, his voice low and dark. It was the way he talked to her in bed, when they were pressed skin to skin and mouth to mouth. 'I think that's when I fell in love with you.'

'What?' Eliza asked, trying to ignore the want that was uncurling, warm and heavy, in her belly.

Gabriel gave her a knowing look. 'When you trod on my feet during that first dance. Your aunt was watching us as if I might eat you alive, and yet you stamped right on my feet anyway.'

'Hmm… That's when we came up with my list,' said Eliza.

'Eating cakes, gambling and drinking brandy,' said Gabriel. 'I think you've crossed those off your list several times over.'

Eliza stepped closer to her husband, dancing in a proximity that propriety would never allow. 'I've been thinking,' she said, looking up into his eyes. 'There's no reason why we shouldn't continue with my curriculum.'

She went up on tiptoe to whisper in her husband's ear. Gabriel immediately missed a step, and found that it was his turn to tread on Eliza's feet.

'We're leaving,' he said, his eyes hot. 'Right now.'

Eliza smiled serenely up at him. 'It'll cause gossip…'

Gabriel pulled her flush against him, and Eliza didn't care who was watching.

'To hell with the gossip,' he murmured, and kissed her.

Over the long years of their marriage, the Duke and Duchess of Vane became known for their scandals. They were forever racing around on horseback—with the Duchess rather disreputably dressed—or stumbling out of closets and falling out of trees. As the years progressed, those who knew them were forced to concede that the couple were a living testament to the fact that living happily and well was, in truth, the best revenge.

* * * * *

A Duke for the Wallflower's Revenge
*is Casey Dubose's debut, look out
for her next book coming soon!*